Long Enough to Love You

Long Enough to Love You

KIRSTEN PURSELL

atmosphere press

To my dad, for always believing in me . . .

Tell me, what is it you plan to do
With your one wild and precious life?
—Mary Oliver

1

On Opening Doors

I paused at the front door, not wanting to turn the handle, knowing I would be met by the sounds of silence. It was an empty feeling. One I had known was coming but did not want to confront. It was the reality my normally busy, bustling house was now empty, and the vacancy would never fully be filled again.

That was the way it was supposed to be all along. If Mark and I did our job right as parents, our children would leave and make their own way in the world. We succeeded on that front, sending them off to college with the tools needed to navigate their own waters away from the safe harbor of home, far from my protective mom wings. Every part of me was truly beaming with pride knowing Max and Maya were doing what they were supposed to be doing. But it begged a bigger question: What was I supposed to be doing?

I also knew on the other side of that door was a conversation waiting to happen that had been years in the making. It was the one where we had to figure out if we liked each other without the normal of the past quarter century. Were we capable of being together and happy as two? Or was it time to acquiesce to this part of our journey together ending?

It was a hard conclusion to reach when there was no real explosive moment or event that triggered the desire to move on and be happy, perhaps even happier, in the ever after of being an empty nest. The thoughts circulated in my head like a tornado, constantly churning. There was never a calm. After the tornado passed through and the thoughts subsided and turned to gentle winds, the destruction had been unleashed. I couldn't go back to before because the constant nagging question of what my happiness looked like lingered in the back of my mind. And, when it lingered, it was unresolved.

Cleaning the wreckage caused by a tornado was a monumental task. You didn't just sweep it away. You brought in bulldozers, backhoe loaders, and heavy equipment essential to clean up. That seemed simple compared to managing the damage spinning in my head. But I was resolved; I needed to believe I was more than a heap of trash after a storm.

I saw my reflection in the door's glass as I went to grab the handle. It was that of the woman I wanted to be staring back at me. She was confident, capable, fearless, and independent. I knew her once, and I wanted to be her again. I acknowledged her with a gentle smile, offering support for what was to come.

With my head playing out scenarios it clearly did not know the answer to, I took a deep breath and reached for the door handle, feeling simultaneously apprehensive and excited. I was ready to walk in and confront my future, the one I envisioned without Mark. I reached for the handle only to find the door yanked from my hand and Mark standing on the other side.

"Jesus, Jenn, where've you been? I've been texting and calling, and you haven't replied." Mark was a hard man to read, but he didn't get mad often and berating me was not usually his style.

"What the hell, Mark? You stalking me?" My voice was unsteady, strangely defensive, and echoed loudly in the foyer of our home. Another reminder of the empty inside.

He looked confused. "No. What?"

Instead of me blindsiding him, he blindsided me. I looked

at him, wanting to hate him for taking my momentum away, sensing full well he had nothing to do with it. I wanted to reply that I was lost in my own head trying to figure out how to have this long-overdue conversation, but that quickly dissipated when I saw the expression on his face. It was not that of a man anticipating his world was about to come crashing down on him for reasons unknown, but rather the look of a man overcome by grief. It was a grief much deeper than that. And it scared me more than the conversation I thought we were going to have.

"What's wrong?" I asked, panicked something might have happened to one of our kids.

"It's your mom, Jenn," he said somberly. "She's gone."

"Gone where? What are you talking about?" I was confused, unable to fully process what I was hearing. The words did not make sense.

From behind him I made out the shadow of a man. It was my dad. I hurried to be by his side. Grabbing him. Hugging him. In that moment, realizing the implication of the words.

"Dad, why didn't you call? I would have come to you."

He looked at me, confused. His thinning hair hadn't been combed, his big blue eyes were bloodshot, and the buttons on his shirt misaligned adding to his disheveled look. He struggled to say his words as if trying to speak a foreign language.

"I couldn't figure out how to use the phone to call you. Your mom always did that. I didn't have your number. But I could remember how to get here."

"Oh, Dad. That must have been such a long, hard drive."

"It's alright. Nothing I can do for her now, anyways."

"But you called someone for her?"

"I called 911. They got there and said she was gone. There was nothing they could do. Someone came, took her body. Carol came and offered to call you, but I said I would let you know."

"Carol has my number, Dad."

"Oh. I suppose I should have let her call you then." In that moment, he seemed so fragile and forlorn.

"That's okay. I'm glad you got here safely." I gave him a long hug, holding back the tears I wanted to let flow freely. I did not want to cry tears for my mother. I knew those would still come. It would be a process. And I knew those moments would find me when I least expected them to. A reminder here. A picture there. These tears would be the ones which came with the realization my dad was alone without my mom and that he was mentally and, quite honestly, physically a fragment of the strong, gregarious man who had been the backbone of our family.

My sadness quotient had doubled in a matter of minutes. My resolve to be strong for myself, to do right by me faded as this new curve ball was thrown in my direction. Even in this moment, I found myself annoyed by Mark thinking he just got off the hook again, avoiding a heavy conversation.

There were times, many times, over the years where I had questioned staying. I would be the first to admit I chose safe and simple. Safe and simple meant not worrying about money. It meant being cared for in superficial ways. But it did not guarantee happy. Safe and simple did not ensure I would be seen for who I am. It just meant ninety percent would be satisfying with the other ten percent being up for grabs. Some would say ninety percent was amazing. I challenged that assumption.

I chose a man who didn't show me daily he loved me with words or affection, but he was honest, faithful, loyal, and dedicated to our family and dreams. He supported me when I walked away from a career on the upward trajectory to be a stay-at-home mom. He let me be independent without checks and balances. I was able to overachieve just like the old days. Only this time it was through my involvement in the world of PTA, school, and youth sports.

If anyone would have told me the next twenty years of my life would be over in a flash, I would have laughed. I was so busy in those moments I could not ever imagine them coming to an end. I lived in those moments, relished them, found peace and glory in them. I created two amazing human beings, and they did not disappoint. Of course, I am biased. I am supposed to be. Even if they weren't perfect, I would profess to nothing less. That was my job as their mom.

When my youngest started becoming less dependent on me, I found myself trying to imagine my life after she left. I was always an overachiever. I wondered what I could pour my energy into next. Writing, my passion, had been fleeting at best over the years. Maybe I would dust off the old notes, find the files buried somewhere on my computer of ideas I jotted down but never fully pursued over the years, and write that novel.

I was beginning to find excitement in the idea of doing things *I* wanted to do again. It was going to be my turn to be the center of attention after giving all of mine to everyone else all those years. There was a chance I would be accused of being selfish or ungrateful if I suddenly shifted gears. I could count on some people to encourage me to pursue my passions, do what was best for me, find things which gave me joy independent of my role as a mom. But there would be detractors too. There were always those I told myself. Were they the *bitter Betties* of the world, too chicken to do something for themselves, too afraid of being alone, too dependent on the lifestyle they had?

But, if I truly stood back and weighed the options of my

situation, I could understand them. Why rock the boat when you could do anything you wanted and still live your life comfortably? Those conversations with myself had become exceedingly loud voices in the last couple years. Now it felt like they were screaming at me.

Somewhere in between those voices arguing pros and cons, contemplating what-ifs, it led me to address the elephant in the room. While I was anticipating the "what next" part of my life, I began to question what my happiness looked like. For so long, it had been defined by my family's contentment. With them gone, the focus began to shift to me. And it occurred to me I deserved to be happy. And so did he. We both did. But would I be better off and happier when he was no longer my safety net? How do you know it's the right decision? So many times, I imagined just once he would do something so wrong that I could not forgive him. It would be so much easier. Having to deal with roller-coaster emotions predicated on nothing but an uneasy, unfulfilled feeling in my gut was exhausting.

But safe and simple meant I would be the bad guy even if, in the end, it was for the greater good of all. Reluctantly, I had been grappling with how to own that, be confident with that, and move forward in the present knowing the future would be a big, fat unknown with zero guarantee what I felt had been missing or lacking would magically appear on the other side. I was fully aware that the grass was not always greener on the other side. But what if the grass wasn't really that green on your side anyways? If the grass was already an off-shade of brown, did it matter if it was brown on the other side too?

Every conversation I had planned and played out in my mind was suddenly buried in the realization that my mom had just died. It was unexpected. She had been a healthy eighty-year-old woman. It might sound like an oxymoron. But she still walked with her friends daily. She did her Jazzercize class at the senior center several times a week. She played bridge. Her mind was sharp and her body still agile. Her heart, however, had a different story. While she went quickly, it saddened me to think of Dad finding her. And then wondering how he kept himself composed enough to make the call to 911. He would get in his car and drive several hours to tell me. How? There were so many thoughts running through my mind simultaneously.

I watched as Dad fiddled around in his pockets like he was looking for something.

"What are you looking for, Dad?" I asked.

"My keys," he said absently. "I need to get back and take care of things."

That was my dad: Always taking care of things.

"Dad, stay here tonight and I'll go back with you tomorrow. That way we can take care of things together."

He paused and took consideration. I could see the relief come over him. Nodding, he went to the couch, sat down, and began to cry. I walked over to him, grabbing the tissues from the table as I walked by. I had never seen my dad break down before. He was always strong and in control. In that moment, my tears began to flow uncontrollably too. As I sobbed, I found myself wondering if the crying had several meanings: losing my mom, seeing my dad vulnerable, or realizing I had put off a conversation I felt I was ready to have but would now be delayed indefinitely. It was a perfect storm of emotions. The reality was it was a combination of all three, each with their own deeper meaning, all needing to be addressed. Just maybe not in the order I thought or hoped.

2

On Car Rides and Truths

I went to bed that night knowing that I could not start the conversation with Mark. He was upset by my mom's death just as much as Dad and I were. I suppose there was a small part of me that was relieved not to have the conversation just yet. I was ready, but I wasn't ready. I really did not have a plan. I played out parts of what I would say to him, knowing he would be upset, but he wouldn't be angry with me. He was a man of little emotion, except when it came to our children: then the cup runneth over.

Mark was truly a remarkable father. Each of us would likely admit we were better parents to our children, devoted to them on every level, than we were partners to each other. Maybe that was a natural evolution that happens when you have children that consume all your energy and attention. It certainly was in our case. With both kids gone, the past couple of months had been hollow and lonely as we tried to figure out how to be just each other again. It was sometimes awkward. Sometimes sad. Sometimes just two ships in the night meeting on opposite sides of the bed when it came time to sleep. And even then, we slept in opposite directions. I was an earlier to bed, earlier to rise person; he liked late night TV and waiting until the sun rose to wake up.

I found myself reflecting on what it was that drew me to him all those years ago. I may have chosen safe, but there was something sexy and exciting to Mark when we first met. Mark was unlike any man I had dated before. He was quiet and humble, despite being quite remarkable and accomplished. He was the opposite of me in personality. I was the more outgoing and outspoken one. I said what I felt. I knew it bothered him sometimes that I often spoke before I thought. You either loved that about me or didn't. I think, in hindsight, he may have just tolerated that part of me. He was a thinker, not a man of many words and certainly not words that would be perceived as opinionated, unfiltered, or judgmental. Those would be my labels.

It was hard to find anything about Mark to dislike if you were his friend, acquaintance, or just met him. It was the little things that began to pile up, then the resentment sometimes in the moment, sometimes in reflection. And sometimes, every so often, he found ways to indirectly make me feel I was less than perfect. I will own that. I know that. But on the flip side of that was also the need to feel like I was worthy of loving, that he thought me beautiful or sexy or something positive. Compliments were not dispensed with Mark. I think his analytical mind just assumed I was to know those things. Those realizations happened slowly because I was truly happy in those moments in the beginning,

Our relationship started slow. That was different for me, too. I liked things fast and spontaneous. I liked knowing how things were going. I liked knowing how a man felt about me. Mark offered me none of that. He kept me guessing. In my younger days that would have driven me crazy. But with Mark, it kept me on my toes. I could tell he liked me. That part was easy. But his commitment to me and the pursuit of a long-term relationship was often frustrating. There were many times over the three years we were together before he finally proposed that I questioned what I was doing in the relationship. I would ask myself what it was about him that kept me there. And I would ask him what it was about me that kept him in the relationship. He was never able to answer that question. It wasn't that he thought I was beautiful. I do not know if he did. I was a self-assured woman successful in my career. I would tell myself I did not need a man to validate me as a human. Turns out, as the years went by, I was starving for validation from Mark. I wanted to know why he loved me; what was it about me that attracted him to me and what kept him interested in the relationship? He would scoff at the mere mention of those questions. And his inability to answer them festered, grew, and began to burn a form of resentment in my soul.

Mark was five years older than I was. He was established in his career as an attorney, finding success in a small law firm. He liked that the hours weren't overwhelming. He didn't practice law for the money. He did it because he enjoyed helping people. He was, however, not flexible when it came to the idea that maybe we should live somewhere else so that I could pursue other career options, or he could work for a bigger law firm making more money. He was a man who did not embrace change easily. He was content in his idyllic world.

Maybe it was that he was so opposite of me that way. I liked change. I liked spontaneity. While I appreciated time at home, I liked exploring and experiencing the world. He would accommodate my need to travel with annual trips I planned for our family. He never argued or protested that the children should be given the opportunity to explore the world. I required that, I told him. I think he considered it his one great concession. Or maybe it was me getting to have a small piece of the life I so loved before children and their lives became what I lived and breathed.

Mark and I met through a running club my best friend Meg had encouraged, no begged, me to do with her. She thought it would be a great way to meet men in Greenwich since most likely worked in New York City and had good jobs in finance or law. Meg was all about the kind of men you could meet. I reluctantly went with her to a run session. I loved running, but didn't like the idea of someone telling me where to run or how fast I needed to go. I liked the time alone in my head to problem solve or disconnect. If I ran with friends, I knew we would go the same pace and have lots to gossip about and catch up on. Running with strangers was not something I looked forward to let alone with men who would likely try to run faster than me or assume I would not be able to keep up.

But Mark wasn't that kind of man. He ran with the group because it worked with his schedule. It forced him to make time for himself. I do not believe he ran to meet women. On the contrary, I suppose. I think he found it insulting that someone would find it okay to invade his space in an effort to meet him. He was cold and disconnected from the group, but incredibly focused at the same time. I somehow found that oddly sexy.

I did find Mark one of the more attractive men in the group. He was very fit. He often ran without his shirt on and had nice abs. I am a relatively tall woman and I liked that he was taller than me by a significant amount. And his hair was quite remarkable. I found that beautiful hair on a man was starting to become harder to find as thinning hair began to set in. (Mark still has remarkable hair although there are few signs of the dark brown hair it once was, now lost under the gray that it has become.) But it was his light blue eyes that caught my attention first. And the way they would shift away to avoid eye contact. It was clear he was trying to avoid human connection and interaction as much as possible at these running meet ups.

Mark was a deceptively fast runner and one of the few men that I struggled to keep up with on the runs. He had no interest in conversation and I liked that. We both ran near the front of the pack, kept to ourselves, ignored the others, and got in a great run. I appreciated his lack of interest in me, given there was no shortage of men that made their intentions abundantly clear. I did not mind men paying attention to me, quite the contrary. I did, however, mind when it interfered with my ability to focus on my run.

It was on one of those occasions that Mark and I had our first conversation. One of the men in the group had been making it clear his intentions to get my attention. He would run on my feet, then surge ahead, drop back, and try to start a conversation. He did this over the course of several runs. I did my best to brush him off. I was curt. I would slow down or speed up in an obvious attempt to escape him. While he may have been some high stakes Wall Street financier, he was not brilliant at taking a hint or he was just so accustomed to bullying his way into someone's business, that he did not take the subtle (or not so subtle) clues I had been giving him. Even at the end of the runs, this man would huff and puff next to me in an effort to connect. I would point to my phone and walk away. And he'd be back for the next run.

After many runs like this, Mark started catching on to what was happening. I think in some odd way, Mark liked running with me even though we weren't intentionally doing it. I sensed he appreciated the silent, unspoken running partner next to him. On one Friday run, the Wall Street guy would not leave me alone. He was insistent that I meet him for drinks after our run. Finally, I heard Mark tell the guy, "You need to back off." I don't think I had ever heard Mark say more than two words before that.

"Mind your own business," he retorted. I watched as Mark sidled up beside me.

"We have plans tonight," Mark proclaimed nonchalantly. I did a double-take as he said this.

"Really? I have never seen you say one word to her."

"Because we're running," Mark replied.

"You even know her name?" The guy was getting cocky. He clearly had been studying the situation.

I jumped in. "Of course, he knows my name is Jenn."

He looked to Mark for affirmation. "And she knows my name is Mark." The introductions had been made.

"Well, I didn't see that one." That was enough for him to drop back on the run, start chatting up Meg, and that was that.

Mark moved closer to me, and we ran in stride the rest of the way. It was an understood silence. (Silence, I fear, is something I imagined he wished for over the course of our marriage when speaking my mind became unfiltered and often uninvited.) When we finished the run, we walked beside each other, and I thanked him for rescuing me.

"It was probably about time we introduced ourselves anyways." He put out his hand. "I'm Mark."

I took it. "Jenn."

"I like that you can keep up but don't feel the need to talk," he said matter-of-factly, and I laughed.

"I like that you don't try and outrun me to prove a point." He smiled at that.

"Maybe we should make a point to Wall Street guy and get drinks sometime?" He was shy in his asking.

"I would like that," I replied. "But wait, you aren't a Wall Street guy too?"

"Worse. I'm an attorney." He was subtle, which I liked. And I found that sexy too. We exchanged phone numbers and had our first date that weekend. We had a mutual love of running and a shared disdain for Wall Street man whose name was really Charles. Meg would date Charles for two weeks before announcing him selfish in bed and incapable of meaningful conversation that wasn't centered on him.

I hoped sleep would overcome me quickly, stopping the thoughts that made me feel like I was swimming against the current. My head hurt and my eyes burned from wiping away the tears. My mom was dead. My dad was struggling. And I wanted out of my marriage. At least I thought I did. I was a good swimmer. I could swim parallel to shore, keep my head above water, and eventually make my way to safety. I might get banged up a little, maybe even need the life preserver to keep me floating in high seas, but the high tide always subsided, and I would figure out what to do and how. Thankfully, my children weren't currently in crisis. That was my one saving grace.

When I came downstairs in the darkness that next morning, I found Dad sitting at the kitchen table with an empty coffee mug. I kissed him on the cheek as I walked into the kitchen.

"Morning, Dad. You're up early," I said in my chipper morning tone.

"I couldn't sleep. I want to get home to your mother," he said sadly.

"Dad, she's gone. There's nothing we can do. Let me make you some coffee." I took the mug from his hand and walked to the Keurig.

"I couldn't find your coffee maker."

"I don't have a potted coffee machine, Dad. Just the Keurig."

"Oh, that damn thing. I don't know how those things work."

"Sure you do, Dad. I've shown you many times."

He looked sadder, more confused. "Oh, I'm just old and forgetful." I handed him the fresh cup of coffee. He took a sip.

"Careful, Dad. It's hot."

"I like my coffee hot. You know that." He did not bat an eye as he took his first couple of sips. "This is good. I just forgot how. I'm sorry."

"Don't apologize. Let me take care of you, Dad." I sat at the table with him. "Let's have a nice breakfast then head back home."

"Okay. I like that. I'll drive my car."

"No, I'll drive your car. I can take the train back when everything is taken care of. Or Mark can come get me. We'll figure it out. Let's just get you back home."

He nodded in sad agreement. I had just lost my mother. Though I did not see that coming, losing our parents was obviously inevitable at some point. That Mom went before Dad was not predictable. While Dad was still here with me, I felt this strange sensation that he was slipping quickly as well. I wanted to be wrong. I hoped to be wrong. I wanted my dad to be able to find some happy again in his life. It had to be difficult to be married to my mother. She was never an easy woman. But he was loyal, tolerated her mood swings, and loved her faithfully. At least, that was how it appeared.

Dad and I left shortly before noon for the drive up the coast to his home on the Cape. Fall was my favorite season, and I found a new appreciation for the changing leaves and gentle winds that swirled just above the tree line. The nip in the air a reminder that winter was standing at the door, ready to rear its ugly head with sleet and snow. Fall was the pleasant calm before the storm. The irony of that suddenly a metaphor for my life.

I would try to remind myself of that as Dad often tested my patience on the drive. He liked to tell me which way to go, when I should turn, reminded me the light was yellow and I should slow down. I suppose it gave him something to focus on that wasn't about Mom dying.

Halfway through the drive home, Dad became oddly quiet. I looked to see if he had fallen asleep, but he was simply staring out the window.

"Dad, you okay?" I asked. He seemed startled by the question.

"Just thinking," he said.

"About Mom?"

"About Randy," he answered.

"Who's Randy?" I wanted to know. He never stopped staring out the window like he was lost in time.

"Randy was the one your mother really wanted to marry." I saw him wipe a tear from his eye.

"You okay?"

"I just got something in my eye." He pulled a tissue from his pocket and wiped at it. I could tell he was choked up.

"It's alright to be sad, Dad. You two were together for fifty-five years."

"I hope I made your mother happy. You think I made her happy?"

"Mom was not a happy woman." She wasn't. She walked through life like it had cheated her. Maybe now I was beginning to understand why.

"Who was Randy? Mom never talked about him." To be honest, Mom did not talk about much unless it was about her garden or her bridge club. She asked few questions about her grandchildren and certainly was not going to be bothered by any life issues my brother or I might have had. She was present, but absent.

"Randy was your mother's first love. They were engaged when she was just eighteen. And then he went away to Vietnam. He never came back home."

"So he died?" I asked. "You think she would accept that over time."

Dad explained that he did not die. In fact, he returned from the war. He never told my mother until she learned from his younger sister that he was living in Hawaii and had married a girl he met while on leave there. There was no Dear John, or in this case Dear Sally, letter. He simply vanished. Mom was rightfully crushed.

Dad went on to tell me that Randy had actually gotten the girl pregnant while on leave and his parents made him marry her out of respect for her as well as to preserve the family's dignity. His family essentially exiled him to Hawaii as the girl was Polynesian and that flew in the face of the family's strong Catholic faith and, while unspoken, disdain for interracial relationships.

"Your mother was ready to get on a plane to Hawaii to take him back, but her parents said she would be disowned from the family if she did. And you know your grandparents. They were always pretentious and self-righteous."

My mind was spinning. I didn't know these things about her. She never talked about herself like that. Mostly she just complained about life, which was amazing because Dad had given her an incredible one. But it started to make sense to me.

"So when did you meet Mom, then?" I thought I had asked this question over the years, but I couldn't recall the answer.

"We had always known each other. You know how tight the Cape is." Yes, I did. Everyone knew each other's business.

"Your mother's parents and my parents decided to set us up. I had just graduated from Yale. This was a bit of a sticky point for Sally's parents. Your grandfather was a Harvard man through and through."

"You don't have to remind me. I can still see the disappointment on his face when I decided not to go there."

"You didn't get in," Dad reminded me.

"Ouch, Dad. That hurts." It made him chuckle.

"You know I was happy you went to Yale. That old curmudgeon would have found fault with anything." I knew Dad wasn't fond of Grandpa, but I could hear the bitterness even now.

"So it was an arranged thing?" I asked.

"Only the first date. She was so pretty. And such a knockout figure. But so sad too."

"It must have been hard knowing you were a backup."

"You know me, Jenn. I'm an optimist. I thought I was the luckiest guy in the world dating her."

Dad went on to tell me that they "courted" for a year before he asked her to marry him. They had a small wedding, unlike most of the summer spectacles on the Cape.

"Wow. So she was okay with settling?"

"She married me. We made you and your brother. We traveled the world. We had friends. I was a lucky man especially since . . ." He stopped. His sentence trailing off before he could finish the words.

"Since what?" Now I really needed to know.

"We all have history, honey. None of our stories are as simple as they seem." That was a loaded statement, but I could tell he didn't seem ready to tell that part of the story yet. But then he surprised me.

"I had someone else once too."

"You dog, you," I kidded.

"We were married at eighteen. And she died in childbirth, along with our son, a year later."

"Why didn't I know this?" I was stunned by this revelation.

"Because your mother didn't want to destroy our family with my history."

"Oh my God, Dad. You had a whole other life, and it was tragic and sad, and she blamed you for it? How do you choose to stay with, no, to marry even, someone who was ashamed of you?"

"It was different times. We had to protect the integrity of the families."

"So you chose Mom and all her crazy and gave up on having your own happily ever after?"

"Your mom wasn't crazy. And I loved her. I did. And she loved me the best she knew how. I knew she would never be

able to love me like she loved him. But she loved me enough."
I felt a part of my own heart shudder at hearing the exact
words I had felt about my own marriage.

"That makes me sad, Dad, thinking that you felt you were
second best for her."

"I always thought I won the prize when she agreed to
marry me especially after what happened. She was beautiful.
And so smart."

"But she was never kind to you, at least not in front of us,"
I admitted. She was cold and distant and not a loving woman
to him. She loved us in her own way. And I reflect now realizing that Mom was always a little checked out, like she was
looking in the distance for something that she could not quite
make out.

"She was grateful. I know she was. Her heart had been
broken."

"Your heart had been broken," I reminded him.

He defended her. I'm not sure I could have married her
knowing that I may never be enough. But maybe her resentment wasn't just towards Randy, but actually towards Dad and
the fact that he knew love before her too. He had married his
love and she tragically died. It was not a decision she made to
leave him. He must have been devastated and crushed. I wondered if he ever felt he was responsible for his wife's death and
that of his child. I couldn't ask that question. I think in my
heart I knew the answer. And maybe marrying Mom was how
he could make things better in his mind. I ached for him. In
those days and from those families, they weren't always allowed to make decisions of the heart. Both of my parents, in
their own ways, had settled.

I reflected on my own marriage and realized I did not settle. I knew I loved Mark when I married him. I knew exactly
the kind of man he was. He made it abundantly clear he would
never change who he was for anyone, and to be with him I

would have to accept that. At the time, I was fine with it. I had my career. And then I had the kids. The fact that parts of me were left empty and unfulfilled did not occur to me until the time and distance between us grew greater, and the reality that we were so completely different hit hard. I thought about all the times I had asked for little things but was met with disapproval because, as he would say, it was not consistent with his character. I would shrug it off and then bury it in the coffin of my soul. The resentment growing with each reminder that I was not worth making small changes for. I would have tried for Mark if he would have asked me to do things. But he only occasionally complained about something I said or did, and then would chalk it up to that's just how I was.

I often found myself wondering over the years if, when I asked him to do something, he did the exact opposite on purpose. It was his passive-aggressive way of confronting me without actually verbalizing it. I put a laundry basket by his side of the bed so the pile on the floor wouldn't grow. He didn't use it. He would get mad when he couldn't find the tools he was looking for because he didn't put them back after using them. I stopped helping him look over time. Ask him to put the dishes in the dishwasher instead of the sink meant extra dishes would be left behind. Small little things hammering the nail in the coffin. Stupid, small little things. And my takeaway was I was simply not worth doing those things for. He was meticulous at his job. He crossed every "t," dotted every "i," left no stone unturned. I was the uncrossed t, the undotted i, and stone that was not worth turning. It stung more as the years went on.

I looked back at my parents' relationship and was reminded that their love wasn't perfect. They both had so much pain from events that happened when they were younger. I struggled to understand how you choose that. Dad loved her, yes. But I have to wonder why he thought he wasn't worth more. He stayed with my mom even though he knew she would never love him like she loved that other man. It made me sad for him. And it made me sad for my mom. Was she the unhappy person she was because she settled in her life? She was offered a safe path and took it.

I could always feel her bitterness, her sadness, her resentment. Did I ever feel her love? I wondered in retrospect. Saying I love you was not a form of expression she used towards Dad, my brother, or me. I know I am not like her at all. I saw those things and made it a point to be more like my dad with his affection and endearing words. But maybe there was a small part of me that I suddenly recognized as being like her.

The reflection of resignation had been staring back at me. And I realized that maybe it was her I saw reflected. If I chose to stay, am I just like her? Choosing a life that looks good on the surface, but is hollow and sad on the inside? The thought of that triggered a powerful sensation in my chest, as if I were being crushed, suffocating, and gasping for air.

I asked myself what made me be okay with safe? I chose safe even though I would not have labeled it that at the time. Why did I choose safe? Because reckless was dangerous and ultimately unfulfilling. I chronicled it all in journals throughout college and my early working years. In great detail. I wanted to remember those moments. I wanted to look back and understand what I was thinking when I was doing all those wild and crazy things. I stored them in the bottom of my closet at home.

It was amusing to remember the fun me, the wild me, the carefree me. I don't think Mark would have liked that me. He never asked about my past escapades. Perhaps he was afraid to know the answers. Meg and I would chat about some of our experiences when we had too much wine or needed to feel young again. We'd reference the journals, but we never actually pored over the pages again. Too cringey, maybe. I told myself they were reminders of why I married in the first place: I felt it was time to be an adult. And Mark was the perfect man to provide stability, maturity, and safety for me.

I suppose that's what we all want when we get married. We want to know there is a place to call home with someone who shares our ideas and values and loves you just enough to not question. Would I want my children in relationships where it's just enough? Or would I want them to find someone who fills them, challenges them, completes parts of them with the love they so deserve? I knew the answer to that one. Why wouldn't I want that for myself too? Dammit. Why am I asking myself this now? And it comes around full circle: I chose safe because it was just enough when my life was full.

My life with Mark had been a hundred miles an hour since the day we started dating. He had his practice. I was finishing grad school while working as a consultant for a boutique agency in Greenwich. We expanded our running to include races on the weekends, sometimes even training for marathons and traveling to compete in them. We did that until I got pregnant two years after we were married. I worked up until the day Max was born. And then I worked up until the day Maya was born. They were two years apart, which is exactly as I had planned it.

What I had not planned was the overwhelming feeling of love for these little humans I created. I had no doubt I would love them. But I did not have the kind of motherly role model that would have suggested I would want to sacrifice my career and success for babies. But they sucked me in, and all I wanted to do was be their mom.

The timing to leave corporate America was also perfect. I had become stagnant in my career. I was itching to do new things. But the opportunities in Greenwich were limited. Mark suggested I look in the city. Commuting before kids was not something I wanted to do. We could afford the city, but Mark didn't want to leave the safe sanctuary of Greenwich. And I most certainly did not want to commute when I had small children at home. Maybe my decision was impulsive. Maybe it was out of spite. But whatever my deep-rooted reasoning, I chose to stay home with them and do the suburban housewife thing.

Meg laughed at me when I told her.

"Where'd you go?" she asked me.

"To the world of snot and poop," I said as I threw one of Max's diapers in the diaper Genie.

Meg knew me better than anyone. We had met in college and our connection was instant. We were roommates all four of our undergraduate years and then when we first started our careers. We were each other's wing(wo)man in the early dating years, matchmakers as we expanded our circles, and confidants in every sense of the word. When I told her I was considering leaving Mark, her reaction was not one of shock or disapproval, but rather, "It's about time. He treats you like shit."

"He does not," I snapped back.

"No, he doesn't. He's the nicest guy in the whole world. He doesn't treat you like anything. And that might be worse than shit." God, she knew how to lay it on when she needed to. I appreciated her candor and blunt execution of the facts even if it stung.

Her reaction was not much different when I told her all those years ago that I was leaving my job to raise my kids. She asked if Mark made me do it. And I told her that was not the case.

"You really want to just be a mom?" she asked.

"I really do," I said. "Because if I can't have the kind of career I want and be good at that, then I want to be good at raising my kids. I don't want anyone else to get credit for fucking them up if something goes wrong along the way."

We both laughed at that.

She looked at me seriously then and said, "I think you're a bad ass mom and these kids are so lucky you're going to be home with them. Knowing you, you'll go out and be some sort of PTA queen running the show, telling everyone else what to do. It'll be a different kind of career. And you'll kill at that too."

She was a good friend. And she knew exactly the words I needed to hear. Mark's response, on the other hand, was, "That'll be nice for the kids." No deep, meaningful conversation about what that meant for me and what I would be giving up. It wasn't in his nature to look at it as me sacrificing something. And, in hindsight, I would make the same decision again. I suppose I just would have liked for him to consider the implications for me and my psyche at that time. I was a professional. He knew that, but he never questioned what walking away meant to me. So many signs I saw now.

I had been so bogged down in the details of my life, living in each moment with an eye to the future. Not my future, of course. But that of my children. You don't walk away from a career thinking that twenty years in full-time mom mode will abruptly stop. One goes to college. Then the next. And you're suddenly left wondering how you are supposed to reinvent yourself now.

For those years, I buried myself in my kids. I was the PTA queen. I created and executed more programs for their schools and sports teams. It was like a full-time job. The kind of job where you are taken for granted, friendships are opportunistic, and pats on the back few and far in between the backstabbing manipulations of the suburban housewives I would associate with.

Meg married a much older man during those years and never had children. Max and Maya were surrogate children to her. I think she liked spoiling them, but giving them back at the end of the day. Only rarely did I envy her that.

"Turn," I heard Dad yell.

"Oh, shit!" I barely made the turn for the exit. Only one car honked, displayed an unkind hand gesture, but was fine. I had been so lost inside my head I forgot where I was.

"Sorry, Dad."

"That's okay. We're almost home." I could see his mood lighten the closer we got. He had an odd sense of anticipation about him. He seemed at ease. Maybe telling me about his past and Mom's past lifted his spirits. We rounded the turn to his house and saw Carol, my parents' long-time neighbor, waving hello as we drove past. We pulled into the driveway and began to unload my bags when Carol walked up. She gave me a big hug and offered condolences for Mom's passing. I thanked her. She was looking at Dad now. The smile on Dad's face was an unfamiliar one. It was so full of warmth and love. There was mutual affection between them. It was heartwarming. I did not connect the dots then. But it would be obvious to me later.

3

On Funerals and Diaries

Dad and I would spend the next several days planning Mom's funeral. Carol was a constant and provided needed reprieve for Dad. She always made him smile and laugh. Her husband had passed away several years ago and she seemed to understand what Dad was going through. Occasionally, I would see him reach his hand out to hers and she would take it and hold it to her face. It was endearing. Mom would never have done that. He may be at the end of his life, but it was nice to see him finding joy with another woman. And after learning the story of their relationship, I found myself wanting to believe that he could be happy, truly happy, for the rest of his days. I wished that for him more than anything. I wished that for me . . . more than anything.

Mom was a highly organized woman, yet it was frustrating how scattered all her things were. Dad was of no help. She clearly had been the record keeper in the family. While Dad worked hard in his job and was meticulous in managing those transactions, Mom took care of the household matters. She paid the bills. She knew the various bank accounts they had. Dad knew where the investments were, thankfully. He was an investment banker, so at least that would make sense. But, then again, Mom could have decided she knew better and controlled that as well. However, she did not.

I created a large pile of all my findings in Dad's office. After several days, I had everything sorted, labeled, and marked with what needed to be done. I felt very accomplished. I knew there were also piles of papers that could be eliminated and I found joy in purging them. I cleared Mom's things from her bedside table. For years, she had slept in the guest room complaining that Dad's snoring made it difficult to sleep.

Mark snored on occasion so I could understand the importance of getting a good night's rest. I just put ear plugs in or covered my head with the pillow. I only ever left the room if either one of us had a cold or too much to drink, knowing that it would not be a good night for either of us. Mark, on the other hand, could have slept through anything. On occasion, he would accuse me of snoring. I had a tough time believing it since I was such a light sleeper. I always wondered if he made it up as his way of chiding me, since I was so adamant that I did not snore.

As I was clearing out Mom's nightstand, I came across a journal buried underneath a pile of magazines. I had never seen it before. It looked old with funky sixties graphics across the front. If she was trying to hide something, this would not have been the subtle journal you kept. Or maybe that was exactly why she kept it. No one would have suspected anything. *Was she hiding something in plain sight?* I needed to know.

It felt a little weird opening the journal. I hoped it would just be an old diary where she tracked appointments and lunch dates. Simple things that she did on a daily basis. Upon reading the first few pages, that's what it appeared to be. But inside those pages was so much more. And I had to sit down as I found myself engrossed in the pages, wondering if my mother had actually lived these moments or fantasized about them. They were explicit entries about various men that she had affairs with over a twenty-year period, starting when I was in elementary school. I could just see it. She would drop Jason and me off at school, hurry home, put on her make-up, maybe sexy lingerie, and then meet these men.

The thought of her cheating on my dad like that made me nauseous. I can't pretend to know what it was like to be either of my parents in their marriage, but that my mother would keep a journal covering twenty years' worth of affairs was almost unfathomable. Simple little entries like "Al at Motel 6. Makes me feel like I am the most beautiful woman in the world" or "Steve touches me in ways I did not know possible." My mother. A sexual deviant. And my dad? Did he know? He had to. How could he not? Or did he just turn a blind eye because all the stigmas and scandals surrounding divorce were so much more toxic than accepting you were not enough sexually for your wife? I closed the journal. I wanted to burn it, or at least hide it. But Dad walked in before I could do either.

He seemed startled to see me there. He glanced down at the journal I was holding. "You shouldn't read that."

"I was just cleaning out her nightstand."

"She was very private about that, you know."

"No, Dad, I did not know. How could I know?" I held up the journal. I wanted to be mad at him. "You knew?" I asked, more disgusted I suppose than shocked.

He paused, seeming at a loss for words. I could see the wheels spinning as he tried to formulate his response.

"Why, Dad? Why did you put up with it?"

"Because your mother made it very clear to me that I did not satisfy her in all the ways she wanted and needed to be satisfied."

"And you were okay with her having these affairs for all those years?"

"We couldn't divorce. She knew that. I knew that. We were both stuck, Jenn."

He gave some consideration to the next thing he said.

"We were stuck, and we couldn't make each other happy in all the ways a husband and wife should. So we agreed that sometimes we might need something from other people."

"You *both* agreed?" I stuttered.

He came and sat beside me on the bed. He grabbed the journal from me.

"We can burn this. No one needs to know. But don't pity me, Jenn, because I was not innocent either."

With those words, I felt an actual sigh of relief. It was a bit of a shock to learn not just one but both of your parents had been living secret lives for so many years, that they could fake it to the rest of the world, but in the end stayed together. I do believe my father loved my mother more than she loved him. She must have loved him on some level. Her parents died years ago, so any scandal associated with divorce wouldn't have mattered.

In that moment, I felt myself missing my mom. I wished I would have known her. I wished I could ask her now what she was feeling in those moments, why she chose to stay and not leave, and if she had to do it all over again, would she? I never felt my mom was there for me in life's difficult moments. I think she would have judged me harshly for wanting to leave Mark. I did not have a lover. I never had. I had never been unfaithful. I was simply no longer happy in my present. Maybe she would have understood me after all. But then the voice in my head reminded me that was highly improbable.

Dad got up from the bed and handed the journal back to me.

"You know your old diaries are still out in the garage. Might be fun for you to take a look back at your life during that time too." I had forgotten about my diaries. I loved them. They were where I kept my biggest secrets, hopes, and dreams during my teenage years before college. They were a friend I could trust not to tell anyone.

I dropped Mom's journal in the recyclable bin. That part of her history did not need to be saved. It was just another reminder of the mother I never truly knew.

I headed to the garage and found my old storage chest tucked back in the corner behind all of Jason's trophies, stacks of records, old sports equipment, and boxes that I needed to go through some day. I opened my chest and found two diaries from the eighties near the top. I felt a little excited by the find. I wondered if I had any secrets I had forgotten about. I knew I didn't have the time now to read through them. There was a funeral to plan. My diaries would have to wait. And after today's additional revelations, I was feeling so overwhelmed by my parents' pasts that resurrecting mine was not something I wanted to do at that moment. I grabbed the diaries, closed my chest back up, and headed to my room where I stashed the diaries to read later.

The funeral took place the following weekend. We were able to plan it so that the kids could be there. I was grateful that Max and Maya were able to come. And Mark, of course. I would return home with him. I found I had not thought about him and our situation much during this time. I had been busy planning the funeral, making sure Dad was taken care of, discovering dark secrets, and realizing I didn't know my parents after all.

Mark, as usual, was helpful when he wanted to be. He ran errands for us. He made phone calls and picked up flowers and food. He was a good, reliable man. That part of him I did find endearing. I felt myself sad at times watching him, realizing that I struggled to find that enough. Most women would be grateful for a man like Mark. But there was a void in my heart. There was a part of me that felt empty and incomplete. And I did not know if Mark would be able to fill that.

After so many years, I had been running on empty emotionally with him. I found ways to overlook the parts I was starved for. I fed them with busy. Busy was good. Until busy wasn't good enough. Perhaps learning what I did about my parents would serve as some sort of catalyst that I needed and deserved more than feeding my starving heart with busy.

The funeral was quite beautiful. Mom had a lot of friends. And knew even more. She was involved in many things, and it seems her contributions to those organizations earned her the respect she so desired and needed. She thrived on outward appearances and the adulation of those in her inner circle. I took my seat last and felt a sense of pride in putting together an event even she would have been proud of. Despite her generally cold nature, I did love my mother. She did the best she could. I did not pity her, but maybe now I understood her a little better. It must have been hard to hide the pain all those years. Not just for her though, but for Dad as well.

I don't recall the words of the pastor. I found myself lost in trying to imagine her life during the years she was married to Dad, the man I worshiped and idolized. And I found myself comparing her situation to mine. Was Dad Mark? Did he check all the boxes, provide for her, give her a safe existence so that she could live the life she wanted? God, was I just like my mother? Except I never cheated. And I'm confident Mark had never needed to either. But now I didn't know. Did we really know the people we loved and surrounded ourselves with? That question was gnawing at me when I felt Maya nudge me.

"Mom, your turn to speak."

It was like I was awoken from a deep sleep. I felt disoriented and confused. At least it was a funeral. No one was going to judge me for appearing out of it.

"Shit. Sorry." I put my hand on her leg and looked at her. I wondered what she saw when she looked at me. I hoped someone so different from what I saw when I looked at my own mother.

"I love you, Maya."

"I know, Mom. I love you too."

I straightened my dress and walked to the front of the chapel with my notes in hand. I had made a speech up about what an amazing woman my mother was, what a picture of strength and courage, how she lived her life for her husband and children. I think it was the speech I wanted to be real. It was, I suppose in many ways, what I had imagined my life with her would have been like had it been idyllic. With the exception of Dad, Jason, and me, I imagined it was the world that most of her friends saw her living.

I got to the podium. I put the cards down and looked up at Dad sitting contentedly next to Carol. He smiled at me. And then he winked. It made me smile. And it made me grateful in that moment that I did not know all their secrets until now. But I didn't want to say things I didn't feel in my heart. So I took the easy way out.

"Thank you, everyone, for coming today. I think Mom would have been impressed to know that she had so many friends and people that cared about her. She was a remarkable woman. She had a way about her that made her quite unforgettable. But I think you all know that."

I looked up briefly and then laughed out loud.

"You know, it's kind of funny, actually. She had such a need to control and be in charge. I truly have to believe she did not see her death coming otherwise she probably would have scripted her eulogy and made all the arrangements so that she could impress you all one last time."

I could hear laughter and I looked up to see smiling faces nodding in agreement. My brother gave me a thumbs up, indicating I couldn't have nailed that better if I actually stuck to my script. "I'd like to think we all made her proud today. She will be missed."

As I left the podium after speaking, I surveyed the room. I

was grateful for the friends, acquaintances, and relatives that had come to show their support. Despite her cold nature, Mom had a loyal contingent of friends. I recognized most everyone. However, I spotted an elderly man in the back row who looked oddly uncomfortable and out of place. He was there with a beautiful woman of mixed race. I thought it odd, but I didn't dwell on it.

After the service, everyone left the church and gathered at our house one last time. Mom liked showing off her home. It was elegant in all the right ways. She made sure it was always ready for guests. And a fitting closure to remember her there as well.

I waited until everyone had left before heading home. I wanted those few moments where I didn't have to talk to anyone. As I made way to leave, the man from the back suddenly appeared, startling me.

"I'm sorry. I didn't want to scare you."

"That's okay." I paused. "Were you a friend of my mom?"

"We knew each other so long ago. And I never got the chance to say goodbye to her. My sister told me she died, and I knew this was it, my last chance."

It clicked. "You must be Randy." His eyes lit up that I knew who he was.

"I am."

"I'm sorry you didn't get to see her. I think she would have really liked that."

He turned back to see if the woman was nearby. She was not.

"Your mother was my first love so long ago. I know I broke her heart, but I didn't have a choice. And I could never face her. It is my great regret in life."

"Those were different times," I said. "Is that your daughter? She's beautiful."

"She is the most important person in my world. She made

35

all the pain worthwhile." He motioned for her to join us.

I was introduced to Randy's daughter, Kalani. She was a stunning creature. She would go on to tell me that her mother had divorced Randy and left him to raise her on his own. I wondered why they wouldn't have moved back to the Cape if that were the case. His family was here after all.

"They disowned him," Kalani answered. "The only person he ever kept in touch with was his sister. By the time his parents had passed away, he didn't feel there was anything left here to come home to."

"That had to be awfully hard on him all those years, knowing his family didn't want him here. My mother never mentioned you to me, Randy. But my father only recently shared the story with me." I could feel the pain of all three. Mom for loving a man so much but being forbidden to be with him. Randy for loving my mother but being forbidden to be with her because of an illegitimate child. And my dad. My poor dad. His first love, his first wife, died while giving birth to his first child. The magnitude of their collective pain was overwhelming. Did any of them ever get to feel happy? Or did they just resign themselves to the life they had been given?

He looked sad as he registered that Mom had kept their relationship from her children. Maybe in those years I was a teenager and thought myself in love with so many boys she could have shared the story. But she never did. She was so private it was almost infuriating.

Kalani took her father by the hand and squeezed it. "You okay, Dad?"

"I wish I could have told her myself. Tell her that, please. Tell her when you see her how much I loved her. That I never stopped loving her," he said, obviously confused.

"Dad, Sally is dead. This is her funeral, remember?"

"Oh, I forget. I just wish I could have told her." He looked at me. "Was she happy? Did she have a good life? My sister said she was."

I wanted to tell him that my mother was a miserable woman who pretended on the outside to be happy and pleasant while being angry and irritable on the inside. I understood so much more about her now. But I could not tell him this.

"She had a good life, Randy. My dad loved her very much." That was not a lie. She had both those things.

"Oh, that makes me happy. We loved each other very much."

"Okay, Dad. You ready to head out?" Kalani interrupted before his words and discombobulation became uncomfortable.

He shook his head yes. "You have her eyes. You have her beautiful blue eyes."

I smiled at him. "You are right, Randy. I do have her eyes. I think they were her greatest gift to me." It was all I could think of; her love was not. But I understood better now why that was not the case. She let herself love so deeply once before that it destroyed all further ability to love deeply ever again. Randy had been a blessing and a curse in the life of Sally Northridge.

Randy and Kalani said their goodbyes. I walked slowly to my car, processing what had just happened. I wished I would have known my mother better. I wished she would have let me in. I found myself with so many more questions about her and her life. But they would be buried with her. I did feel a sense of closure, though, in learning of her past with Randy.

The rest of the afternoon was a blur as the condolences played out on repeat. I found myself looking at her friends differently, wondering how many of them knew her story. Most of them seemed as cold on the surface as she did. I could not imagine them having intimate, meaningful conversations about their lives, let alone life altering events that changed their lives forever.

My dad seemed at ease throughout the day. I would look at him and see a weight had been lifted. I wondered if it was because I now knew their stories. He had no more secrets to keep hidden within to appease Mom. He stood confidently with Max and Maya, enjoying their company.

With Max living and working in New York City, and Maya finishing her senior year of college in Miami, there was little opportunity for them to catch up with him. He did not understand technology enough to text or email. And using the phone was an obsolete art for them. I cherished my calls with my children, but they were less frequent, generally when they were in crisis for some reason or another. But the texts were daily and that allowed me to feel connected. It was a simple way to feel like I was still part of their lives.

Mark was the loyal supporter. He stood by my side and that of my brother, Jason, as the day progressed. Jason was three years older than I was, although he had married years after I did and was still in the throes of the teenage years with his two children. Jason's wife, Cali, chose not to fly out from California and that was fine by all of us. She used the excuse that it would disturb their children's academics and they couldn't afford to have that happen given the critical time in their education. Mark and I both rolled our eyes when Jason shared that with us.

Cali was not a house favorite. When she was present, Jason was guarded and cold. He did not laugh or smile like when we were younger. She seemed to have a hold on him. But when she wasn't there, the old, fun Jason would make himself known. It was in those rare moments I realized how much I missed my brother. Today, however, it made me feel a little sad that maybe he too wasn't in the best place in his marriage.

We had a brief moment together in the kitchen when I finally talked with him alone.

"Everything good?" I asked.

"Yea, great. Considering. Why?"

"We haven't had a chance to talk since Mom died. It all happened so fast. Just making sure you're good."

"I am." He paused. "Is it horrible if I admit to being a little relieved?" I knew he meant about our mom, but there was this part of me that wanted to ask if he was relieved Cali wasn't here with him.

"About Mom?" I bit my tongue and asked.

"Of course about Mom. What else?" He looked at me knowing that Cali was a topic we did not discuss because it never went well. "Never mind."

"No, Jason. It's not bad. I have been feeling the same thing the whole time." I poured us both a fresh cup of coffee and wondered how much about our parents past he knew. "Did you know about her first love? Or Dad's for that matter?"

"They were each other's first loves. What are you talking about?" With that, I gave him the Cliff notes edition of what Dad had shared with me.

"That kind of does explain a lot why Mom was always so cold and distant growing up." I nodded in agreement. I wondered if he recognized that Cali was similar to Mom. I looked at him closely.

"You happy in your life, Jason?"

"Of course I am. Why?"

"I don't know. I see the old you, the happy you. The fun you. When Cali's with you, you aren't that person."

"Jesus, Jenn, why do you hate her so much?"

And it dawned on me in that moment. "Because she reminds me of Mom. And I don't want that for you."

"She is nothing like Mom. And you're one to talk. You've

hardly said two words to Mark the whole time we've been here. You're fluttering around, talking to everyone, smiling, laughing with Max and Maya, but when you're near Mark, it's as if he doesn't exist."

Had I been that obvious? Had I been passive-aggressively acting out what my brain was trying to figure out? And I wondered if Max and Maya saw it. Did Mark see it? I wanted to say he was probably clueless, but I had felt him reach out to me, and I let myself pull away as if distracted by something else. I did not want to start seeing sides of him that I hadn't seen in a long time, the side that could show he cared about my feelings.

"It's complicated," I said. "I'm trying to figure things out."

"Okay, figure it out. But don't use my wife as a scapegoat for your own marriage." He started to walk out of the kitchen, paused, and turned around. "By the way, you'll never guess who I ran into today?"

"Who?" I said still feeling the sting from his last words.

"Tripp. Remember him?" My heart skipped a beat at the mention of that name. I had not heard Tripp's name since his father died shortly after I graduated from college. "He asked about you."

"Tripp? Wow. I haven't heard his name in forever."

"Yea. It was kind of weird. He was always a good guy, though. Not sure why we didn't stay in touch."

"Life, I suppose. We all went our own directions." I found myself trying to remember Tripp again. "Where did you see him?"

Tripp was in town to move his mother to an assisted living facility. She had Alzheimer's. Now that I thought about it, it would explain why she wasn't at the funeral today. I knew his sister had moved to Europe right after college. She married some wealthy Eastern European who made a fortune when the Eastern bloc crumbled, and built a life for herself there.

That much I knew from my mother. The only information she ever bothered to share about Tripp was that his family was not happy with his life choices. Mom would just laugh and say, "Better their family has a black sheep than ours."

"What does that even mean, Mom?" I remember asking her.

It made me curious, but never enough to make me want to know what she meant by that. I was living my own life, happy working, enjoying new relationships, discovering who I wanted to be. And realizing now, how lost I have become, how far I have deviated from where I started so long ago. The map that had charted my path was suddenly not giving me directions anymore. I was lost. And I needed to find my way back on that road to somewhere.

"I told him about today, but he was heading back home when I bumped into him. He sends his condolences."

I suddenly found myself remembering, wishing I had run into him instead of Jason. It had been decades. I wondered what he looked like. Was he married? Where did he live? Did he have a family? Was he fat? Was he bald? Why did he ask about me? So many questions. And it was as if Jason could read me.

"He looked good. Happy. Lives in Florida somewhere." He paused. "I told him you were good too."

"That's nice." It was all I had. And then I remembered the diaries I had tucked away in my bag to take back home. I found myself wanting to remember again. There were parts of Tripp that hadn't totally left me. But there were so many parts of Tripp I had forgotten. I would wonder on occasion what happened to him. I would Google him sometimes out of curiosity. He was not all over the internet and, from what I could tell, did not use social media. I adopted it years ago to stay connected with old friends and to keep tabs on the kids. But Tripp seemed to have evaded that. But, then again, I did not try very hard to unlock the mystery of his existence. It was more a curiosity than a need to know.

4

On Crickets and Conversations

Jason, Mark, Maya, Max, and I would spend the rest of the weekend with Dad. We organized, purged, laughed, cried, and found a way to remember Mom more for her good qualities than the ones we resented for so long. In the overall scheme of life, she had made it a good life for all of us. I could see why Dad stayed, why he found a way to love her, but also why he needed his own vices. When we packed our things to go our opposite directions, Dad stood in the driveway next to Carol. He did not look defeated. He looked refreshed. He looked like a man who wanted to keep on living. He did not have an expiration date stamped across his heart. He would live his life. And he would be happy doing it.

I gave him a long hug and he whispered in my ear, "Be happy, Jenn. Be true to you. I am so proud of the woman you are. So proud of your family. I just want you to be happy."

"Thanks, Dad. I know. I'm good."

He pulled back. "You don't think I see things. But I do. He's a good man, Jenn. But follow your heart."

I looked at him for a long moment. "I will, Dad. I love you."

Mark and I left Dad to finally make our way back home. I was flooded with the realization that the conversation I was going to have two weeks ago was going to have to take place now. And I wasn't sure how I was supposed to tackle it. Time changes things. Or maybe time makes us see things differently.

The confidence I felt to leave was suddenly beginning to play games with my head. I questioned my reasoning. I wondered if I was just having a bad day. If I stepped back outside of myself and looked in, would I actually see a marriage that I could stay in? Could I somehow fill that hole in my heart with him? All I saw when I asked myself those questions was empty. I rationalized that there had been more good than bad. What if I just took away expectations? If I did that, would everything suddenly be fine?

I was lost in my thoughts when I heard Mark in an unfamiliar, confrontative tone blurt out, "What's going on with you?"

"What do you mean?" His eyes never moved. They just kept looking forward. I wanted to say, "Ha, you can't even look at me to ask me this?" But I did not.

"You are obviously pissed off about something. What did I do?"

"You didn't do anything."

"Bullshit. You've been avoiding me. Hardly saying two words to me all weekend. Short with me. Doesn't matter what I say or do, your reaction is the same."

Mark was more perceptive than I thought. And, quite honestly, I thought I had done a better job of concealing what I was feeling. I took a deep breath.

"I think we need a break from each other."

"What does that even mean?"

"I think we need to separate." His jaw clenched. It was like I had just blindsided him with a sharp left hook. "You can't tell me you don't sense all this between us?"

"No, Jenn. I don't." He just shook his head. He was silent for a long moment then took a breath. "Where did this come from?"

"God, Mark, from years of us just coming and going, living two separate lives. Pretending to like each other as more than the parents of our children."

"Jesus, that's because that's what we were doing all those years."

"No, Mark. I still existed. I still wanted to be seen. But you have never seen me."

"That's not true." He was in denial. Or just did not see it.

"Mark, you have never seen me for who I am. You have no interest in me as a person. I am so much more than just the mother of your children."

"What does that even mean? Of course you are. I see you."

I wanted to ask why he fell in love with me all those years ago. What was it about me that he liked? When I asked those questions over the years, he would laugh it off and say it was a silly question. It hurt then when he did it. And it hurt now that he did not understand it. Maybe I should have demanded he give me an answer. Today, though, I was not going to be complicit in what happened. I was telling him what I needed to start the process of ending. It was going to be painful. It was going to hurt. I had no doubt I would question what I was do-ing. I already was doing that. It shook me to the core to say those words to him. Could he truly have been that unaware of the state of our marriage? I supposed his obligations at work kept him occupied enough to not allow the trivial moments when I got angry or annoyed with his inaction or his inability to compliment me—even sometimes, even just a little—to be-come an issue.

When I did not offer an immediate response, all he gave me back was, "Fine. If that's what you want."

"I don't know what I want, Mark. I need to figure that out. I think we both deserve to be happy. And I need to figure out if that's us together or apart."

"Whatever." He was done talking. He turned up the radio like it would tune me out. Maybe he hoped I would somehow get lost in the words as they bellowed from the speakers. My mind was spinning. I had done it. I had started the conversation. I had let him know I had doubts about us and our future together.

The car ride home felt endless. The silence was excruciating. I could tell he was angry. Silence was his greatest form of retaliation. The impact of that left hook still reverberating. I wondered how he did not see it coming. How was he so blind to the cold and distance between us? There were so many signs. The words "I love you" rarely spoken anymore. When, then more as a conditioned response than genuinely meaning those words. Conversations were curt. There was little laughter anymore. God, I missed laughing. I missed feeling his touch, any touch, really. I could have sought it out. He knew I needed it and liked it, but he left the box unchecked time and time again. On occasion, a forced hug. And sex he knew I loved, needed, desired. It had become sporadic, mechanical, and always the same. It was routine just like everything else in our lives. How did all those signs get lost on him?

We pulled into the garage without a word. He grabbed his bag from the back and went straight to his study. Normally, he would have taken my bag in too. But he left it for me. I carried it upstairs, feeling the weight of our marriage on my shoulders. I felt guilt and sadness set in. I am not sure how I could have said it any differently. I never intended to hurt him like that. And I told him as much. I wanted to cry. But I couldn't. I could feel part of me coming back to the surface after having released that heavy weight from my chest.

I had been gone two weeks. I had so much to unpack and

sort through. I sat next to my bags not wanting to tackle the task at hand. It had been an exhausting time and the silent drive home nearly unbearable. I was about to abandon the task until I remembered the diaries. I needed a distraction right now. I dug through my overnight bag and found the one from my senior year. That was such a defining year for me. It was about college decisions. If I didn't get into an Ivy as was pretty much mandated by my family history, where would I go? It had to be East coast. It had to be pretentious. My parents were not keen on backup plan conversations. They just figured legacy would provide for me well. And they were right. Once Harvard said no and Yale yes, it was much less about that than just muddling through the last few months of high school. I was a good kid. I did not find trouble and trouble did not find me. My parents and I both knew as much.

I opened the diary and started skimming the pages. There were funny entries about sneaking Boones Farm into the movie theater only to lose control of the bottle and hear it clanking as it rolled down to the front movie screen. We laughed so hard I'm sure we peed our pants. We ran out before the usher could catch us. I wrote about following boys at the mall who pretended to ignore us. I talked about kissing Mikey Nichols at a bonfire. He was dreamy but so dumb. So many little moments I did not recall. But reading about them made me remember, and I smiled thinking back on those times.

Then there was graduation and all the freedom that represented. I had an entire summer to play and have fun on the Cape before setting off for college. I was so excited to get to read books and listen to music all day long. Jason would be home from college for most of it. Instead of doing an internship that summer, he told my parents he planned to lifeguard and "chill." That got a chilly reception and Dad promptly found him a part-time internship at a boutique brokerage house not far from our summer home. I forgot about that too.

Jason did not become a stockbroker. He was too smart for that. After chasing his college sweetheart to California and quickly realizing she was not worth the required effort, he landed a job on the ground floor of a tech start up in Silicon Valley. Jason was smart like that. I loved that he willingly defied convention and life's prescriptions. Unlike me, Jason did get into Harvard. And with that was quickly my grandfather's favorite grandchild.

The walk down memory lane had taken my mind off my current situation. I thought about putting it away and coming back to it later, but then I turned the page and there he was: Tripp. All the details from that summer poured out on those pages.

It all began with four simple words: "I met a boy." I followed that with: "No, I met a man." How perceptive I was to see the difference right off the bat. I wanted to keep reading now. I wanted to remember Tripp like I lived Tripp in those moments when I was seventeen. I turned a few more pages to discover a picture of him taped to the page and his name written in bubble letters with hearts. He had become buried in my mind, hidden deep in my memory bank. I was not sure I had ever planned to remember him the way I wrote about him. But life didn't always go according to plan. I never planned to want to leave Mark so that I might know some other version of happiness—if there was such a thing.

I had to take a break, though. It was getting dark out and I needed to consider making dinner. Or ordering it at least. Then I heard the door slam shut. I looked out the window to see Mark driving off. A few seconds later my phone pinged. It was Mark. "I won't be home for dinner." That was all. I suppose I did not expect an explanation. He was upset.

I left my things unpacked. I would get to it eventually. My usual need for order put by the wayside as I felt the pull of my diary to keep reading. I grabbed it and walked downstairs. I opened a bottle of my favorite pinot noir and poured myself a tall glass. I foraged through the refrigerator in hopes of finding something I could call dinner. I did not have much of an appetite tonight. My stomach was in knots. There was a block of cheddar in the refrigerator and some crackers in the pantry that hadn't been opened yet. That would be my dinner. I sliced the cheddar and opened the crackers. They were satisfying with my glass of pinot. I sat down at the kitchen counter, grabbed the diary, and opened to where I had left off.

5

On Seventeen and First Love

Summers in the Cape were always magical. We left life in the city and headed to the coast. We were lucky that my grandparents invested early and built their dream summer home on the waters where the haves would play and everyone else would wish they were us. Even today, that hasn't changed. My parents would eventually move to the Cape full time when Dad retired. It had always been their dream to move away from the fast-paced, hustle and bustle that was city life. I liked the yin-yang of that existence. I loved that my own children were able to spend time playing on the same beaches I did. It was close enough to our home in Greenwich to allow for frequent retreats in the warm summer months. It was something I never tired of, and my children seemed to relish that time as well.

And there was no summer like the one after my senior year. The last great hurrah before college. It was the summer of Tripp. The one when I realized Tripp was no longer a boy but a man who had somehow gone unnoticed by me. In fairness, though, Tripp had not been to the Cape for many summers. He had been working for his dad in the summers he went to college. This summer, though, he was headed into his senior year and knew it was his last chance to play before the adult world called.

The first time I saw him sitting on the beach with Jason, I did not recognize him. I watched him from the deck as he and my brother seemed to be catching up on their lives. They were the same age, had been friends for an eternity, but had not seen each other since they graduated high school. I headed down to the water hoping Jason would introduce me to his friend. When I got to them, I was so struck by the magnificence of the man he was talking to. I had no idea who he was. He did not look familiar. I could feel my face flush when my brother said, "Jenn, you remember Tripp?"

Tripp just smiled and said, "Hey, Jenn. You grew up."

I did not know what to say. He took my breath away. And my words. I had none. My mind raced to come up with something clever or cute. But I was at a loss for words; no clue what I was supposed to say.

The best I managed was a simple, "Hey." And then I put my head down and beat myself up the entire way down to the water. All I could think walking away was when did Tripp Porter become such a man?

I could not get down to the ocean fast enough. I didn't care if the water was still a little cold. My face was burning. I could not get over how beautiful that man was. And that he was gangly, dorky Tripp. I took my shorts and T-shirt off, wanting to put them on my towel, but I had absentmindedly left it by Jason and Tripp. Crap. I couldn't go back now as I looked back to see if maybe they had gone. They had not, and that's when I saw Tripp watching me over my brother's shoulder. He smirked. I melted, turned towards the ocean, and did my best to nonchalantly enter the water, hoping I wouldn't trip getting in, but feeling this strange sense of joy: he had been watching me.

I stayed in the water a long time after that. I was afraid to turn around and see if he was still there. There was this part of me that wanted him to be and the other part that was too afraid that he might be. I wouldn't know what to say to him if he started talking to me. And I certainly couldn't start a conversation with him. Jason would no doubt be a jerk about it, find a way to tease me. My mind was going crazy. I played out conversations in my head. And then I would reel it in with the reminder that he was three years older than me, already in college, and that he would never be interested in the girl who just graduated from high school.

Eventually, I began to shiver and decided it was time to go in. I turned around and did not see him. I felt a tinge of disappointment while simultaneously feeling relief. I left the water, looking down while adjusting my suit. There was nothing worse than discovering half of your boob was hanging out the bottom of your top or that some of your pubic hair might be coming out the side of your high-rise bottoms. I loved that swimsuit: my neon green Body Glove bikini. I rocked that suit back then. It fit me perfect in all the right places. While I never felt like I was the prettiest girl, I was an athletic one and my body was fit and mature for my age, so I had been told.

Once I made sure everything was where it was supposed to be, I headed up the beach towards my clothes. I grabbed them from where I rashly dropped them earlier. I tried not to get them wet, wishing I had thought to bring my towel to the water with me. That's when I saw him: Tripp was walking towards the water with my towel.

"Here," he said, handing me the towel. "I thought you might need this."

I took it from him. "Thanks. You didn't need to." I wrapped it around me and continued to walk up the beach, trying to maintain some semblance of cool.

"I know. I wanted to." I smiled at him. "Actually, I wanted to see if maybe you'd want to hang out tonight?"

"I'm sure Jason would find that a little annoying having his little sister around."

"Not with Jason."

"Oh. I'm confused." I really was.

"I thought maybe you and I could just hang out. You like bonfires?" He was direct. I liked that. Most boys my age didn't know the first thing about talking to girls let alone directly asking one out.

"Yes." I kept my answer succinct. I didn't want him to read into my confusion as to why he was asking me, Jason's little sister, to a bonfire.

"Then a bonfire it is. I'll come by and get you around eight." He was so self-assured.

"But Jason."

"Jason won't be an issue. Jessica's here." Turns out Jason would be seeing Jessica Miller, his perpetual summer fling. Theirs was truly just a summer thing every single summer since junior year of high school. He never talked about her after the summer ended. They were familiar and enjoyed each other's company, at least sexually. Jason would not tell me that's what they did. But he glowed when he saw her. I imagine I was glowing just about now with the realization that Tripp had just asked me to go to a bonfire with him. He walked me to the back door of my house, touched my arm and said, "I'll see you at eight."

I smiled and tried to act calm. "Sounds good." He walked away. I walked inside and closed the door behind me, careful not to let anyone hear my squeal of joy as I lost all ability to contain myself anymore.

I remember running upstairs and grabbing my diary. I needed to tell someone. This strange sensation had taken over me. There was something about Tripp. And I would write those words:

I met a boy. I mean I met a man. What a man. He took my breath away. And my words. I had none. Not a clue what I was supposed to say to him. That does not happen to me ever. But he asked me to a bonfire. I won't question why me? I won't wonder why he decided to ask me. I will just hope that he has seen that I am not a little girl anymore. Just like he is not a boy anymore either.

That first night with Tripp was perfect. We talked like we had known each other forever. His ability to have conversation was refreshing compared to boys my age. He was easy to talk to, and we laughed about silly things we remembered about summers on the Cape. We liked the same music. I had no inhibitions around him. The time with him flew as would that entire summer.

At just before midnight on that first night in June, Tripp would kiss me for the first time. It started slow and burned from there. And then he stopped. He looked at me. "You sure aren't that little girl anymore, Jenn." He definitely was not the boy I remembered either. He walked me to the door, gave me another kiss. This one more deliberate, and I could feel my feet lift from the ground below me. No one had ever kissed me like that before.

"See you tomorrow." He turned to leave and followed it up with, "At the beach. If you want."

My brilliant response, "Okay."

I was giddy when I walked in the door. Until I saw Jason standing there, clearly pissed. "What the hell, Jenn? Tripp? Really?"

"What's wrong with Tripp?"

"For one thing, he's three years older than you. And for another, he's one of my best friends."

"You haven't seen him for years so, no, he's not. And three years isn't anything these days."

"You do know his reputation, right?"

"How would you know his reputation?"

"People talk. Guys talk. Girls talk."

"Well, I don't. And I haven't heard anyone talk about

Tripp. Ever."

"It's because you're just a kid. They don't talk around you."

I was irritated. He was trying to burst my bubble. "I'm sure you're just looking out for me, but I can take care of myself." And with that I walked up to my room and closed the door, wanting to feel Tripp's kisses all over again. It was a beautiful night. And the beginning of the summer of my first love.

Tripp and I quickly became inseparable. We spent the days together on the beach and our evenings at bonfires or walking along the strand. We never struggled with things to say. It never felt like there were awkward pauses. It flowed with us. There was nothing we couldn't discuss in depth. He said I was smarter than most college girls he knew. He liked that I wasn't boring or too into myself, and that I wasn't intimidated by topics. Everything between us came with such ease.

Over the course of that summer, Tripp would be my first. Maybe not my first kiss. I had had those. Maybe not the first time someone had touched me in intimate places. But he would be my world of discovery. He would teach me how to love and how to be loved. I didn't question his experience. I devoured what he taught me.

I had always imagined that Tripp would want to have sex as soon as I would let him. I knew I was desperate to know what it was like. And for a man, not boy, like Tripp to show me was beyond my wildest imagination. But instead of going fast with me, pushing me to have sex with him, it was me doing the asking. I longed for his touch. And he would tease me. Tell me I needed to be patient. That he wanted my first time to be perfect. He was building the anticipation.

I had no expectations or romantic notions about the first time I had sex. Before Tripp, I had just wanted to get it over with, to know what it was like, to say that I did. My friends were starting to have sex. It was pretty much all we talked about. To actually lose my virginity to Tripp took a totally different meaning, though. There were times when I would find myself in disbelief that Tripp would want me. But he did. And I let him, falling hard, fast, and deliberate in those moments.

He was methodical, almost calculated in how he pursued me sexually. One night he might be kissing me passionately, stopping before moving his lips down my neck, then kissing along my bra line or the inside of my thighs just inside my short seams, gently moving his fingers along the edges to expose my skin enough for him to explore. I would burn inside. He was building the moment for me.

Then there was the night when it finally happened. We were kissing on the sand. He had unsnapped my bra and his hands found their way to my breasts. I remember him slowly lifting my shirt to expose them, stopping to take them in, loving them with his eyes. He would begin kissing them, licking them, sucking on them, and then occasionally playfully nibbling at them. My body was in overdrive. He was in control, and I was the passenger begging him to run the light and drive faster. He did just that. His fingers undid the button on my shorts, easily moved the zipper down, and then his fingers slowly made their way inside my underwear, where he toyed with me gently. Without me saying a word, he looked at me, playing with me, smirking, and adding, "Not yet, Jenn."

Then he moved his hand, rolled over on top of me, kissed me with such passion, and began moving his hips as if he were inside me. I could feel his hardness as he moved up and down.

"I want you to know this is what it will be like, me on top of you, us moving together." He stopped.

"Don't stop," I said.

"I want you so bad, Jenn."

"Then don't stop. Let me feel you, Tripp."

"Not here. Not on the beach."

"Yes, here. I need you," I begged. I was dying to be one

with him. It was dark. No one was around.

"You sure?" he asked.

"I've never been surer of anything." And then he took my shorts off, made me tremble as he went down on me, doing things I didn't know could be done. He unbuttoned his shorts, exposing himself, and gently moved inside of me. I gasped, but not in pain. It was slow and easy. I watched him as he waited for my reaction. "Don't stop," I said. He didn't. It would not last long and he would apologize. In that moment, I did not know why or what for.

I would learn that summer that Tripp was a beautiful, passionate lover. He was consumed by me. Me, of all people. I loved learning how to have sex and all its nuances with Tripp. There was nothing I was afraid to try if he asked. He was addicting.

Long after we would be together, I would replay those magical moments, only to have them erased and replaced with the next time we were together. Sometimes I just wanted to scream out in ecstasy. How did he know how to touch me like he did? The places. The things. Oh my God, the things he did. I didn't know then that so much more could be done.

The reality was we evolve as lovers. There was a process of discovery during which you learned the things you liked, things that made you uncomfortable, and the things that made your body respond uncontrollably. It was the beauty of that summer. In those moments, we did not feel rushed to love each other. We could take our time not realizing that the clock was ticking and cruelly not in our favor. We knew every part of each other's bodies. It was a great exploration, a beautiful discovery, learning each other's triggers. You uncovered those things sometimes on purpose, sometimes on accident.

I can look back now and wonder why we didn't do this or do that. But then I realized I was so invested in those moments we did have, perfecting our movements, being in sync with him as we evolved as lovers that I would not have known all the things we had yet to do. In the end, though, Tripp would teach me what an unselfish lover was and how to please him. He would say I made him a better lover, too. Maybe because I was eager to please him, to be taught, to love him like he wanted me to love him. We were compatible sexually and intellectually. Being with him was beautiful in every sense of the word. Tripp would teach me at a young age to be in touch with my body, to listen to it, and know what it was capable of. (No doubt, a gift to the men in my future as well.)

We also had our music. Maybe that was what brought us together more than anything. We could sit in my room or his for hours listening to the newest music, discussing the lyrics, wondering what they really meant. Sometimes he would tell me a certain song could be our song. He liked to watch me dance. Music would make my feet move like magic. I was the most comfortable in my own skin when I was dancing. It was my happy place, my escape, whenever I needed to shut the world out.

We both loved alternative rock, the quick tempo, the upbeat rhythms, the perfect beat to dance to. But there were slow songs, too, and he would hold me tight as we moved to the music. We wouldn't talk about those songs. We would just live them by moving together, our hearts beating as one. I loved hearing his heart gently beating as my ear rested on his chest. Other times he would stop, take my face in his hands, stare intently in my eyes, and kiss me so intensely I knew there was no way we wouldn't find our way beneath the covers, risking being caught in those moments. He made everything so exciting. I look back now and think how lucky I was to have someone be so patient with me, so willing to teach me, to love me like Tripp did. Love like that should not be wasted on a seventeen-year-old. But it was.

Our summer together was not totally perfect. We had our

hiccups. We both had made commitments to be other places over the summer. I would spend two weeks in Europe with friends as a graduation gift. He would spend a week in the city visiting his friends on a couple of occasions. It felt like we were constantly counting down. Countdown to leave. Countdown until we'd be together again. It was sometimes weeks, sometimes days, and even sometimes hours. It was heartbreaking always counting. The anticipation of seeing him again was always overwhelming. But summer would wind down faster than either of us was ready for. The clock had run out and there would be no more countdowns. Time finally won out and stopped in our summer love story.

Our last night together, we would fall asleep on the beach in each other's arms after making love. It was different that night. Sad. Slow. Deliberate. Like maybe inside we knew it would be the last time. We woke the next morning to the orange hues of the sun rising.

I liked waking up next to him. I studied him. Hair in his face. Mouth slightly open. I kissed him. He smiled and pulled me in tight.

"I have to go. My parents are going to kill me."

"I don't want you to go." His words were sad and heavy.

I remember looking out over the water. "This is my favorite time of day."

"Mine too. And it's how I'll always hold on to you." He pulled out his camera and snapped a picture of us.

"We're not breaking up, Tripp. We're just going back to school."

"I know," he said. And he knew so much more than I did at that moment.

"I love you," I blurted out as the tears came rolling down my face. I got up and left. He came running after me, tears running down his face too. He held me for the last time. Kissed me with intention.

"God, I love you." And that was our goodbye.

I held it together long enough to run inside the house. I fell to the floor and began to sob inconsolably. I could barely breathe. I loved Tripp more than I thought humanly possible. For a moment, I wanted to forget about college, forget about my future, forget about my dreams, and just run away wherever he wanted me to go. Then there was the rational part of me that realized I had so many dreams, so many things I needed to do. If I didn't do those things, I would only resent Tripp—and myself—for choosing him. I pulled myself up off the floor, blew my nose, wiped my eyes, and walked upstairs to my room. I needed my diary. I needed to hear myself rationalize the pain away. In that moment, I could not though. I found myself sobbing more and soaking the pages of my diary to the point I could not even write in it.

I left for college that day with a very heavy heart. And for the first few weeks, I was missing him. But with every day, I found myself adjusting to college life. I made friends. I went to parties. I started to notice other boys. And I noticed other boys noticing me. I think Tripp had given me a sense of confidence in myself that I did not have before, that I didn't exude to the world. Now, in college, I felt like a confident woman. I knew what I wanted to do with my life and nothing or no one would stop me.

When I finally did sit down to write in my diary again, I wrote of the heartache of leaving him. I wrote of my fear of letting go. I never questioned he would continue loving me. I was confident he would. It was a crazy, emotional, incredibly erotic time for both of us. But I was quickly realizing that we were on different paths. I let myself be open to the college experience. I wanted to be free to live and explore, have fun, figure out who I was supposed to be without Tripp. It hurt, but I knew it was right. How insightful I was to ask this simple question as I wrote of breaking it off with Tripp:

At seventeen, am I really supposed to believe that a love could be forever? We both have dreams we need to turn into reality.

The romantic in me now wants to scream at that girl. She wants to say he was worth it. He loved you like no other. But the realist in me recognized that neither of us would be who we were if we had not lived our lives independent of each other. Those dreams would have been impossible, against all odds at that moment in our lives had we stayed together. We were meant to grow into the people we were to become independent of the other's influence.

I found myself wondering as I read my diary entries if we should never have loved each other. Time, distance, and reality were always one step away from engulfing us. But maybe knowing that time was not always in our favor, it fueled our desire to be together even more. It made the experience of loving each other so raw, primal, almost desperate. We needed each other that summer.

I was struck as I read the degree to which I found myself in love with him, how much I had forgotten, and how deeply I had buried the memory of Tripp. Why would I repress that? I knew the answer. It was simple: I was seventeen.

I was exhausted remembering. I somehow managed to finish the entire bottle of pinot. I suppose I was less surprised by that given I had been reading for hours. I was consumed by my words, unearthing those moments, trying to remember them as I lived them. They were beautiful moments, the magnitude of which I managed to bury deep in my psyche. I did not remember Tripp like I wrote about Tripp. But reading my words was like unlocking a vault to my mind's past. Why would I bury such a treasure?

I was too exhausted to even begin unraveling that mystery. It had been a long two weeks and an even longer day. It was ten at night and Mark still had not returned. I put my wine glass in the sink, grabbed my diary, turned out the lights, and headed upstairs for bed.

I could not hit my pillow fast enough. But instead of falling asleep, my head was spinning. I don't know if it was the wine, the realization I had announced I wanted to separate, or the onslaught of memories I had just rediscovered. I was alone in my big house. It felt empty and, at that moment, I realized what I was feeling: lost.

6

On Bumps in the Night

I heard Mark come home around midnight. He did not come to our room. I saw the light switch on in Max's old room, now our guest room. He sounded drunk. And that was confirmed when there was a large thud as he hit his toe against the bed. "Shit," I heard him say. Mark did not cuss. I did. Cussing was an art form to me. The f-word was a perfect modifier for most anything. It was rare to hear Mark use profanity. If he did, he had either been drinking or something didn't go his way when he expected it should. Tonight likely involved both those things.

After a few more minutes of him banging around in an unfamiliar room, he shut the door and turned out the light. I will not pretend that it didn't hurt a little to have him sleep in the other room, for him to make no effort to see me. We have gone to bed many nights without one or the other saying anything. It was usually not a result of one of us being overly upset. We just tended to have different sleep schedules. Even if we had sex at night, I would usually stay in bed, falling asleep, while he would get up and go back about his business. There was no cuddling. We did not have intimate conversations. We did not discuss our wants and desires anymore. I don't even recall a time when we really did that anyway. Strange when I think about that now. Were we always too busy that sex was just about the satisfaction and less about the emotional connection? I suppose that was a function of all those years hurrying so we wouldn't be caught, which ultimately led to a sex life of quickly satisfying the other person and then getting on with it.

The depth of love and affection left then too. There were no "I love yous" or compliments. I love you was an afterthought as we were running out the door.

Would a fly on the wall be laughing at our love life all these years? Or would that fly be wagging its finger at me saying "Girlfriend, it's about time you saw the signs"? I would tell that fly I wasn't blind, but that my vision was blurred by the chaos in my life that put me second. I wanted to be first. I was determined to do this for me. Would that fly cheer my decision or suddenly accuse me of being selfish? I wanted to swat that fly and make it disappear.

I did not expect Mark to come home, drunk or otherwise, march into our room and declare that he loved me so much he couldn't bear the thought of losing me. That would have been a totally different man had he done that. It would have been nice to think that maybe reality would have hit him hard enough to realize that was the case. But it was not how Mark functions. And it was not how we have functioned as a couple. We might function, this much is true. There were many things we have done well together. We were great parents together. But a couple? Together as one? United on all fronts? We were more yin and yang; hot and cold; yes then no.

There have been so many times looking back over the course of my marriage that I questioned my purpose in it. But the years got away from me. The career, the graduate degree, the endless events surrounding raising children that took over as soon as I walked away from my career. The career, the one thing up until that point which had defined me. The career suddenly replaced by a new role as a full-time mom. I embraced that role and never thought it would ever come to an end. Over the years, as the kids were home less, then mostly gone, the silence surrounding me was sometimes deafening. The voices in my head I had suppressed came to the forefront, taunting me to reassess, to evaluate, to question, to face what I had been trying to avoid for as long as possible.

Every year the realization grew that I had been avoiding the inevitable. My safe and comfortable marriage was not bringing me joy. I had given up parts of myself to play the part of housewife and mom. I still cringed when I thought of myself as a housewife or homemaker. Those terms were so seemingly outdated. I had a nice home, but I was not a good cook, at least I did not enjoy it. I did the minimal to keep my house clean. Mark always said I should hire a house cleaner, but I felt guilty doing that when I knew I could just as easily get it done even if I didn't like it. I did not want to be labeled one of those typical Greenwich housewives who hung out at the country club and started drinking at noon.

I did not entirely miss the old me. I had played hard for years enjoying longer-term relationships, playing around in between, living maybe a little more dangerously than what would give me comfort in a long-term relationship, the one I would want to raise a family with. I know there was nothing wrong with safe and simple. It was the right decision for so many years. The old me, the one who liked playing a little on the edge, who was open to adventure in every way possible, quickly got lost, buried, forgotten, in all the newness marriage and motherhood presented me.

The suppressed voices in my head had no more reasons to be silenced. I tried hard not to listen at first. I did not want to destroy my idyllic life, the one that looked so perfect on paper. I did not want to be judged and outcast by my own community. I laughed at that, too. A community, like most communities, where half the couples got divorced, plenty had affairs, and the odds of success were almost as good as winning the lottery.

When I made the decision to tell Mark I wanted to separate what felt like months ago, instead of two weeks, I had carefully laid out all the pros and cons in my head. I was confident it was the right decision to make. Meg and I talked in great detail about the implications. She was a supportive friend. She did not judge me, but she knew me well enough to give it to me straight.

Meg had always been my person over the years. She served as a reality check when my vision was blurred, or my blood alcohol level high. I felt she was the only one I could share my thoughts and emotions with and my struggles to make the decision. Her answer to me was always she wanted me to be happy and good with myself. That one always hurt because I never thought I wasn't good with myself.

"You deserve to be loved, to feel loved," she would say.

My argument that I had always known Mark loved me enough was seen as sad resignation by her.

"No one should ever feel like they're only worth loving just enough."

"I don't think he knows how to do anything more." I defended his position.

"You've told him over the years that he sometimes needs to give more emotionally."

"He has tried," I blurted out, realizing I was once again defending him.

"A day or two is not trying. He can't keep it up. It doesn't make him a bad person. It just doesn't mean he's the right person for you for the rest of your life."

I knew it was sometimes easier looking from the outside in. She knew me better than I knew myself at times.

"You could always try counseling." I rolled my eyes. I was not a huge fan of airing my dirty laundry to a complete stranger who has learned to say, "I understand" and "Thank you for sharing. I know that must have been painful" ad infinitum.

"I know you don't like parts of it. But if it gets Mark to open up and see what an amazing woman you are, then maybe it's worth it. I just want you to be happy."

"I know. And I want to be happy. I will be the bad guy. I already know that."

"The only person that says that is you."

"I hate it when you're right," I conceded.

"It's why you love me."

"Fuck you." We both laughed. I knew she was right.

I woke up the next morning to the sound of running water. Mark had made his way to the shower. I felt a knot in my stomach. I wondered if I should get up and head downstairs or wait in bed for him to emerge. My inner fight or flight response wanted me to get up quickly, but I was not the one running away; he was. I got up, brushed my teeth and hair, and had started to get dressed when he opened the door. I startled him.

"Sorry. I didn't mean to wake you," he said in a monotone voice.

"I need to get up. I didn't get anything done last night," I said.

He stood there in his towel. I thought for a moment he still looked good without his clothes on. He was a sexy man in his own way. Maybe I should have told him that more. I think I shut off the compliments to him because I wasn't getting any. I know life does not always have to be a two-way street and I could have kept on giving, but at some point, it becomes exhausting to be the only one to acknowledge the other's existence.

Somewhere over the course of the years, me telling him I

loved his body or the feel of my fingers running through his hair dissipated. Compliments no longer existed for either of us unless they were solicited. And even that was exhausting. I showered all my compliments on my children. And I watched them turn into adults who easily gave compliments to others and openly showed their affection with girlfriends and boyfriends over the years. I made it a point to remind Max to always let girls know how he felt and to compliment them. As for Maya, I wanted her to know a man needs to see her for who she is and acknowledge her for that.

"A man should make you feel like you're the most beautiful person in the room, if not the world," I told her.

"Eww. You don't think that's a little cliché?" she would ask me back.

"No. I think the man you're with needs to love you like you are the only person in his world."

"Does Dad make you feel that way?" she asked me once when she started dating her last boyfriend. I did not answer right away. And then I was honest with her.

"No. But I knew what I was marrying when I married him. It doesn't mean you shouldn't have more than I did."

"It's funny you say that, Mom. I've always thought you deserve for him to show you he loves you so much more than he does." I held back tears when she said those words.

"You are a perceptive child, aren't you, Maya?"

"No. I just think you're a really cool person and you have so much love in you. With me and Max gone, I always wonder where the love goes?"

"It doesn't. You guys still need me. And I'm lucky I get to love you two." I ended that conversation there. It was not easy to hear your teenage daughter recognize what you have desperately been trying to avoid acknowledging over the years.

Mark moved past me in the bathroom. He could not even make eye contact with me.

"So you're just going to act like nothing happened?" I asked.

He continued to get dressed. "No. I just don't know what to say."

"You don't need to say anything. But at some point, we need to address the elephant in the room."

"Fine. You want to separate, then leave. But I'm not going anywhere."

"Wow. So, no conversation? You're just going to give up?"

"I don't want to lose you, Jenn. But I feel like I don't even stand a chance, like you've already decided. Do I even have a shot?"

I was dumbfounded when I realized Mark never saw this coming.

"I don't understand how you think things are fine."

"What do you mean? You have never complained."

"Oh my God, Mark. Did you hear what you just said? I have asked for so much from you over the years. And you just tell me you won't change or be a different person. I was always the one giving to make things work."

"That's bullshit."

"No, that's how you see it. Because you don't ever want to think that something could be wrong."

"Fine." He threw his towel in the hamper and started to walk out of the room. "So, you're just going to go? Do what you need to do. I don't even know what to say."

"I don't know. I'm trying to figure this all out. I'd like to talk about it. And the reality is we have things we have to do together. It makes it hard for me to just leave, right?" I paused. "Maybe what I'm saying is we should try counseling." We had been married for twenty-five years. Inside, I knew I owed it to the marriage to try. I honestly believed I knew the answer, but I started to realize I would have a hard time reconciling my decision to leave if I didn't know I tried to do everything I could to make it work.

"You hate counseling." He was right.

"But I'm willing to try. I don't want you to think I'm just going to throw it all away."

He shook his head at me.

"What?" I asked.

"Doesn't counseling just mean you've reached the end and it's over? If you have to ask someone else to tell you about your marriage, that there isn't hope anyways?"

"I don't know what the success rate is on that. But I'm telling you I'm willing to try."

"Whatever."

In my best sarcastic tone, I told him, "I'm glad you think I'm worth fighting for after all."

He shook his head and walked out of the room. I suppose it could have been worse. Or it could have been different. He could have decided I wasn't worth the effort at all. I was so confident I wanted to be out of this marriage. That I acquiesced to counseling was a great capitulation on my part.

I got dressed and went downstairs. I made myself a cup of coffee and sat down at the table with Mark. He did not look up from his tablet as he read the news. He was tense and uncomfortable with me there.

"I'll start looking for a therapist," I offered. He didn't say anything, but I could tell he was processing.

"What is it exactly you need me to be that I haven't been?" he said after a few long moments of silence.

"I need you to see me."

"That again."

"Seriously, Mark. You never give me a compliment. You

never talk to me about things I might be interested in. I know you told me you would never change who you are for anyone, but some of the trivial things should be worth it if I am."

"I swear you want to live in this fairy-tale world where husbands tell their wives they're beautiful every day and kiss them good morning and good night."

"First of all, I can count on one hand the number of times you have ever said I was beautiful."

"That's not true."

"It is. And you know it. But I knew that when I married you. It still doesn't make it hurt any less. I know I have always been confident enough in my own skin. But, of all the people in the world I want to see me as beautiful, it's you." I felt myself holding back my tears, struggling to finish my thought. "And you're the one person who doesn't. Even if I was the ugliest person in the world, I would expect you to still see me as beautiful."

"I do. I have always thought that of you."

"I know you think I want to live in this fairy-tale world, but there is nothing wrong with wanting Prince Charming. Even a little bit."

"But now I can't even say anything because you'll think it's forced."

"Right."

"So I can't win."

"Yup."

"Well, then what's the point of all this if I am in a hole so deep I won't be able to come out?"

"The point is, you try. If I'm worth it to you." I stopped, waiting for him to say something more, but he didn't. "Do you even know why you fell in love with me in the first place? I've asked you before, but you never answer. You just laugh it off like I should know the answer." He said nothing. "I've always known the things about you I fell in love with."

"Like?"

"Like your humility. I loved how there was nothing you couldn't do and how easy you made things look. You're passionate about things you like to do, like running and law. You have always been a genuinely nice person. I thought you were sexy." I added that with a smile, but it did nothing for him.

He got up from the table. As was typical Mark, he decided when he was done talking.

"I really don't get it, Jenn. All of a sudden. But I'll do whatever you say."

With that, he left the kitchen, and I was left sitting there with a cold cup of coffee, feeling more frustrated than when the conversation started, realizing I was negotiating with a cement wall. He was acting defeated but also telling me he'd do whatever it took for me. I wondered what that looked like to him. And, more importantly, how long that would even last.

7

On Playing Hide and Seek

Mark spent the morning in his office catching up on his clients from the few days he had spent at Mom's funeral. I spent the morning buying groceries and running a few errands. I unpacked my suitcase. I started to do Mark's as well, but decided he could do it himself. One of those things he took for granted, I reminded myself. He was a grown man after all.

I had the diary by my bedside. It was hard for me to distract myself from wanting to read what I had written, especially about Tripp. But I needed to be in a better frame of mind. Reminiscing, remembering that time was beautiful. My stomach was in knots from my morning interaction with Mark. I was both livid and dumbfounded by his reaction. He was such a brilliant man, but so out of touch with his feelings—and mine.

I decided to go for a run. There was nothing better to clear my head than a few miles in the fresh air, breathing deep, feeling my muscles burn, disconnecting from my life. I put in my headphones, hit play on my phone, picking a playlist that was my happy go to. Music was still that thing I could turn to when I just needed to let go.

Five miles later, I was back home. Mark's car was gone. I checked my phone for messages, but there were none. I was not going to dwell on it. I was actually hoping he'd be gone for a while so I could be in my big, quiet house in peace without worry or consideration that I might say or do something that would set Mark off.

I showered, threw on my favorite sweats, grabbed my diary, and began reading where I had left off. This was the sad part. The part after my great revelation that at seventeen we're too young for one person. I knew I loved him. I did not write as if I believed we would be together forever once I got to college. I hoped he would not forget me. I rationalized in my writing all the reasons we shouldn't be together. I sounded quite mature for a just turned eighteen-year-old college freshman.

Stapled to the page where I wrote of telling Tripp we should see other people was a letter from him. I opened it up. A picture of us I did not remember was included. We were at the beach. It was from our last morning together. He was giving me a kiss on the cheek as we lay there together. My expression said this was what love looked like. Even I could read that now. I could feel the color slowly drain from my face as I read his words over and over again.

> Dear Jenn,
>
> God, I am so in love with you. I know you know that. I did not think I would fall for you as hard as I did. After our summer together and we both went back to school, I was counting days until I could see you again. I was so invested in you. I want to understand and support the fact you need to grow as a person. I don't want to let you go though. I can't imagine my life without you in it. But, because I love you so much, I will let you go as much as I can. I mean, in the sense that you live your life, and you do the things you need to do to be you. I wish I could convince you otherwise, but I know you well enough to know that you are a strong-willed woman. No matter how much we love each other, it doesn't seem like we're in the same place. And there is nothing I want more. I would do

*anything for you, Jenn. But even then, I know it is not
enough. I know in my heart I will always love you.*
Tripp

I was sobbing reading that. I always remembered we loved
each other. And I remembered having such a heavy heart
when I told him I thought we needed to break up. I do not
think I considered the impact my breaking up would have on
him. Why would I? I was in college, free to do what I wanted
with whomever I wanted. I did not need a boy to hold me back.
I buried Tripp then. I buried the memory of him deep enough
that I wouldn't allow it to resurface, and I would certainly not
allow him to get in the way of me enjoying my college experience.

I never saw Tripp again after that summer. He spent his
last summer interning at a hospital. After that, he went to
medical school. Mom shared that much with me. That made
me smile mostly because I knew his parents did not want him
to become a doctor. Good for him, I thought back then. His dad
died shortly after that, and his mom became reclusive. Jason
had lost contact with him as well. Then Tripp just disappeared.
I had busied myself in college, discovered I liked partying and
playing hard. The education was a necessary component that
I actually came to enjoy and appreciate. Yale, it turns out, was
the perfect fit for me.

I finished reading through my diary. After I broke things
off with Tripp, I never mentioned him again. A brief comment
comparing him to another guy I had slept with was the extent
of reference. Reading back on it now, it makes me a little sad
at how cold I appeared in my breakup with him. It was so clear
by his last letter that he truly loved me. He loved me enough
to let me go do all the things I needed to do. Damn him, I
thought now, for not proving to me I was wrong!

I did not intend to find the memories I had tucked away in that diary. I remember storing my diaries and various keepsakes from my younger days when my parents made the permanent move to the Cape. I had hastily thrown them in a box not thinking I'd ever really have use for them, but knowing I was not ready to part with them either. Like the prolific writer I was back then, I could not just throw away my words.

I had long stopped putting words to paper to express my emotions. I was a corporate climber when I packed them away. But maybe I knew I might need those words as a reminder in my future. Even then, I put them in a place where it was not meant to be easily found so that the urge to remember as it really was stayed locked away.

I have so many memories of my childhood. Memories are an amazing thing. They allow us to hold on to a part of our past in powerful ways. We can remember painful events, beautiful moments, influential experiences, and trivial details. We can change how we remember things to fit our narrative of what happened.

Reading the pages so well documented brought back the memories of how I really felt at that time. I had tucked those away. I have always treasured that Tripp was my first love. But I forgot the intensity of our relationship, how much I learned from him about unconditional love—both giving and receiving. I did not remember the pain of my decision to leave for college, the back and forth of my emotions, and my stubborn will to do what I wanted. And, ultimately, I did not regret that.

By reading my diaries, I dove deep into my own story, the one I had so unknowingly buried. If I dug further into my story with Tripp, would it open old wounds? Tear at the seams I had so tightly woven? Rip the bandage off what I didn't want to be reminded of? Or simply remind me that life had been so simple once, but youth made it complicated?

The diaries had brought so much to the surface. I felt compelled to reach out to him. I wanted to know how he was beyond what Jason had told me. I wanted to know what he did with his life. I wanted to know on so many levels. I did not expect Tripp to tell me I had been important in his life. I know in those moments I was. I was genuinely curious about what had happened to my first love. The thought of a second chance with him was not something that crossed my mind in those moments.

I told myself we might both be disappointed in how we turned out all these years later. It was the first time I questioned if he might think I was a disappointment not doing all the things I wanted to do, all the things that I could not have done had we stayed together. I reminded myself I had not even found him yet and who knew if he even remembered me like that. If I forgot so much about him, it's equally likely he forgot much about me.

I pulled out my phone and got on Facebook. I had so many questions since Jason's revelation that he had run into him. At first, I was disappointed not to find him. My quick little searches over the years when his family's name would come up in conversation never amounted to much, but my efforts were minimal at best. I would become distracted and move on.

I guess there was a part of me that did not want to know what happened to him beyond what was said on our occasional visits to the Cape. We had all moved on and become buried in the details of our own lives. When you have your own family, gossip became less a thing you did on purpose but stumbled into instead. My children were my focus. Tripp was my past. A long-ago past that I had tucked away in the pages of my diary.

This time, though, I didn't have an excuse not to look him up. My diary reminded me of that. My empty nest did as well. And, sadly, the current state of unknowing in my marriage. It was a perfect storm of reasons to find Tripp. I wanted to know what happened to him. He was my first love. And my first true heartbreak. He was a beautiful memory that had become faded and maybe even lost with time.

I began my search to find him. He didn't appear to have Facebook. Or Instagram. Or even LinkedIn. A Google search left me without answers too. At first, I was stumped. My enthusiasm that I might instantly reconnect waning. Why couldn't I find him? He was a doctor. He lived in Florida. That much I knew. And then the switch flipped. Tripp was not his actual name. He likely went by his real name: Thomas Robert Porter.

I have always been fascinated by names and the process of naming conventions. Why do some people have ordinary names and others unusual ones or distinctive monikers? I am Jennifer. Jenn for short. And should there have been any discussion of using my initials to create a unique nickname, that would have been easy. I was born Jennifer Evelyn Northridge. Yes, JEN. I guess you could credit my parents with hedging their bets I would be called anything else. They did allow for the addition of the extra "n." That would be as edgy as they would get.

I was not sure why it didn't register at first. I knew the story of his name. He hated always having to explain it to people, but he obliged me when I asked that summer. No one names their child Tripp on purpose. At least not in the sixties and seventies. Thomas Robert Porter was a noble enough name. In fact, he was the fourth in his family to have been born with it. His dad went by Tom. His grandfather was Thomas. His initials spelled out sounded like Tripp and with that his name was established. For the East coast, Tripp was an appropriately arrogant sounding nickname. Except there was no part about Tripp that was arrogant.

I started the search over once I made the realization. I still could not find him on social media. But I was finally able to start connecting some dots. Finding him took some effort. He did not look the same. The pictures I did uncover were blurry, or he was part of a larger group. He was not recognizable to me. But as I dug, I found more. Finally, I found a clip from a local news program he had done as a spokesperson offering his expert medical advice. I still wasn't sure I recognized him. His beautiful hair had thinned. He was thicker than when we were younger. But weren't we all? His eyes remained that same shade of blue. It was his voice, however, that confirmed it was really him.

I always remembered his voice, the cadence with which he spoke. He was excitable and upbeat when he talked, his enthusiasm front and center of whatever he was discussing. I loved watching him when we were together. He was a light when he spoke. He could convince anyone to do anything. He was confident, but not arrogant. He prided himself on his ability to gain favor.

I viewed the clip several times. Each time I watched, I started seeing more of him. It was definitely Tripp. I had found him. I found myself feeling excited by this discovery. He was suddenly becoming real again, more than just the boy from my diaries. He was a man now with a lifetime lived since we last saw each other. Now I had to figure out how to reconnect.

Mark did not come home until I had finished supper. I left him food on the table. He offered only the smallest of explanations.

"I got caught up in a case at the office. Sorry I didn't let you know." His tone was tired and somber.

"I had a busy afternoon. It's fine." I sat in silence with him while he ate. Eating in silence was not new to either of us. Our standard six-foot long dining room table often felt like we were hundreds of feet apart. Yet, the reality was we sat close enough to hear the other person chew, swallow, and breath. Today those sounds felt even louder and the silence that separated us was stifling. There was no attempt at conversation. I did not have words. I could not tell him I spent the afternoon searching for my first love after being reminded how wonderful it was. That would only be spiteful. Finally, he spoke.

"Oh, yeah. What did you do?" I was caught off guard that he would even ask me.

"I went for a run. Went through some of Mom's papers I brought back. Caught up on some reading. Nothing special. It just went by quickly."

"That's nice. I'll look through your parents' stuff tomorrow at the office."

"I'm sure it's all fine. You're the one that put their estate together."

He stared at me for a long moment.

"Did you find a therapist?"

"I didn't look. I'll do that tomorrow."

He got up from the table and put his dishes in the sink. It irritated me that he didn't think to rinse them off and put them in the dishwasher. That was my job, in his mind. He turned around, walked over to me as I stood to push in both our chairs. He put his arms around me from behind, catching me off guard. I felt myself stiffen at his touch. He held me awkwardly and whispered in my ear.

"I love you, Jenn. I don't want to lose you. I can be happy with us together. You are my happy. And I'll do whatever it takes to prove it to you." He kissed me on the cheek.

"Okay. Thank you." That was all I had in response. I appreciated the effort. I didn't know if it was too late or not. All I could think in that moment was I couldn't wait to continue my search for Tripp.

I went to bed that night satisfied in the knowledge that I had at least located him.

I did not hear Mark wake the next morning and head off to work. That was unusual for me. I chalked it up to my utter exhaustion from life's last two weeks. I had been running on fumes between Mom's funeral, ensuring Dad was taken care of, and the realities of my own situation at home. I was emotionally and physically spent. I awoke finding myself surprisingly refreshed. A look at the clock told me why: I had been asleep for nearly twelve hours. I never did that.

I showered, got dressed, and headed downstairs for a much-needed cup of coffee. I grabbed my laptop, sat at the kitchen table, read a few emails, and scanned Facebook. I continually found myself disappointed with it, though. So little posting about people's lives. I knew they were living, but I suppose people were always more interested in learning what other people were doing rather than sharing what was happening in their own lives.

I always found irony in the fact we all posted happy pictures of perfect families. Even more amazing to me was the number of "friends" who went on vacations with large groups.

I didn't even know that many people, let alone know that many I would ever want to vacation with. I would ask myself if I was somehow envious of those people living lives so different from mine. Then I reminded myself that I had a nice group of friends I relied on. We didn't need to vacation in the Bahamas together or ski in the Alps. We had coffee once a month and caught up. I didn't post about those things. And the pictures I did post often told a story so different from the one I was living in that moment. The reality is no one posts pictures when they're unhappy and miserable. We are all smiling, telling the story we want the world to see, not necessarily our reality.

I used Messenger on Facebook sporadically. I preferred texting. However, I was good about checking my notifications. Maya had sent me a link to an article. Meg sent me a picture from our college days. PayPal reminded me I made a payment.

Today, for no good reason, I just kept scrolling. The chance that on this day I would decide to go through all my old messages was a coincidence. I forgot that I had reached out to certain people, disappointed to some degree that they had not replied. There were random old messages I never deleted and a few missed messages. Sometimes, though, there were things that defy explanation. For me, it was the sudden realization that I had missed a message from seven years ago. Maybe I was too new to it then and didn't check frequently enough, never noticing as the years went by. The message sat there unread all these years.

That one message was one of those little triggers that sets off a chain of events you cannot anticipate or ever in your wildest dreams foresee. My heart quietly skipped a beat when I saw a message from Thomas Porter. I quickly did a search on Facebook. How did I miss him? Easy. He was at the bottom of thirty people sharing his name. I had scanned right past him yesterday when I looked. His picture so blurry and unrecognizable.

I never would have viewed his profile. I proceeded to click the message from him.

"Hey Jenn. It's Tripp. I always wondered what happened to you. Beautiful family. How are you?"

He had looked for me. He tried to reach out to me all those years ago. He had thought about me. I wasn't just vanished from his memory. I found myself eager to reply. I was strangely nervous. After all these years, what if he didn't respond to me? It didn't matter. I was just happy to know he was out there somewhere. And that he did not forget about me. My response was simple:

"OMG. I just saw this from SEVEN years ago. So sorry I missed it. How are you?"

Like many of my previous lovers, I was genuinely interested in knowing how he was. It had been three and a half decades. I had so many questions for him. I knew he was alive. Thankfully. I would have been devastated if he were not. I found him in Florida. I knew he was accomplished. But was he fat? Just how much hair had he really lost? Was he married? Divorced? Did he have a family? I wanted to know.

I was not sure what I expected his reaction to be. Did he remember me like I was recently reminded we were? Did I want his first response to be that he remembered me, the girl who broke his heart in a million pieces, making it hard to love another for a long time? Selfishly, maybe. But I hoped not.

I found myself wondering how it was that I missed his message. Was it fate, coincidence, divine intervention that it should happen now? It didn't feel real. So many unanswered questions. Would I have had the same reaction to him then as I find myself having now? Maybe I didn't see the message then because I wouldn't have been ready to reconnect with him; it was simply a sign from some higher power I didn't subscribe to reminding me that fate was funny sometimes. Had I not found him or him me, would I simply have let it go over time, realizing we weren't meant to reconnect. I would have wondered forever like a couple other people in my formative years what had become of him. But I didn't need to wonder.

Messenger pinged. It was Tripp replying.

Maybe people come back into our life unexpectedly, unseen for the simple reason to help us live again, to find that piece of yourself that went into remission, but had been seeking to resurface, to let you be whole again. A simple reminder they existed, that they were a significant part of your story. Then a "Hello. How are you?" Proof they've gone on living their life in a full and meaningful way, just like you had gone on to do when you severed that tie. But what happened when you did reconnect and a part of you began to ache at the knowledge this person still existed? And you to him?

8

On Ghosts and Beating Hearts

Tripp and I had reconnected and began texting. I did not expect to have any reaction to him at all beyond gratitude that we were able to catch up on our lives. He gave me the abridged version: became a doctor, married, has two teenagers, lives in Florida. I found myself feeling genuinely happy for him. I did not share details of my life other than I was married for twenty-five years, had two amazing kids who were off in the world, and that I had walked away from my career to raise them.

"Wow. I thought for sure you'd be a CEO somewhere running the show."

That made me smile that he remembered my ambitions from so long ago.

"I did do the corporate thing for a long time. Then I had kids. It changed everything." I sent that text then quickly shot off a follow-up one: "I can't help but think you're disappointed I didn't become the person you thought I would."

"No, not at all. Just surprised." He texted back.

"I loved being a mom. I was lucky I got to stay home." I defended myself. I didn't need to. I knew that. Here was the one person in the world I wanted to remember me as something bigger than I might have actually been, and I felt like I had let him down.

He read what I wrote but did not respond. Then I saw the ellipses begin to move. He was typing.

"Remember the pix you gave me?"

"Which one?" I asked.

"In your striped top?"

"The Esprit one? I loved that shirt."

There was a pause. He sent the picture complete with his thumb holding it. My heart skipped a beat. I studied the picture, remembering how much I loved that shirt. I looked happy in it too. He sent a second picture, which were the words I had written on the back. I told him how much I loved him and hoped that we would always be together even when we were apart.

"Wow. I can't believe you saved that," I replied, even though I was so glad he did. It made me feel like I had been important enough to him to hold on to that photo.

He replied with an embarrassed smiley emoji.

I pulled out the picture from my diary of us on that last day together and sent it to him. There was a very long pause. Then finally I saw the three dots indicating he was typing; then they stopped. And finally, a text came through:

"I sent you the only copy I had of that picture because it was too much for me to hold on to. I forgot about it." He sent a second text: "Thank you for reminding me."

Why did I feel my heart starting to beat a little faster just at those words? Had all I uncovered in that diary reignited something inside me and now he was fueling that fire? It was a strange sensation to think that I could have had that much of an effect on him.

I sent him a heart emoji back.

"So much to catch up on. Can I call you?" he asked.

"Of course."

We both realized that a lifetime is a lot of words in texts.

The phone rang. I felt myself nervous to answer. What if we didn't have anything to say to each other? What if the conversation was awkward and forced? I picked up on the third ring.

"Hey, stranger," I said.

And there it was. That familiar laugh. And his distinguishable voice.

"How surreal is this?" were his first words.

"Very," I admitted.

"I can't believe it's you. I have so many questions."

With that a lifetime of questions, filling in blanks. We talked for nearly an hour barely able to brush the surface of what the last several decades had entailed for both of us.

I learned his story and shared mine in return. Tripp, the boy from the pretentious East coast family, would defy all their stigmas and norms. He shunned finance, choosing instead to do it his way. His mother cast him as the black sheep of the family, although I would hardly call being a doctor that. He chose to work in poor countries around the world, spending the bulk of his years working for Doctors Without Borders. He said he loved seeing the world and helping people. It also meant he didn't have to spend too much time listening to his mother complain about his life choices, since regular phone communication was difficult. That made me laugh. I remembered his mother vividly and imagined that did not go over well with her.

He shared with me that it wasn't until he was forty that the thought occurred to him it might be time to settle down, lay roots, maybe even start a family. And he did. He was in the thick of it with two teenagers at home and a much younger, yet equally ambitious wife. I was happy for him, but maybe, admittedly a little disappointed that his life appeared perfect and there would be no opportunity knocking on the door to the past.

Talking to Tripp was surreal. But also felt as if time hadn't stopped for either of us. It was easy and fluid. Like it had always been. He was familiar in so many ways. I could feel his presence. He had become a ghost that was suddenly taking shape again. There was this part of me that sensed neither one of us wanted to hang up yet, both caught up in our lives, and remembering what we had once been together.

"I don't want to hang up, but . . ." I started to say knowing that if I didn't get off the phone soon, I would want to keep hearing his voice.

"I know. Me too. I'm so glad you reached out. So much I still want to ask." He paused for a second. "I feel like we could talk for hours and that still wouldn't be enough time."

"But at the same time, it feels like we never stopped over the years," I added.

"Yea. It was always easy to talk to you. I'm glad that hasn't changed."

When we finally did hang up, I felt a rush of emotions sloshing about in my head and heart. I did not think I would have the reaction to him that I did. It was unexpected. And so much more than I had bargained for.

I was content with the realization Tripp and I were "friends" again. I could watch him on Facebook just as he could watch me. I hoped there would be more conversations to follow. There were still so many questions I had for him. We did end it with we would stay in touch.

"Now that I've found you, I'm not letting you go again," he said as we were saying our goodbyes. I knew he meant nothing more by it. He was sincerely excited to have caught up again. Just as I was happy in the knowledge we were reconnected. It was as if we had both been packed up and tucked away in boxes. We were opening those boxes now and being reminded what was inside them. It made me realize I was always present, just beneath the surface in his life. I only hoped I would be strong enough to stay the course to figure things out in my own marriage and not become distracted by this.

9

On Therapy
and Concessions

I attempted to tuck Tripp back away, knowing full well I wouldn't be able to just forget about him. I had buried the memory of him for so long. Bringing it all back was exciting. I liked remembering that someone could love me so much once. I reminded myself he was the first, but not the only one. There were others. And there was Mark. I owed it to our twenty-five years of marriage to figure out if I could find happiness in it.

I found myself battling the voices in my head that told me I was too old to worry about happily ever after anymore. The other voice told me that I still had so much of life to live and so much love to give. I wasn't sure I could give it to Mark anymore, not organically, and I wasn't certain he could consistently give me what I felt I needed either.

But Mark made it clear he wanted to try. He said he would do whatever it took to keep me. There were things he knew I wanted. I wanted to be seen. I wanted him to compliment me. I wanted him to initiate sex with me. I wanted him to be interested in my day and the occasional side projects I did. I had written several articles over the years for local publications. He read none of them. When I would press him on why he didn't, he would say he spent so much time reading during the day, he found it tedious to read if he didn't have to. My takeaway from that: I was tedious. Those were the big things. The things I needed to feel whole, like he saw me. I did not think it was unreasonable.

Therapy was the logical next step. I knew I likely needed to talk to someone about my own issues and we, as a couple, needed to go together to see if there was a chance for us. The thought of over sharing made me cringe a little inside. But I had been bottling up my own emotions for so long, I often felt I could just explode. A therapist might reassure me . . . or not.

I was lucky to have found a therapist with availability. I heard it would not be easy, but this one could see me within days and see us as a couple the following week. I needed to move forward; waiting was not something I was ever good at. I felt relieved to have this scheduled.

I have never really been a believer that someone could ask you a few questions and come to conclusions about your relationship and the status of your marriage. I was a bit hesitant at first, but Tracy was warm and kind and did not judge me. She listened as I told her my struggles.

I enjoyed the conversations I had one on one. I felt like I could make her believe whatever I was feeling was the right thing. I told her I didn't see us together in a year. And I have told him I don't know either. She validated my issues on every front. I assumed that was what she was supposed to do, but she also scared me. She said if I was looking for something better than Mark, I might be disappointed. She said all the good ones were taken. What did that even mean? That frightened me. Maybe they were. But I knew I was a good one. And I knew Mark was a good one. We just weren't good together anymore. If that was the case for us, wouldn't that be the case for lots of couples?

If I thought the grass might be greener, she made it quite clear it could very well not be. I stuck with my premise that if the grass is brown where you're standing, it cannot be any worse on the other side either. I had to believe her experiences would not necessarily be mine. It planted a seed of doubt, nonetheless. It was her job, I told myself, to remind me to consider everything before leaving.

I had hoped therapy on my own would help me better define what I needed. It was clear I already knew what I was missing. She could hear the pain in my voice when I explained events over the course of our marriage. My happy-go-lucky exterior broke under her questioning.

On the verge of tears, I explained to Tracy exactly how I felt:

"I am like a donut. I am whole on the outside. But I am missing the middle." I used my hands to create a visual. "I am that ninety percent that is happy and loving life. But it is the ten percent that evades me, that rips me apart on the inside. There are the two voices dueling with each other: one saying ninety percent is amazing and should be enough, while the other side says ten percent is too much empty."

She asked me a simple question: "Do you think Mark can give you that ten percent?"

I knew the answer. "No. If I did, I wouldn't be here."

"Well," she continued. "Let's see if Mark knows there's something missing and if he has any thoughts on how to get you there."

"Fair enough."

I was a strong woman. I was also a very emotional woman. I wore my heart on my sleeve. I loved deeply. To not feel like I was loved the same in return had taken its toll on me and I didn't even know it. I had given so much of myself to my children that I failed to recognize the love I needed in return from

Mark. I somehow believed the narrative that Mark loved me enough not to leave. I didn't want to be loved enough anymore. I wanted to be truly loved for all of me: my talents, my brains, and to believe Mark loved even my looks. My happy personality hid the pain I felt at not being seen by him. I knew that about him. I did. But being so busy in those moments allowed me to forget the important little things that made me feel whole by him.

I liked Tracy. She didn't just listen but provided the perspective I needed. Even after one visit, I think she knew that staying in this marriage was not my happy, but she applauded my resolve to not just quit.

I talked with a therapist years ago. I reflected on that and wondered why the topic of my marriage never came up. I even remember thinking that. But in those moments, I was struggling as a parent. Both Max and Maya were extremely bright and gifted children with stubborn streaks that ran deep. Efforts to talk with Mark were met with "you're doing great" or "they're just kids." It was easier for him. He was no one's punching bag or carpet to wipe their feet. That was my job.

Mark and I visited Tracy together the following week. We created a united front walking into therapy together. Her office was crowded with books on relationships and mental illness. I wondered to myself how much she might put labels on her patients, thinking we were all a little more messed up than what we went there for.

There was a plain gray sofa and matching chair placed neatly across from where Tracy took her spot. Soft pillows for added comfort were neatly placed on each end of the sofa. A blanket was hanging over the back of the chair. I wondered if people sometimes napped there or if they needed them for comfort. She motioned for us to sit. I sat on the couch, assuming Mark would sit next to me, but he moved to the chair instead. I did my best to hide my disappointment.

"Really?" I whispered.

He got up and moved to the other end of the couch. If I was Tracy, it would be hard not to read into this statement. He might as well have stayed on that chair; there were a million miles between us.

I wish I could say it went well. To me it was like watching Mark in court. He was ready for battle. He came with a prepared defensive opening statement and arguments. When I added my two cents, he told Tracy, "I feel I don't even have a chance here. I'm in a hole so deep."

Tracy asked him if he thought the effort to get out of the hole was worth it.

"That's a stupid question. I wouldn't be here if I thought otherwise."

"Okay, Mark, then tell me what you think will make Jenn happy."

He was flustered. "Geez, I don't know. Tell her I love her. Make sure she has lots of things to do so she's busy."

I jumped in on that one.

"Of all the things I've told you I need, your answer to my happy is busy?"

"Isn't it?"

"I am happy when I am busy, yes. But I want to find happy in the moments when I am not busy. When I can sit there with you and think, wow, this man really loves me. And I really love him. Or I can sit there by myself and not wonder what I said that was so wrong or why I might look mad to you even when I'm not. Because honestly, Mark, the only time you ever seem to comment on my appearance is when you think I'm mad— so looking ugly."

I paused. And tears started to form. "Do you know there have been times over the years I have hidden my face under the pillow because I didn't want you to see how ugly I was when I was sleeping?"

"That's just stupid."

"Maybe. But it's how I felt in those moments. It's how you made me feel. And you didn't even know or notice. Because you only ever notice me when I point it out to you."

"I don't even know what to say to that. It's such bullshit."

"Only to you. But to me it's always this painful reminder that I was never worth being seen by you in moments when I needed it. You've never shown me I should feel otherwise. So, busy is good because then I don't think about you seeing me. But the kids are gone now. You have your work. And I don't know what I have. But I'm trying to figure it out because I don't know if what we have is going to be me being happy for the rest of my life."

He took a deep breath and offered, "I love you, Jenn. I don't say it enough."

"Ever."

"That's a two-way street."

"I guess there are parts of me that have become like you, then. I don't like those parts." I looked at him. "I know you love me, Mark. You've always loved me just enough. And maybe just enough isn't enough anymore."

He had nothing more to add. It was his silence that hurt me. I wasn't cold or uncaring. If I was those things, I would not be sitting here with a stranger dumping my marriage trash at her feet. It was equally painful for me to watch him suffer. While he was not an emotional man, I could see that this process hurt him. I imagine Mark always thought because I didn't complain often about the things that drove me crazy, that I had some magical superpower to overlook them time and again. Instead, they were building inside me, and I was a dam ready to burst. My superpower strength could no longer quell the surge of emotions I had been holding back for so long. It was sudden to him, but a long brewing storm for me. My superpower was no more. I was no longer bulletproof. Instead, I was shooting bullets, and he was the target.

We left therapy in silence. I said what needed to be said. I could only hope Mark heard me. It was a start. Or maybe it was just the beginning of the end.

I couldn't fall asleep. My head ricocheting thoughts. Questioning myself. Feeling petty. Realizing so much of my discontent was the accumulation of little things. So many little things. When I dissect that list, I feel trivial and small. Is it unfair to end something because someone doesn't tell you they love you enough? Or tell you in small ways that you are meaningful? And, even if I am not the most beautiful woman in the world, shouldn't I feel that way with him? He chose me. We chose each other. For different reasons, of course. But we managed nearly thirty years together as a couple. I realized it was me who let it continue. It was me who was okay with being loved just enough because there was so much else happening around us in those moments. Why, when the house emptied of noise, did I hear silence that was deafening?

10

On Opening Doors When Opportunity Knocks

I hadn't heard from Tripp since our last phone call. I found myself wanting to reach out with random questions, just for ways to stay top of mind and not lose that connection. I could not find any legitimate reason until I heard a song that took me back.

Tripp and I would spend countless hours listening to music. I loved Depeche Mode with their music for every mood. He loved the happy sounds of Oingo Boingo. I loved to dance, and he loved to watch me dance. When we danced together, the world was perfect. It didn't matter if the music was slow or fast, we always found a way to move together. Much like our lovemaking, it was effortless.

I wondered if he still loved music. I know that music has always been a part of me. There were songs for every phase in my life, for moments and moods, for short runs and long hauls on the road. Much like running or writing, music supplemented everything I did. We had shared that back then.

I was in the process of checking out at my favorite clothing store when "I'll Stop The World (And Melt With You)" by Modern English came on the radio. There is no song I can recall that always makes me want to stop what I am doing and dance. I found myself singing the lyrics and moving to the music. The cashier shot me a look like I was too old to be doing that.

"It's a classic," I told her as I finished paying. "It takes me back."

"Okay. Whatever." She handed me my bag. "Have a nice day."

I pulled out my phone and sent Tripp a message. "Modern English was just playing. Reminded me of you. You still love music?"

I did it. I sent it. The reply was almost immediate.

"Yes, I still love music. I even learned guitar."

I wanted to tell him that was sexy. If he would have said he became a drummer, even sexier. But I did not. He did not ask me anything back, but I wasn't ready for the conversation to end. I liked his words. Or maybe it was that I just liked knowing he was on the other side of the conversation, a real person. And then I got a text with a song attached. It was "Stay" by Justin Bieber and The Kid LAROI.

"Funny. I have that on my current playlist," I replied.

"You still have good taste."

"Haha."

"That could have been our song back then."

The tone suddenly felt different.

"Maybe. Except neither of us was staying," I responded.

"Maybe."

"We both had dreams," I reminded him.

"You were my dream then. Staying was all I wanted."

Why was he doing this? Why would he tell me that? Did I dare ask him the state of his marriage or share with him the state of mine? He didn't give me time to reply.

"Too much. Sorry."

"Not too much. Just not sure what to do with that."

"You happy in your life?" he asked.

It was such a loaded question, but almost as if he could read my mind. Just like he used to be able to do all those lifetimes ago. Was I that transparent even in a text?

"I'm empty nesting. It's a struggle." I couldn't bring myself to burden him with the truth.

"I can't even imagine at this point."

"It goes fast."

There were parts of our conversation that felt like an invitation. I would not be far from Tripp when I went to visit Maya for her sorority mother-daughter event. Would he want to see me if I asked? I felt emboldened so I did.

"I'll be near you next weekend. Want to catch up in person?"

He did not reply. I knew it. I had crossed the line. I misread the conversation. But when he did respond, the reply told me otherwise.

"I have a conference next weekend. What about Friday?"

"Perfect."

"I'll let you know where. Excited to see you."

Smiley face emoji. They didn't have one for giddy woman jumping up and down.

I spent the next week trying to distract myself. Mark had buried himself in a case he was defending. We had work to do on our marriage but no time to do it. Excuses made real by reality. I was, however, grateful for this week where he would work long hours and I could busy myself for the weekend with Maya.

Maya was the sorority girl I never was. I loved that she liked pretty dresses and events which gave me occasion to wear them too. Formal legal events with Mark meant uptight suits and my hair pulled back. I played the part of the loyal wife well and truthfully enjoyed being by his side. He knew how to charm a room. Everyone loved him, couldn't say enough good things about him. I sometimes found myself looking at him in those moments thinking, '*where is this man at home?*' It was also the voice in my head now that reminded me; I will be the bad guy if this relationship ends. He will always be the good guy. I struggled with how to reconcile that in my head.

We were picture-perfect on the outside. The world did not see through the smiles, laughs, and exterior walls. They were not privy to the struggles when the lights went out and I was left empty and alone on the inside. I have never liked the dark. I craved sunlight. Needed the warmth the light brought. Max and Maya were always my light. And for the moment, the thought of seeing Tripp in a few days proved to be a light as well.

Trying not to think about seeing Tripp again for the first time in thirty-five years proved to be a challenge. As each day drew closer, I could feel butterflies. I felt the excitement building. It was the simple idea that I would no longer have to imagine what he looked like; I would actually see him. Touch him in a hug. I had no expectations. We were grown-ups now, living very different lives than we had when we were young and in love. Back then, the outside world only interjected itself when we needed doses of reality to remind us that our time together would be finite. When those reminders came, we hurried even more, allowing ourselves to fall deeper into each other.

Tripp and I agreed to meet at a local tap house not far from his office. It was a bit of a drive for me from Maya's university, but I permitted myself plenty of time to make it early. I wondered if I would instantly recognize him when he pulled up.

Would he recognize me? Granted, we both had the luxury of Facebook posts with recent pictures, but reality does not always resemble the photographs.

When Tripp did pull up, he instantly flashed his smile at me. It was that boyish, coy one that had melted me into submission so many times so long ago. He waited for me on the curb as I got out of my car. I studied him as I did. My reaction to Tripp was not a physical one. I do not believe I would have recognized him had our paths crossed. Save for his magnetic blue eyes, he was not the man I remembered. His hair had thinned and grayed. He kept it trimmed short now. Not the longer dark hair it had once been. He was fit but there were a few pounds on him. He had filled out over the years. He was taller than I remembered. His blue eyes still sparkled. And the embrace was firm and lingered. I instantly remembered that touch.

But more than anything, it was his words. It was how easy it was for us to just start talking like there hadn't been a lapse in time. There were no awkward pauses as we jumped from subject-to-subject alternating between the past and the present. We were laughing and remembering. Only once was there a silence, and that was when I caught him staring at me.

"What?" I asked, instinctively wiping around my mouth. "Do I have something on my face?"

"I forgot how pretty your eyes are." Already a compliment. Mark has never told me my eyes are pretty.

"I never forgot yours," I said. Our eyes caught for a long moment.

"I can't believe you're here," he finally said, shifting his eyes away from mine.

"Like a ghost, right?" But it wasn't really. It felt like time had stopped in that moment, like we had found a way to bridge time.

"One more question then, Caspar." I laughed when he

called me that.

"Just one? Okay."

He reached for my hair, pulling a strand towards him. I usually wore my hair down and straight when it wasn't in a ponytail or pulled up in a bun. I wasn't one of those women that could be bothered with having perfect hair every day. With hair that went halfway down my back when straight, it overwhelmed me at times. But I liked how it looked when it was down.

"You had curly hair. And it was darker, right?"

"Yes, and yes." I loved that he remembered. I hated my curly hair growing up. It was unruly and unmanageable. I always felt like a wet poodle in the summers on the Cape. Curly hair and humidity are not good together.

"I loved your curls."

"God, I hated them. My hair is still curly. They just have amazing straighteners these days. And I'd be gray or some off-shade of white if I didn't color my hair. Blonde makes it easier. I'm fighting looking old with whatever tools are available."

He laughed at that. "You aged well," he said.

"As did you, Tripp."

A glass of beer quickly turned into two hours of laughter and conversation and the realization that he was very real. *He was so very real.* No longer some ghost or a figment of my imagination. The afternoon was surreal, never quite feeling like it was actually happening. It was hard to ignore the chemistry between us, talk and laughter fluid and never awkward. It was like time had never stopped for us, as if we just picked up where we had ended our last conversation. Our connection seemingly not lost to time, age, and experiences.

The familiarity of our conversation made it difficult to stay closed off to emotions resurfacing. And in my precarious marriage situation, Tripp was the perfect elixir to stir up old feelings that were raw and deep so long ago. I did not want the time with him to end, but Maya would be waiting for me, and the drive was at least an hour in Friday traffic. I looked at my watch, but he spoke first.

"I know. You have to go." I nodded. "I do too. Gotta figure out dinner."

"Yes. And Maya's waiting for me."

"I'm so glad we did this, Jenn. I don't think you realize how much you meant to me back then and how much you changed my life."

"I'm pretty sure I crushed you." I smiled coyly when I said it. "I was seventeen. Love like that shouldn't be wasted on kids."

He laughed at that. "But it's the kind of love everyone should get to have at least once in their lives."

"You only get first love once. You were mine." I'm pretty sure I was not his first love. But I knew I was the first love that was deeper, the kind that stayed with you long after the breakup.

"I was lucky," he said.

"We both were."

He started to get up from the table and I followed suit. I did not want it to end. The thought that I might never see him again saddened me. But I knew this was likely it. He gave me a hug goodbye. I don't think either of us wanted to let go. He pulled away first. And began to walk to his car.

"Can I ask you a personal question?" he asked.

"Sure." I hate that question. I always wondered if anyone ever says no. Depends, maybe. But never no.

"You are happy in your life, right?"

How was I supposed to answer that? I wondered. How much did he really need to know? Why was he asking me? I know I did not act like I was unhappy.

"That's a loaded question." I thought about how to phrase it. "I have had an amazing life. I have no regrets."

KIRSTEN PURSELL

"That's not what I asked."

"I am as happy as I can be right now. And, if I'm totally honest, I'm trying to figure out what happy is supposed to look like for me from here on out."

"I want you to be happy. I want to know you are happy," he said.

"Thank you. Are you? Happy, that is?" I asked.

"As a clam." I'm glad I had not tried to read anything more into our conversation. He said he was happy, and I wanted to believe him.

I watched Tripp as he got into his car. He waved goodbye as he drove away from me. On the drive back to Maya, I replayed our conversation over in my head. I was smiling at his memory. I was happy for him and the man he had become and the life he had made for himself. Tripp was even more as a man than as that boy I fell in love with so long ago. I realize now how lucky I was to have been loved by him. It was a beautiful first love.

My evening with Maya proved a nice distraction from both Mark and Tripp. Maya had blossomed since starting college. She was self-assured, knew what she wanted, and enjoyed our conversations. There was nothing she wouldn't share with me. I reveled in the gossip, otherwise known as "tea," she dispensed. I sometimes cringed at her sexual escapade confessions, but remembered all too well what sexual freedom in college meant. Even back when I went to college, it seemed there were two types of situations: the couple that dated forever and those that just had casual sex. I suppose there was a third type: the ones who didn't do either. I wasn't sure which one Max was. As a male, he did not share those things with me. If he shared them with Mark, Mark did not pass it on to me. If Max needed my advice, he knew I was all too keen to dispense it.

The rest of the weekend was a blur. It was a constant flurry of activities with Maya, her sorority sisters, and their mothers. I was exhausted once I got to the airport for my flight home. I had given little thought to Tripp and even less thought to my relationship with Mark. Now, though, it was time for home and the realities of my real life. The one I wasn't sure what it was supposed to look like. I dreaded the impending conversations, but I dreaded the silence even more.

Just as I was about to board the plane, my phone pinged. It was a text from Tripp with a link to the song "Beautiful Mistakes" by Maroon 5. And the simple words: "This is why we live a thousand miles apart."

I knew the song too. It was on my playlist; our music tastes still aligned. I'm not sure I had ever really paid attention to the lyrics before. I liked the music, the beat, the singing. Now the words took on a whole new meaning. I find that with songs, though. Songs resonate when there is implied meaning. Until now, that song had none beyond a catchy tune. I would never be able to listen to it again and not think of Tripp. I played it as I boarded my flight. My stomach turned. My heart raced. Damn you, Tripp. Then I answered his text.

"Why? Because we were unfinished business?" I replied. It was a true statement. Our love had been defined by a time that would not allow us to move forward.

"Because you would be hard to resist." I did not know how to respond. I didn't see that coming despite the connection we had as recently as two days ago.

"I like that," I said. "Makes me glad that I can still have that effect on you." I added a smiley face emoji to take some of the heavy meaning away.

"You were exactly as I remembered you."

"Old, wrinkled, and sagging?" I joked.

"Beautiful, witty, and smart." Goddam him. What was happening?

"You still looked good, too. If I didn't say it then."

"Thank you."

"You're making this hard for me," I confessed.

I was testing him now.

"I didn't mean to. It's just a cool song. And it reminded me of you."

This was the part where I toyed with telling him my struggles. He was like a ghost from my past, disappeared for thirty some years, to resurface. But in some ways, it was like time stood still. The years went by but our connection to one another had remained unbroken. It was an eerie feeling to have it feel so easy especially after all these years.

"Getting on a plane now." Send.

"Confession: My marriage is not great. So your words have more meaning than you can imagine." Send.

Dot. Dot. Dot. "Sorry. Didn't know." Received. Dot. Dot. Dot.

"But the song still holds true. Have a good flight."

I switched to airplane mode. Closed my eyes. It wasn't just me. That was all I could think. That and I wished I was his beautiful mistake.

11

On Football and Hail Marys

Walking into my home had become a dreaded task. It meant awkward silence. Contrived conversations. Mark walking on eggshells in fear he might set me off. Given that I was not prone to explosive fits of rage, I found it strange he would approach me now with kid gloves. I know he wanted to try for the sake of our marriage. It meant that parts of him needed to be someone different than he had been. I knew it wouldn't be instant. If at all.

There's that moment in any great football game where the quarterback has a few remaining seconds to make the pass of a lifetime all the way down the field. It's the one where the receiver miraculously makes the catch despite two men clawing at him to keep from getting the ball. It's that Hail Mary moment that no one ever forgets. Can there be such a thing in a marriage?

Men can be funny like that. They think they've played the game right, followed all the rules, made necessary adjustments. Yet, that doesn't always yield victory. Instead, a sort of panic sets in as they are suddenly faced with the prospect of losing the game, that maybe they should have given a little more in the moments before the Hail Mary was needed. After all, what are the odds the ball is going to be caught in those final seconds?

That is how it felt with Mark. We were living in this new reality. I had laid out to him what I felt was missing. My list felt trivial at times, but necessary. I wanted him to compliment me without being asked. I wanted him to tell me he loved me without me saying it first. The reality is neither of us had told the other we loved them in a very long time.

It was easy for us to tell our children we loved them. It used to be easy to tell Mark that. But when you are the only one giving, the only one saying, at some point you tire of the words, they lose their meaning, and you just stop. I wanted to hear it. I wanted to feel it. I wanted to believe it. I just didn't know if I could.

While my revelations to Mark may have felt like news to him, these feelings in me had been churning for years, growing in a cauldron of despair, waiting to be poured out like some witch's brew to cast a spell. The spell would either make or break us. Did witches ever cast magic spells in the name of happy? Or was that reserved just for fairies?

I told myself I would try. He was at least willing to concede to some of my demands. I wanted to believe that the concessions, the willingness to give me some of those things that had been missing, that they would magically make up for the void I felt inside.

And then I would reflect, and flashes of our marriage played out in slow motion in my head. This wasn't new to me. This had been building for so long. Was it any wonder I could feel myself starting to well up with frustration, that the littlest thing would set me off? Things that I might laugh at before suddenly felt like fingernails on the chalkboard. Of course, the counter voice was whispering in my head, *"You really don't think another man will have idiosyncrasies that drive you crazy? And you him? We're older now. Set in our ways. What makes you think a better version is out there?"* Stupid voice of

reason always sits there lurking in the shadows to say something to throw me off my forward progress.

So I stay in this land between heaven and hell, not sure
where I will land or if the middle is just always going to be
what can be expected. Maybe this is why so many people don't
leave a marriage that is mostly good, but unfulfilling in other
ways. Maybe this is why, at fifty-four, I struggle wondering if
the other side will be better. And am I willing to go it alone?
Hence, my own little purgatory.

The voices reminded me of my wedding vows. The part
where we said we'd be there for each other in sickness and
health, good times and bad. But what about the part when we
stopped loving each other on a deeper level? What about the
part where maybe we were only meant to love each other for
a finite period of time? I loved others. They ended. In a marriage, though, you aren't supposed to just quit and walk away.
If he said he would fix things you needed to be fixed, then don't
you let him try? I made no promises it would work. But I told
him what I needed, and it was up to him to follow through.

At first, Mark tried. If I wore my hair down, he told me it
looked nice. If I got a new dress, he'd say it looked good.
Funny. The hair and the clothes look good. What about me? I
wondered if he got it, if he understood the hair and the clothes
aren't what I want him to see. I want him to see me and to tell
me I look pretty with my hair that way or I look beautiful in
that dress. What part of that execution was so hard to understand? He was a brilliant man but lacked some basic understanding of how to communicate—at least, with me.

Nonetheless, I did appreciate the compliments. It meant he
was trying.

"I love you," he said as he was leaving for work one morning. It was followed by a kiss and a hug. That was better than
the quick peck on the lips where contact was barely made as
he flew out the door to the office.

I did not say it back when he did. I didn't know if I loved him like that anymore. And I didn't want to give him a false sense of hope. Yes, I said I wanted it. I understood the hypocrisy. I felt like he was the one that needed to prove to me why I should stay, that he was worth staying for, that he would love me in all the ways I had wanted. All these years of loving and giving to everyone else left me desiring so much more attention than I had been given. It was not unreasonable, the therapist said, for me to want and expect that. Making it clear to Mark was my job, she said.

I knew Mark was capable of saying the words. He had always told our children he loved them. Every phone call ended with the words. When they were home, they did not go to sleep or out with friends before hearing the words from both of us. I was thankful that he told them he loved them. So thankful for that. But he didn't tell me. And it was stupid if he didn't say it because he thought I wouldn't. That just made it worse for me. He was supposed to be fighting for me. Instead, he approached everything about me with caution, making it feel like he was just waiting for a bomb to drop.

When I did not tell Mark I loved him in return, he got upset.

"Really?"

"You say it once and want it back?" I retorted.

"I thought that's how this worked."

"No. I need you to remind me you love me."

"That goes both ways," he said as he walked out the door.

In many ways, I knew he was right. Was that just my affirmation that I had already made up my mind? Was I just going through the motions to say I did?

Mark came home from work that night and apologized, which surprised me. He said he overreacted. "It hurt not to have you say it back. But then I realized your hurt from me not saying it as much as I should." *Or at all*, I thought to myself. I had to give him credit for the apology and seeing the error of his ways. Score one for Mark. He was trying.

He even initiated sex. Even though we had been empty nesting off and on for quite some time, didn't have the same worries we used to, he did not stray from the course. Sex was predictable with Mark but at least he was trying to deviate from the norm.

Two scores in one night for him. We had sex for the first time since my mom had died. I wondered if he processed it had been that long. In my mind, I already knew it would be fast. They say seven minutes is the average. I would occasionally joke with Mark that our seven minutes included taking off our clothes and putting them back on. He would laugh. I'm not sure he appreciated it.

We never called it making love. I will concede that was a strange term for both of us. It sounded like something the smooth radio voice would say over the airwaves. Most of the time, we spoke in innuendos when it came to our love life. If I wanted sex, I simply walked around in my underwear or naked. If he wanted it, he would suddenly appear when I got out of the shower. Or he would get in the shower with me. The last many years, sex was routine and infrequent. A victim of our busy lives, an easy excuse not to have it.

Our sex life had been good in the beginning. I'm convinced I always liked it more than he did. Or maybe it was that I needed it more than he did.

Mark and I had great sex our first years together. With kids, sex became something you did when you had a few minutes at the end of the day when you weren't worried they'd walk in your room. Of course, as they got older and went to bed after we did, that became a challenge. We would sometimes go entire summers without sex because the kids' schedules and our schedules were so crazy, we barely had two minutes together. Sleeping in the same bed was for just that:

sleeping. We might have sex before he left for the office if the kids were off to camp early. Their routines became our routines, which meant sex became less and less.

Somehow, when the house emptied, my desire to have sex again returned in force. I don't know if my body started coming alive at the thought of Tripp or if it had just been missing sex for so long. I found myself wanting it constantly. My body hadn't been allowed to want it whenever it desired it. Now, I should be able to have it whenever the mood struck. The idea of uninhibited sex was exciting. We could have it anywhere. Go places we hadn't been in a very long time. The thoughts were exciting, and I looked forward to exploring this with Mark. Until I didn't.

When nothing changed in the bedroom, even if I tried something different, I ultimately felt defeated that my effort had not been appreciated—if he even noticed at all. It would usually end the same way, with the same results. Orgasms? Mostly. I would fake it on occasion. Easy to do as a woman. Satisfaction? Some. Intimacy? *What's that look like*, I wondered? It was not happening like I had hoped.

The things I had come to realize were missing were not coming back. Asking for it now felt awkward in ways. I wanted him to want things, to get creative in the bedroom. That was what I told myself I wanted over the years. But did I really want him doing those things to me? Or was there a reality I knew I did not find myself attracted to him in that way anymore? That's normal too, right?

This too, I knew, meant I had to tell him in no uncertain terms what I wanted. I wanted him to go down on me. I could do some landscaping, clean up that mess to welcome him back. That thought was kind of exciting. I would give him a blow job again. I could do that. He never asked. But he never asked for anything. Maybe we could introduce toys in the bedroom. I read articles. It's normal for couples to play. I say normal and it makes me feel like nothing we did in the bedroom was normal anymore. It was routine. Boring.

I know not every man is driven the same way in the bedroom. The same can be said for women too. Not every woman is comfortable exposing herself for ultimate pleasure if it means she has to figure it out on her own, explain what she needs, and might just possibly end up disappointed because her lover can't deliver, or her body doesn't react. I knew all my body's triggers. Over the years, I had become comfortable with pleasing myself. It was sometimes easier and more convenient than waiting and hoping for Mark to satisfy me. I needed those orgasms. I wondered if over time they were how I kept my body alive, reminding it of pleasure that was different from my usual orgasms with Mark.

At some point along the way, I let go of the me that liked to have a lot of sex, liked to challenge a man to pleasure me, and became comfortable with the ordinary. I was having sex and with that most of the time orgasms. Throughout those many years, just doing that with the day to day of life was an accomplishment.

Now, though, I realized I was guilty of accepting the status quo. I did not challenge the assumptions that it could be better. If neither of you complained, didn't it mean it was fine? Or did it mean you gave up in the bedroom too? Maybe I was even ready to be better off alone than faking orgasms on occasion or wishing that he was doing something slightly different to me.

I had missed kissing. Really kissing someone. I loved the years before sex. The teenage years when you're too young to go beyond Frenching and getting felt up by a boy. It was not impossible to kiss for hours. Now I just wanted to be kissed for seconds. Feel his tongue again. Know that passion a kiss can ignite.

And that night he kissed me like he used to. But I didn't feel that spark anymore. I tried to feel it. It was almost as if he was trying too hard. I know I used to love the way Mark kissed me. Now it felt awkward and forced.

I wanted things and he was trying to do them. He heard me when I said I missed being kissed. He even did the neck thing. Oh, how I loved when a man would gently hold your neck in his hands while he pulled you in close to kiss you. It was so movie cliché, but there's a reason we women swoon at those moments in movies: we wish for that exact same magic. For some men, it's natural. Or they at least paid attention to women's reactions in those moments. I had to tell Mark I liked that. Spotty execution over the years. But, then again, passionate kissing was something left behind as soon as life commandeered us.

I tried to find the magic we once shared in the bedroom. But in that quest, I realized there were so many things that got lost in the process. We started to have conversations about sex. He liked the idea. He wanted to please me. Moving away from the routine, the usual positions, bringing lubes and maybe even toys into the bedroom excited him. At the same time, though, I think it frightened him.

It was sometimes sad watching him in the bedroom as he tried to put all the pieces together. Our conversations over the past days made me realize how much he hid his insecurities in the bedroom.

"I don't understand how you never said anything about being insecure," I said, as we were having one of our better conversations. "Because I never complained?"

"Maybe. But no man wants to admit he feels inadequate in the bedroom."

"You have been apologizing to me for years for how fast sex is. You've even said that's just how it is, so I need to get used to that."

"I know. That was wrong." He looked at me. "I've done a lot wrong, Jenn. I know."

"I didn't say you've done a lot wrong. But I would think you would want to please me and if that means getting help down there, then it shouldn't be some admission of guilt on your part."

"You're right. I want to satisfy you. You just never said anything."

"Over the years, I was just happy when we could have sex. But now I want sex all the time." I tried to lighten the mood. "I've read it's normal for women in their fifties to experience heightened sexual desires."

He snickered at that. "I'll look at Viagra."

I thought that a small victory in the overall scheme of things. A few days later, a small, discreet package arrived in the mail. Quick fixes were available on the internet these days. And Mark knew that. I tried to be positive in my assessment: he admitted an issue and sought out a solution. The dark voice in my head said *he knew there was a fix all along; wasn't I worth it before?*

Now I had this heightened desire for sex, and he wanted to please me. I even revealed my great secret, one that I did not want to reveal but thought maybe it was how I could meet him halfway. I had told him that my sexual needs were always so much greater than his, so I would just satisfy myself.

He asked if I meant toys, and I had to reluctantly admit I had a vibrator. This was my great secret. I liked having it. If I gave this part of my sexuality to him, too, what would I have left just for me? I stepped back, reminding myself that I was supposed to want to save this marriage, not hide opportunities where they might exist, especially in the bedroom where my body was yearning to be touched, wanted, satisfied.

I was surprised to learn he got himself off on occasion too. At first it bothered me since I was always willing. But then I realized that was not entirely true. I admittedly had phases where I didn't want him touching me for lots of reasons: I felt fat or ugly or gross or repulsed by him for whatever reason. I was complicit there too.

Mark was excited by the prospect of toys in the bedroom. And that gave me hope in return. But when it came time to add toys to the mix, he was awkward. It was sad to see a grown man fumble in the bedroom. I am not sure that most men would know what to do if in the same situation after thirty years with the same woman. But it saddened me. Made me wonder if I really could try for that much longer. There was never a guarantee that sex would be different or better with someone else. God knows, that scared me to death. But I wasn't sure I would be okay for the rest of my life with effort, not enthusiasm.

Instead of healing my broken pieces, the more we seemed to try, the more obvious it became to me that we were just trying to fix things with band-aids.

It was easier said than done ripping off band-aids. You could peel them off slowly, hoping it only gently pulls at the skin it's adhered to; or you could yank it quickly, hoping for a sting that ends quickly. But pulling, yanking, peeling, they all hurt in one way or another. I tried to peel slowly to make the pain less for both of us. But Mark would not let me finish before he would start to stick it back on.

When I tried yanking quickly, he tried desperately to be parts of what I needed. But it felt irreparable; like the band-aid would not adhere again even with the best intention. The stick was gone. And all that was left was to throw the band-aid in the trash, let the wound feel the newness of the air on its outer edges. Let the sore find a way to heal without the protective layer of the band-aid. If I bumped it and it started to bleed again or it became infected, I would have to find a way to mask the pain without relying on the band-aid to fix it.

I believed he wanted to try to be all the things I needed. I could live with good sex, yes. I knew as I got older the need for sex would wane. But what ate at my core was the realization that Mark was trying now only because he realized the end was potentially near. Why not have tried harder all those years when he knew the little things I needed?

12

On Selfies
and Second Chances

His text came. I had not heard from Tripp since the weekend I confessed my situation. It was unexpected. His initial lack of response a sign he would leave well enough alone, not open any doors, lead me on, give me hope.

"I can't stop thinking about what you said."

I scanned through my messages to find what he meant. It had to be about my marriage.

"????" I replied. The last thing I wanted to do was assume.

"Your confession."

"Oh. And?" It felt like an eternal pause.

"Do you still run?" he asked. That was a random change of topic completely out of the blue.

"Yes. Why?"

"There's a race next month in Miami."

"Are you asking me to meet you? Because I think you already know I'll say yes." I was being assertive. I could feel my heart beating faster.

"That's exactly what I'm asking. Meet me in Miami."

"Yes." This was sudden and unexpected, and I felt like he needed to explain himself a little more. I did not see this coming despite some benign flirtations. If I really thought about it, though, there was still chemistry between us. It would not have been that easy when we reconnected had there not been.

"But you have to call me," I said. I wanted to hear his voice. I needed to be reassured that I was not dreaming all of this.

"Okay. Now work?" I replied yes and waited for my phone to ring. I don't think I took a breath during that time. I gasped for air when it did finally ring.

I answered, hoping the nervousness in my voice was not obvious. He was smooth and calm. Was he seasoned at this sort of thing? He was asking me to have an affair with him. How could he be so put together?

I knew his marriage could not have been perfect. I would not have been a temptation if he was truly content in his life. I had believed him when he said he was happy. And that he wished me nothing but happiness.

I had never cheated on Mark. No man had even made a pass at me over the years. Harmless flirtations now and then. I had avoided opportunity. I had been a loyal and faithful wife. Until now, when I was about to engage in a conversation with a man from my past who wanted me. I was so nervous.

"So, you know me, straight to the point: I would have thought you were off limits to me."

"I know. I don't know what changed. It wasn't one thing. I just started thinking. And the songs kept playing." He paused. "It's that it's you, Jenn. More than that I don't know."

"I like that. I like that it's you," I said. "But it's cheating, right?" That was classic me. I didn't beat around the bush. I called things like I saw them. If he was going to do this with me, I wanted to know what he was really thinking.

"I know." He didn't sound down about it. His voice never changed inflection or cadence.

"Is it cheating if you've already been with that person?" I tried to joke. Both of us knowing cheating was not something to be taken lightly.

"I'm pretty sure it is."

"You've never done this before?"

"No." I needed to believe him. I wanted to believe I was worth risking everything for. It was for sex. I liked that he would be the first man to touch me in three decades.

"Me either."

"Good. I'm excited to take you on this journey, Jenn. I'll see you next month."

"Just give me the details and I'll be there." Then we hung up. And I was floating on top of the world. I sat there for a very long moment wondering what had just happened. How had it happened? So fast without a real warning. I heard myself under my breath: *You are going to be his beautiful mistake after all.* No wonder I loved music so much: Sometimes the power of suggestion transcended beyond the words being spoken as a call to action.

I felt like that young seventeen-year-old girl the first time Tripp noticed me. I was excited, nervous, but equally apprehensive. There was this part of me that doubted it was really going to happen. In those first moments, though, I ignored that voice of reason and just enjoyed the feelings of excitement for what was coming next.

Because I couldn't scream it from the rooftops, I had to call Meg as soon as I committed to meeting Tripp.

"What do I do?" I asked.

"You fucking go!" she said.

"Thank God you said that. I told him I would."

"I didn't think you would do anything else. You're ready for this."

"I know. But . . ."

"There are no buts, Jenn. This is exactly what you need to help you move on."

As always, she was right. She was always right. It was both a blessing and curse to have a best friend that knew the right thing to say every time.

I was thankful for my friendship with Meg. I knew I could not go on this journey with Tripp totally alone. I was in foreign territory. I needed a trusted confidant. I wondered if Tripp had someone who knew what he was doing. I would explode if I didn't have somewhere to turn. I hoped he had someone to talk to, a trusted old friend. Someone to help him make sense of what he was feeling. He still had kids at home; no doubt they were a constant reminder to him of what was at stake. And his wife likely did not have the benefit of knowing he was struggling. You do not offer to take someone on a journey unless your own needs are not being met.

I liked talking with Tracy. As my therapist, she was the only other person to know, and validated that point as well. She made me feel better in accepting that no man in a truly happy marriage would do what he did. He would not send songs as reminders. He would not send messages saying he's thought about what you said. He most definitely would not invite you to meet him if he were happy and secure. In my mind, I knew all these things. I'm just not sure he did. Her reminder to me, though, was not that Tripp wanted to have an affair with me, but that another man could want me and make me feel things that had laid dormant for so long. "Even if he changes his mind," she said, "it shouldn't change the fact that you are still a very desirable woman with much to offer a man. And independent of needing or wanting a man, you are a strong woman capable of living the kind of life you want."

She told me words I needed to hear. I would take them in, do my best to absorb them, and hold them to be true. But I still heard those voices wrestling in my head, always lurking, always challenging my forward progress, just one step away from sabotaging my hopes for greener grass.

Meg was the more outspoken voice. She would tell that voice of doubt to shut up and go away. She would tell me not to listen to it. I wished it were that easy.

Most of my life I had been the impulsive, quick to decide, rash person. It annoyed me that Mark couldn't make decisions on the spot. He always had to weigh the pros and cons, research things on the internet, compare options. And then he still couldn't decide half the time. I have made good decisions and some bad ones with my impulsive nature. And I was sometimes quick to judge a man, his intentions, feelings, motives, desires, pretty much everything. If he didn't make an immediate impression, there would likely not be that second chance. It wasn't always right, but it's how I functioned.

For me to still be in my marriage knowing I want out, was a departure from the status quo. At times, I wanted to pat myself on the back and say, "*See, you've evolv*ed." Other times I heard myself saying, "*Stay true to your convictions; you know what you need to do.*"

I liked having a friend who knew me consistently over the years. I realized as my children were growing up that there were different friendships for the different times in our lives. We had lacrosse friends and tennis friends. While our kids may have stayed in touch, the parents mostly moved on. I wondered if it was me, but I know it wasn't. It's just the circle of life. If I really wanted to stay in touch with someone, and vice versa, we would have found ways to stay connected. I suppose, with the introduction of social media, some of us did reconnect, promised to meet for coffee and catch up, but most of those never executed.

I had a very small circle of consistent friends. We met

infrequently but we kept in touch. Our lunches a few times a year were our venue to vent, gossip, and strategize about life. I had always thought we would meet more often once the kids left home. At first, we did. But we were all finding our new normal. Some of them went back to work. Some moved away. Some just disappeared without a goodbye. Others, like me, volunteered and took on projects put on the back burner while the kids were growing up.

There were acquaintances who we heard were getting separated or divorced. We would speculate on the reasons, turning their marital discord into opportunities to gossip. On other occasions, I tried to gauge my friends' reactions to the prospect of leaving a husband, and it was met with complete disdain. Their biggest reaction, *"Why would anyone walk away from our lifestyles?"* made me want to puke. Mostly because I was guilty of having that same reaction sometimes too.

Meg, though, was my tried-and-true friend. She was the one person I knew would accept me and support me. She was not righteous or judgmental of me. Aside from my dad, she was the one person I knew wanted my happiness above all else. If I chose to stay with Mark, she would smile, laugh at his dad jokes, and remain loyal to me. She would reserve comments about our situation for a time and place where I would not hear. That's what a true friend did.

I knew it drove her crazy how fickle I could be. I don't think she realized the effect the situation with Tripp had on me. I had not seen myself as attractive to anyone else over the years. Some women, Meg included, always had men hitting on them. Men did not hit on me. I had never had the opportunity to be unfaithful with anyone in the quarter plus century I'd been with Mark.

"You're just intimidating, that's all," she said to me.

"If men liked a challenge, wouldn't that be encouraging, not discouraging?"

"I don't know the answer to that, but I do know you're still hot," Meg told me. "Craig thinks you're hot." I shot her a twisted side-eye. "What? I'm not threatened." We both laughed.

"I'm so fucking old. How can I be hot? I don't feel it."

"Because Mark never tells you. You think Tripp would have looked twice if you weren't still hot? Ha. Men think with their dicks. You know that. Even in their fifties. And you can still make them think with theirs. Do not ever let that be the reason you won't leave. You are better than all that. There are still plenty of amazing men out there who would give their right arm to even be considered by you."

I wanted to believe her on many levels. I knew I still looked good for my age. It didn't matter that I cheated with the occasional Botox injection or that I colored my hair in defiance of the gray. I was not going to let a number dictate what I could still somewhat control. Gravity was another issue, but there was a bra for every sag. As long as I could exercise, I would stay fit. I needed that for my sanity. It had always been a way of life for me. If I had enough wine in me, I might actually be able to admit that I looked better than most women my age. But I was still in my fifties. And that just felt old.

"Is it worth the effort?" I wondered out loud.

"Shit, Craig may be fifteen years older than me, but he still looks at me like I'm thirty. Well, maybe forty. And he tells me all the time I'm hot. My husband is almost seventy years old, but he can rock my world. You deserve that too."

"But what if the therapist is right? What if the good ones are all gone?"

"You're a good one. Sometimes good doesn't always mean forever. Remember that. We evolve as people and you're not the only person in the world who had an evolution away from their marriage."

I sometimes wondered why I paid a therapist when all I needed was wine and honest conversation with my best friend.

That night the first text from Tripp came. "Excited to see you soon."

"Me too."

"Already imaging rediscovering you." Oh. My. God.

I replied with a blush emoji.

It made me smile knowing the words took on a different meaning now. The tension between us had escalated in those moments from friends to potential lovers.

His words were an invitation to banter. It was fun and exciting. The playful innuendos ensured we were both invested in this. We pushed boundaries, crossed lines. Bantering was like foreplay for when we would meet.

The concept of bantering was new to me. I think we used to call it flirting. And you had to do it in person. Sexual innuendos in text form left much to the imagination. This was new territory . . . all of Tripp was new territory. And I was going to enjoy this.

Before we embarked on this journey, I wanted Tripp to know I wasn't looking for forever. I was looking to find myself, the woman buried.

"I'm excited to be with you again, Tripp. There's something about sex with a ghost," I joked. "But seriously, I want you to know that I'm not looking for a future. I'm not looking to destroy your family."

"I know. I asked you, remember?"

"Very much."

The risk, though, was there. The risk that we were unfinished. That our story wasn't over. You do not pick up a book with the intention of never finishing it, not knowing the ending. That was equally unfulfilling. I let Tripp open the book and turn the pages. If we kept reading, was the risk we would love each other again? I knew that answer. And I imagine he did as well. Whether we wanted to or not.

As long as he wanted to keep turning the pages, I was eager to oblige.

The first request was simple: "How do you feel about sending me a picture of you?"

I sent him a picture of me from the weekend with Maya.

"Like this?"

"That's nice, but maybe a little sexier."

"Lingerie?"

"I like lingerie."

"Do you have a favorite color?" This was fun. Not going to lie.

"Black. Red. TBH I'm sure you look good in anything." He found a way to compliment me even while sexting. Damn him. Damn Mark for not finding a way to compliment me in our marriage.

"Hmmm. Never done that before."

"I'm looking forward to it."

I replied with a kiss emoji. Now to figure out how in the world I'm supposed to take a selfie of myself in lingerie I don't own. One of my black bras and lacy underwear would have to suffice. They were sexy. The bigger question was my ability to pull off sexy while photographing myself.

It was a scary thought taking your clothes off again for

somebody else. Mark had known me, knew what I looked like, knew my idiosyncrasies. Either they didn't bother him, or he never said anything about them. If I had to be honest with myself, the reality was he probably never even noticed them. Now I was being faced with the prospect of exposing all my insecurities to a man who once knew me in my purest form before the scars of pregnancy, childbirth, nursing, and a few pounds here and there, amongst a plethora of other potentially body-altering maladies. I was determined to ignore those. I would not let those things hold me back from embracing the woman that I knew I was still capable of being.

That was until I stood in front of the mirror in that sexy black bra and lacy underwear and assessed what I was about to share with Tripp.

My breasts resigned to gravity and the cruel realities of aging and having nursed my beautiful children from them so long ago. My belly taut but no longer flat and smooth. Babies grew in that space and left permanent reminders. I could find flaws with myself without looking hard. I reminded myself Tripp would not expect me to look seventeen. I was no longer young and thinking I needed to impress with my body or looks.

Men went through the aging process too; their six pack abs replaced quite literally by the six packs of beer they consumed, soft Jell-O bellies that wiggled when they laughed, bulging proudly from their middles like jolly old St. Nick. Tattoos they never should have gotten served as saggy reminders why. Hair, for many, not even a topic of conversation. Funny how the standard for aging seems to be tougher for women than men. I wondered if men worried how they would look in the bedroom the first time with a woman when they were older. Did they have the same conversations in their heads that I did? Was Tripp just as nervous as I was to expose a mature body to me, one that likely no longer looked like when he was twenty?

I moved from my upper body to my lower half. Legs still looked strong. I stopped at my crotch. The excitement, the anticipation abruptly had the brakes slammed. I panicked at the sudden realization that it had been a long time since anyone had been down there. I found myself inundated with not knowing what it was really supposed to look like in the southern hemisphere of my anatomy. We shaved the bikini line then. Now? Young women looked like little girls down there. In my fifties, was I ready, quite literally, for a clean slate? I reminded myself that Tripp wasn't asking for naked. My bra would hold my boobs where they needed to be, and my underwear would hide the jungle beneath it.

I sent the first picture. Awkward. Afraid. But equally a little excited. I wondered if when Tripp saw it, he could tell how clumsy I felt playing contortionist while taking a selfie in my underwear, feeling simultaneously self-conscious and sexy.

He sent the flames emoji. I took that to mean he liked it. I sent the embarrassed emoji back. Sometimes they just worked so much better than words.

"No one has ever done that for me before," he replied. I could hear the lonely in his voice. It said much. It said I may be married but I am empty in parts too.

Why was I the first one to do that for him? He had been sexual for so long. He seemed eager to want to please and to be pleased. I loved pleasing him—then and now. When he chose safe, did he stop asking too? Or, like me, did he just never ask for more not wanting to rock the boat, show discontent or frustration? Or maybe he just stopped wanting exciting in exchange for that safety his marriage, like mine, provided. I don't think we were that different after all. We were just two people whose paths crossed at the wrong time again with one of us open to possibilities while the other was still living in their moment.

After I sent the pictures, I admitted that it turned me on to do it. I told him I masturbated to the thought of him afterwards. I did not tell him how many times I had actually gotten myself off thinking about him. I thought about him even as Mark and I had sex. My body was in overdrive. I needed and wanted to be satisfied. I channeled Tripp through Mark. Once a week, our new ritual, I imagined what being with Tripp would be like again.

Tripp's response was much more powerful than my admission: "I'm glad I'm not alone." Just knowing that he was thinking about me was satisfying.

Mark never questioned my new unbridled enthusiasm in the bedroom. My reality was either I was faking it through my marriage or trying to just figure it all out. Whatever it was, I still had to go through the motions.

I'm sure Mark thought I was coming around. He was open to new positions and old ones we hadn't done in a while. Viagra was a nice addition to the bedroom; it made pretending so much more satisfying. Toys did not make a reprisal. Not for him at least.

But for Tripp, maybe.

I gave him pictures. He gave me words. Hardly seemed a fair exchange. Except the words were so sexually charged. So exact. I could imagine all of it. Wondering at times if you could orgasm at thoughts. Because his words went through me.

On my birthday, he sent a well wish. I asked if that was all. His reply, "I'm working on that gift for when I see you." And then he gave me a graphic description of what that might look like.

"Are mini orgasms a thing?" I asked. He was a doctor. He should know.

"I'll have to look."

"Your words are making me feel things everywhere. Over and over again."

"I like that I can have that effect on you."

"It's going to be hard to top that. Slide is my new favorite word." I was referring to his telling me how he was going to slowly explore every part of my body, stopping long enough to slide into me to feel me, turn me on, arouse me, before sliding back out and continuing his exploration of my body. Slide was a beautiful word.

"I'm sure I can come up with something. So many things I want to do to you."

Then that night, he asked me for something beyond a picture. He asked if I'd video myself masturbating for him. Sitting at my birthday dinner in an upscale steakhouse with Mark, Meg, and Craig, I was trying to visualize how I was going to do that. Food was the furthest thing from my mind.

There was so much I never would have considered myself capable of doing. I was not completely sure I would have confidently done these things in my younger, more self-assured days when I knew my body was a temple and could easily deliver on the expectations. But now, in my fifties, I found myself in the exciting, yet extremely awkward position of being asked to video myself masturbating. How would that even work? I most certainly did not want to see what I looked like when I was pleasuring myself.

I would be the first to admit that I rather enjoyed doing it. I liked the control of determining the speed, pressure, and intensity of a vibrator or my fingers. So why did I blush when Tripp asked me to send him a video, saying he would like that very much? Tripp remembered me as a teenager, figuring out my body, how it worked, what triggered my erogenous zones. Quite honestly, he was the one that awoke those in me. He would not have known that then. And now, after decades of experiencing and loving others, recalling who we were as one would not be something either of us would truly have top of mind anymore.

I did it. I found a way. And I was petrified at what his reaction might be. I suddenly found myself wondering if there was a right or wrong way to masturbate? What if I wasn't what he expected? And, worse, maybe asking me to send him the video was a test, and I failed by actually following through. *Who does that at my age?* kept running through my head. I was caught in a moment, wanting to feel like a part of me was still capable of turning a man on, that he would want to see me at my most intimate. He had always made me weak in all the good ways. I am normally a confident, secure woman who has never needed confirmation of my ability as a lover, but I was suddenly unsure who I was anymore.

I sent the video. I was mortified to watch it be uploaded, only to receive a message failed notification. The file size was too large. Go figure, I took too long to orgasm and now I was being tortured by having to figure out how to divide the video up. That meant actually seeing me doing that. I tried not to watch. Somehow, I knew if I paid too much attention to the details, I would just delete it, embarrassed by what I saw. No part of what I saw looked sexy and like I knew what I was doing.

I edited. I sent. I waited.

Dot. Dot. Dot.

"Oh, my God. That was so hot."

It wasn't like I thought he was actually going to critique me. I didn't know what to expect. Every part of this was foreign to me. I understood none of it. But I liked the challenges he was giving me. And the reactions I was getting.

"Bring the pink toy when we meet," he said.

"For you or me?" I asked.

"For me to use on you." God, this man and his words.

Beyond all the sexual references, Tripp still found a way to remind me that this was my journey. He wanted to please me. He wanted to help me rediscover the woman that I had been so long ago. He would always come back and say he liked something a certain way, but would do whatever I wanted. He asked if I liked certain things or if anything was off limits.

"I am yours in all the ways you can imagine," I replied.

When he asked me what I wanted, my response was simple. I wanted to start at the beginning. I did not want pictures or videos of him. I wanted my imagination. And then I wanted to be able to experience every part of him from the beginning. He would be familiar, but now much more a man than the person he was when we were younger and eager to please. I imagined his body still strong and fit, but with new scars that came with an interesting story or two. His hands would move slower and more deliberately than they did when we were younger and in a hurry. And I knew that he would find ways to awaken in me what had been dormant for so long, hidden because comfort and familiarity were easier than risking disappointment in an already static marriage.

That word *slide*. I have never been more affected by the use of a word in my life. The visuals of him sliding into me. The thought of it. The way he made me feel like this was all for me and about me.

"I can't wait to take you on the journey," he said.

I joked, "You think you have more than one time in you?"

"God, I hope so," he said back. Did that tell me he wasn't having a lot of sex anymore?

"Is it strange that I'm oddly excited to give you a blow job?" I toyed.

"I'm desperate for you to do that," his response.

I was getting comfortable sending him pictures. While he told me he had to delete the first video because he couldn't stop watching it, I knew I could do better. I wanted to do better for him. I felt less clumsy, picked an easier position, knew how I really liked to do it, and went for it. I still couldn't watch it. That was not something I ever wanted to do. Why couples video themselves is beyond me. If I wanted to watch two people having sex, I would much rather watch two people who made it look easy and effortless. I would have been too self-critical.

I texted, "I have a surprise for you. Door number 1, 2, or 3?" I had the new video and two pictures of me wearing new lingerie I had bought for our planned rendezvous. Mark did not need me to wear lingerie. I had feminine, admittedly sexy underwear that I wore all the time. They made me feel good enough.

I knew, though, that Tripp liked the idea of lingerie, so I bought a couple of sexy outfits to test out on him. Had he chosen just door number one it would have been the black bustier with the crotchless underwear. What a concept, I thought. I sometimes wished to be younger and single just to wear some of the exciting, sexy lingerie that was out there. Door number two was a feminine teddy in sheer blue. My favorite really. It made me feel pretty and in control. Door number three was the new video wearing door number one more or less.

His reply, "Yes, please." I laughed at the thought he did not want just one of the doors. He wanted them all. I sent them in order.

"I can feel the bulge in my pants," he answered.

Effective, I thought.

Tripp had been a nice and necessary distraction from my life. I am not sure how I got through my days. They blurred as I counted down moments until we would meet. I started to train for my run. Did I believe either of us would have the energy left to run it? I hoped not. I yearned to be wickedly sore with every part of my body moved by his touch.

I buried myself in home projects. I finished sorting through all of my mom's things. I started planning for Maya's college graduation. That was coming up quickly. I volunteered at the animal shelter.

I loved dogs, but was glad I didn't have one at home anymore. Too much heartbreak because they die way too soon. We had several dogs over the years. When the last one died, I said I couldn't do another one. It was met with moans by everyone. The reality was I took care of the dog. I cleaned the poop. Did the walks. Organized dog sitters when we were gone. I loved them all deeply. But they also ripped my heart in two every time one of them died. I did not want that sadness. Instead, I started volunteering at the animal shelter where I could love on dogs but go home without a care.

Once Max and Maya were in college, I began volunteering five afternoons a week and assumed more of an administrative role as well. Helping animals find homes, places to be loved and wanted, gave me added purpose as well as distraction. It was a nice balance that afforded me flexibility without appearing the privileged wife of a Greenwich attorney.

Tripp and I continued to banter. I usually heard from him once a day. I anticipated those moments my phone would ping. Then my heart would skip a bit like a giddy little schoolgirl crushing on the football quarterback. There were so many parts that felt so surreal, like I had been dreaming the whole thing.

Some mornings I did wake up to dreams of him. I would text him as much.

"Had an amazing dream about you last night."

"Hope I didn't disappoint."

"Not possible. At least in my dream." Wink emoji. "I'm having a hard time waiting."

"Soon. Sooner than you think," he responded.

"I don't know how you're able to wait." But I knew why. He was not living every moment of his life to be with me. He was working. He was taking care of his kids. He was being a dad. And a husband. He was still entrenched in those moments, and I was likely more an afterthought than a driving thought.

"Sorry. I don't want to sound overly excited."

"Haha. I know," he replied.

"You just make it hard not to want it sooner."

This time there was a longer pause in his response. Those always made me nervous. Tripp was quick to reply when we bantered.

"Question for you. You don't expect more from me than this, right?" That was a strange question I thought. I was anxious and eager to be with him, yes, but I wasn't asking him to rescue me and take me in like an abandoned puppy in need of saving.

"I want nothing more than sex," I replied.

"Okay. Good. I can't blow up my family."

There were so many things wrong with that sentence. I sensed he knew the magnitude of what we were about to do. Was he suddenly realizing the danger he could put himself in?

Was he wanting to put on the brakes after he already ran the red light? I became a little nervous. Did I take it too far? I had to remind myself, though, that I didn't start this. I didn't ask him to share pictures or do uncomfortable things. I liked the journey he wanted to take me on. I could stop, reluctantly, maybe, but I could.

"That was never my intention."

"Okay, good. Now that we got that bit of housecleaning out of the way." I wasn't sure how to respond to that. Thankfully, I didn't need to.

"You around next weekend?" he asked without missing a beat.

"For?" After that last exchange, I was afraid to come off too strong.

"Meet me. On video. I have a dinner out of town. Thought it might be fun."

"Get our feet wet?"

"Ha. Yes."

Now a virtual tryst. He was throwing every modern era sexual novelty at me.

"I can make it work, I'm sure," I said and started plotting in my mind how I would sneak away or send Mark away. Didn't matter. I would do it.

"Don't forget the pink toy." Read. Dot. Dot. Dot.

"And I like you in black."

Oh, this man had all the answers.

I plotted, manipulated, and schemed to open up my Saturday night. I needed Mark to leave for a few hours, not that I thought we would be a few hours, but long enough to keep the window of opportunity open.

Meg came to my rescue. Craig, who wasn't necessarily that fond of Mark, but adored me enough to sacrifice, asked him to go to the city to watch a basketball game. I owed him. Mark was none the wiser.

I texted Tripp my expected availability. It sounded more like a business arrangement than whatever this was supposed to be. I had heard of people having phone sex. It was a strange concept to me. With the advent of live video, it opened up a whole new realm. A weird one. But a whole new one, nonetheless.

Tripp's Facetime call came through right on time. I liked just seeing him on the other side of the phone. Hearing his voice. Studying his face. I tried learning more about his life now, but he remained somewhat closed when it came to actually speaking about those things. The most I got was, "It can be hard when you're busy." It was a lonely admission. And then he got right to business.

"Let's do this."

"Okay. I've never done this before. How does it work?" I asked.

"Me either. But let's start with your pants. And we'll go from there."

I removed my leggings while awkwardly trying to hold the phone. I should have thought this out more I told myself. It felt strange taking off my own clothes. I teased him when I was just in my black thong underwear, asking, "Do I stop here?" It was the first time I heard him laugh during our conversation.

"Take your shirt off first." I liked how he knew what he wanted. I took off my shirt, revealing the lacy black bra that gave my breasts more lift than they had without it.

"I like that. Very sexy. But I want you naked." I didn't ask what part of me he wanted to see first. I removed my bra, and I heard him say "Nice" when he saw my breasts.

Then I removed my thong. I had not yet landscaped. That

was on the books for next week, before he would see me in person. I was a grown-out disaster down below in anticipation of waxing. I hoped the lighting was bad enough that he wouldn't be able to tell.

"Now for the toy."

"No. First you take your clothes off."

I wanted to see what he looked like fully exposed. I was no secret to him. I had already shown him every part of me. Seeing another man's penis was also a strange thing. I quickly saw the effect I had on him. Glad, in my mind, that I didn't turn him off. I worried on so many levels about disappointing this man. This man that I knew was not capable of more than this. I knew that.

I could have stared at his body for hours. I desperately wanted to be touching him in that moment, running my hands over every part of him.

"God, I want to be touching you," I told him.

"I know. Me too." He quickly changed his tone. "Where's the toy?"

I reached for my trusted vibrator, showing him, which elicited a smile. I found it strange how much I remembered when he smiled and laughed, wondering if those were things he didn't do that much anymore. This vibrant man felt a little lost, a little distant in this moment of total intimacy. I reminded myself that no one was forcing him to do this; he asked me. He was always the one doing the asking.

I propped my phone up so that Tripp could watch me.

"I want you lying down on the bed." I did as I was told.

"Now, take your vibrator and show me how you like to use it." I turned it on and gently started massaging myself. This was so strange.

"Take your other hand and touch yourself too," he said. And I did that as well.

Tripp guided me through how he wanted to watch me. He

told me all the things he would be doing to me if we were together. How he would pull me to the edge of the bed and explore me with his tongue. He would tease me before he would enter me, he said. And then only long enough to make me need him more before he would stop and turn me over. Taking me more forcefully.

It was easy to imagine those words as I stimulated myself with the pink toy. It was hard to perform with someone watching you. It was oddly disturbing and equally arousing. I would climax after he did. That was both satisfying knowing I could turn him on like that, but also a little sad for me because I wanted to be able to see him be pleased. I wanted to see the look of pleasure on his face caused by me. Me.

I rolled over on the bed comfortable in my nakedness.

"I wish I could have watched you too," I admitted to him. "Next time, you get to go first." He smiled when I said that. And I watched as he moved naked about his hotel room, searching for a towel to wipe himself off. There was no faking that.

"That wasn't too bad for two rookies," I said.

"Yea."

I couldn't tell by his reaction if he was disappointed by me, by the experience, or just regretting maybe a little what just happened. The vibe suddenly shifted, becoming awkward between us for the first time since we reconnected.

"I entered the race," I said.

"I still need to." Was I suddenly hearing a change of heart? "I'll get on it. I've just been a little overwhelmed. Taking the family on a trip next week."

We said goodnight. And that was the last I heard from Tripp. I reached out once after our virtual tryst. I said I had a new picture for him. No reply. No thumbs up. Mute.

The sounds of silence. I hated them. It had been over a week since he ghosted me. I was too old to be ghosted, I thought. I was too old to play games and get caught up like this, I said to myself.

I would feel relief when and if I heard from him. I knew I would be sad if he changed his mind. In those moments, when I was being totally honest with myself, I realized this was what I believed would happen.

My sadness was not because I thought there was a relationship to revisit. My sadness was because I wanted to know that I could be desirable; that a man could want to satisfy me in every way imaginable. There was a chemistry between us. That had been undeniable.

My mind played games with me. It spit out possible reasons, wondering if we went too far and it scared him. I didn't respect the way he just shut me off. He didn't owe me anything; I knew that. I didn't stop him. Just saying the words as opposed to shutting me out without any explanation would seem less petty.

Selfishly, I wanted the time to explore in hopes that it would help me to exit. Maybe because then I could say I was unfaithful, and Mark would not be okay with that. Or maybe he would. If he kept me after being unfaithful, who was the lesser person? It would be me. For staying.

The worst feelings in those long, silent moments were the ones where that nagging voice told me the future was unknown. There was no guarantee that I would ever find love again, or that someone existed who would make me feel whole and give me what I needed. It said you have to be fine without that knowledge. The other voice in my head said it was worth the risk; you deserve happy.

My phone pinged. I felt myself catch my breath. Moments earlier, I had seen the pictures he posted on Facebook from his perfect family vacation that "did not disappoint." Was it

foreshadowing? A cryptic message to me about what was coming next.

"Hey, stranger . . ."

13

On Cold Feet
and Broken Hearts

I wish I could say I knew what happened. One second it was a hundred miles an hour, finding myself in new situations with a ghost from my past. Then it was stone cold silence on the other end.

I knew we weren't in the same place. I had made it clear it was his decision to move forward. It was fast and furious. Doing the unimaginable. We were both enjoying it, pushing the boundaries of comfortable. I told myself the pull of me made him do it. And the fear of me made him stop. I was trying to believe that.

For a moment, he must have been so caught up in the past and wanting to experience sex like we were young again. But, in my mind, I always knew there was the chance that reality would catch up with Tripp. He had waited so long to start his life. The prospect of me was enticing and he momentarily got caught up in that. I only wished I knew what triggered the sudden stop. And why he felt he couldn't tell me that he couldn't go through with it. I was a big girl. I could handle it. It was the silence that was more numbing than the actual rejection, the realization I would be too much for him if we did meet.

I told myself that he was afraid of what might happen. I

told myself that after decades of not seeing, hearing, or knowing each other that he somehow still felt something deep within that could potentially destroy his life as he knew it. It wouldn't matter if I told him that I had those same feelings when I was at that point in my marriage.

I was guilty of letting myself get caught up in those moments. The banter was beautiful. I loved the back and forth that began as playful messages. And then became explicit in every way possible. I loved how he challenged me. And I loved that I could make him feel wanted and needed in those moments when I sensed loneliness and longing in his words.

We let the little things morph into big ones at an accelerated rate. It was the most amazing, spectacular few weeks of my life. Living for those texts. Those small requests. Then the more challenging ones. The sense that something so spectacular could still be felt inside me. Those feelings repressed, lying deep beneath the surface wondering if they'd ever be allowed to be felt again.

Those feelings were allowed to come up for air. And just as quickly were pushed back under, drowning. Did I want to fight my way back up to the surface to breathe or just stay underwater knowing that drowning might be less painful than experiencing the emotional spiral just inflicted upon me?

His text to me seemed sincere, in as much as you can actually interpret tone in a text. He didn't want to "tarnish the memory of us with some half-ass attempt" when he couldn't give more than that weekend. I never wanted more, I reminded him. Selfishly, I knew it might be the straw that broke the camel's back in my marriage, a solid out.

I suppose I believed that he was afraid of more. If he let me in even for a weekend rendezvous, it might make him that much more conflicted. I knew in my heart and head all the reasons. But it still made me feel like shit. I had given so much of myself in so many new ways to him in that short time. I made myself vulnerable. It hurt.

And it made me question every decision I had made up until this point about wanting to leave my safe life behind.

It ended just like that. The pain was so unexpected even though I saw it coming. He was still married, too, but with young children and so much more to consider than I did. I wanted so much to believe that we could do a weekend. That he could make it work. That he could fall into the trap of our shared past long enough to follow through on those explicit texts. I longed for his touch. I longed to remember what it was like to be kissed by him. It had been a lifetime. But I could still feel those moments. They came pouring back to me with the discovery of those diaries. I was truly, beautifully over-whelmed.

But crash and burn. Timing never our story. Never a long-term reality for either of us. I found myself wondering about all the people in the world whose paths I have crossed. I had many relationships before Mark. I had seen some of those men over the years. Others simply vanished. I wondered if seeing them again would elicit a similar response. I knew the answer: it would be insignificant.

The reaction to Tripp went deeper than all that. He was my first love. And I had buried him in that diary. The memo-ries came flooding back when I began turning the pages and started reading my words. The emotions were raw and real and at a level you only get with a first love. All other loves after that are based on the first one, but none quite matches the one that set the bar.

I went to bed that night depressed and feeling more alone than I ever had. When Mark asked what was wrong, I told him

I had a bad headache. The reality of that headache: Tripp was an asshole. My first text breakup. And at my age. How easy it would have been to break it off with boys had we had texts back then. Instead, we actually had to use our words. It was hard, but at least saying the words had meaning and you could feel the emotions.

I felt like that immature teenage girl in those first moments: wanting what she couldn't have; putting her hurt above his.

I tossed and turned as I asked myself a slew of questions: Is it a breakup if we were never in a relationship? Is it called something other than breaking up? Calling it off? Chickening out? Was never going to happen? Fooled you?

Over the next several days I tried to process what had happened. I was totally, completely crushed to the core. I didn't realize there could be a grieving process with just the prospect of having an affair. But I was sad to depths I couldn't fathom. I knew it was not me he was rejecting. I could truly sense that he was hurting, too. I knew that exploring with me was the one thing he would have wanted, but it was not where his heart said he needed to be. I respected that on every level.

I knew the ease of our conversations opened up things neither of us, least of all him, was expecting to feel. I was reliving emotions I had forgotten. They were unleashed slowly, then furiously through our conversations. I knew, too, that he had never forgotten me and had held on to the memories of me. I opened up to those old feelings. And he closed up. I wanted to be okay with the realization Tripp was not where I was. And it was just nice to know how important I had been then.

My mind began to overthink, over-analyze. I had hoped it wasn't some game Tripp had been playing with me with the intent to burn me all along. *Was the score even now?* I found myself wondering. *Was it just some game for him the entire time? Did he just want to exploit me, use me, and then ultimately burn me to teach me a lesson?* In my heart, I knew that was not the kind of man he was. But I wanted a reason to hate him.

Maybe what we had started would not be classified as an affair after all. How do you truly define one? Does just thinking about another person sexually make you unfaithful? I don't believe the answer to that is yes. We all need eye candy at times and fantasy is healthy.

Does it count as an affair if you never actually physically touched each other? *Good one*, I thought. Ask Dear Abby that question and she'll refer you straight to therapy. I knew it was. I knew just saying the things we did in all its many parts and pieces constituted being unfaithful. I was not suffering from guilt. He, on the other hand, must have become engulfed by it.

I did not want more from Tripp than to experience the man he had become. It was clear we still had a connection, and that buried feelings had found a way to resurface. For me at least. Reflecting, I'm not sure that Tripp ever fully forgot about me. Not like I forgot about him.

As much as I hated to admit it, his texts were meaningful. And I suppose they explained things in a strange way. I think he was chickenshit not to tell me in his own voice. He likely knew I would try to convince him otherwise, finding himself torn between loyalty to his family with the opportunity to explore a story that was never really finished. I told myself I haunted him. I had to give myself something.

I imagined he thought long and hard about the right way to say it. I wondered how many times he began to type, then deleted it, only to start again. It didn't matter how he said it, it would not be received well. He had to know that much. I don't believe he intended to inflict pain. He was doing what was best for him in that moment. Just as I did all those years ago when I broke it off with him. At least I did it over the phone. I somehow felt vindicated that I was a bigger person at eighteen than he was now. The lies I told myself.

His words always found a way to be perfect. I have read the text dozens of times, trying to find hidden meanings, subtle clues, something, anything to make me believe I wasn't understanding it correctly. It didn't matter how I read them; they said the same thing. I hated his words for the simple fact that he knew how to use them effectively:

"I loved you so much then. And it took me so long to move on. Thank God social media didn't exist. It would have killed me to see you living without me. There were always reminders anyways. I couldn't escape you like you did me. I can't deny the attraction, but the timing is terrible for both of us . . . I know that you and I deserve one hundred percent and I can't do that. I just can't give more than friendship and it's hard for me not to want to explore what may have been. It's nice to know how important we were to each other. And I will always cherish that."

All these years later when our paths did cross again, it was the same story: One of us open to possibilities while the other was still living in their moment.

"I saw that coming. I still wish we could have had our weekend. I never wanted more from you than that," I replied.

And in a second text I told him to be sure to let his wife know what he needed and wanted from her. "Clearly there is some void, or you never would have entertained me."

I tried to process and rationalize it on my own. But it was not that easy. I hated that I let myself remember. Only to have to ask myself to put it away again.

It was a setback. I was prepared for the change of heart, but I was not prepared for my reaction.

Maybe there was a reason we did safe I found myself

wondering as I slid down the abyss of self-doubt. Was I over-reacting in my loneliness? Safe was lonely perhaps, but it didn't involve exposing yourself, in my case, literally and fig-uratively. Safe meant I had somewhere to be with someone who . . . And that's where I struggled to finish the sentence.

Who was that someone? I was not seen. I was not whole. Safe meant he looked right through the middle of that donut. Safe meant always being a little empty. Safe meant finding joy outside of him to fill that hole. Safe meant robotically moving forward with a man that would always be true to me, always stand by my side because not having me was worse than stay-ing with me even if he knew he did not make me whole. That was safe.

Safe felt oddly comforting in these moments where I just wanted to crawl into a hole and hide. I did not want to figure out my life anymore. I wanted to find strength in myself. I tried to remind myself that I wanted to leave my marriage long before Tripp. I have been empty for so long.

Doubt, my new enemy. Doubt feeding every part of me. Doubt that I am good enough for anyone but Mark. *He is a good man,* I reminded myself. *He gives you everything and asks for little in return,* the voices said. Doubt that another man will find me attractive. Doubt that another man could want me. Doubt that I will ever be good enough. Doubt.

It was easy to curse Tripp for casting that spell of doubt. Or was it what I needed to realize what I had was not that bad after all? That there are men like Tripp out there who will take you in, make you feel things you haven't felt in so long, and then cast you aside to satisfy some hidden agenda of their own. How easy it was to question and doubt.

I needed so much to be more than that in these moments. I wanted to have strength, courage, and conviction. I wanted to be that woman I knew I was. Once upon a time. Where was she now?

I wanted to be able to process what happened on my own. I thought I could do it. I was miserable for days. I jumped at Mark for no good reasons. I found myself on the verge of tears. I was overwhelmed beyond my own abilities to comprehend.

I had mourned my mom's death. I felt empty when my kids both left for college. I was depressed in moments over the years when I questioned my ability to parent my children. I have been sad as I navigate my next steps in life. But the overwhelming sense of emotion associated with a plan that didn't come to fruition was more than I could handle on my own.

I had been moving on auto pilot. I was going through the motions, but accomplishing nothing. I could no longer hold in my feelings. I needed to vent. I wanted someone to tell me what I was feeling was normal. More than anything, I wanted someone to tell me to get my act together.

I found myself at Meg's door.

"Jesus, you look like shit," she said upon seeing me.

"Nailed it. I feel like shit."

I walked in and she gave me a hug. We headed to the kitchen for what I had hoped would be wine, but it was too early for that. Instead, we drank coffee by a cozy fireplace. It did little to offer me comfort as I recounted for her what happened. I let her read the texts from Tripp.

I watched her expression as she read his words. I wondered if she was trying to make sense of it any differently than I did.

"A bigger man would have called, but he was honest," she finally offered.

"I feel like an idiot. And a fool."

"You could not have known," she reminded me.

"Maybe I should have known better. Mark never would have done that to me."

In my moments of self-doubt, I found myself always circling back to Mark and my life with him. I felt myself hiding in the sanctuary of a safe place where I no longer had expectations.

"Listen to yourself. We aren't talking about Mark. Unless it's the part that drove you to even consider Tripp. Then it's Mark that drove you there."

"Mark didn't tell me to have an affair."

"Mark doesn't tell you anything. Remember? He doesn't even know you. You've said you feel like you constantly disappoint him."

I wanted to respond to that. I was going to defend him, again. She shot me a look that said otherwise.

Mark and I have had that discussion. It was the one where I told him I felt like I constantly disappointed him, which he adamantly denied. In fact, he told me he didn't have expectations of me. I wasn't sure if that was a good thing or a bad thing. It made me realize that if I could let go of expectations of him, then maybe I wouldn't be disappointed. If I wanted nothing, he could do no wrong. But I wanted something.

At the end of that conversation, I realized I was the one with expectations of myself. Maybe I didn't disappoint Mark for lack of his expectations; but I disappointed myself for not meeting my own expectations.

"You didn't come here to talk about Mark."

She was right.

"This is hard. It's so hard. I don't think you can even begin to understand how much this has affected me."

I kept asking myself why it affected me so much. I was a mature woman. I was beyond the need to get lost in some trivial thing like a few weeks with a man who used me. At this point, I was convinced that was what he had done. I could take ownership of my role in it if I could ultimately make him out to be the bad guy.

"My head was telling me to proceed with caution. My heart won though. It wanted to believe that we could have that moment."

"Don't be defeated. He wouldn't have gone this far if he were totally happy in his marriage. And he had you to explore that with."

"He had me to scare the shit out of him and head for the hills."

"And you would have done the same thing at that time."

"Would I have though, Meg?" I wondered out loud. Her reply was instant.

"Yes. Because I know you. Family first."

Meg was no stranger to my occasional moments of doubt over the twenty-five years of my marriage. She offered advice, comfort, and reassurance over those many years. She never told me I should leave even at times where it might have been a fleeting thought.

Fleeting thoughts had made their way into my marriage many times over the years. Moments of great frustration met with a flash of divorcing. But I was always brought back by the prospect of not letting my family fall apart. My happiness would play second fiddle to the overall harmony of my family. I sacrificed me for them. And I know that I would do it all over again because it was a beautiful life.

In those moments when I questioned if this was it for the rest of my life, I tried to imagine my life without Mark. I played out different scenarios in my mind. In the end, I always came back to loving him enough not to break our family apart. I loved him enough, just like he has loved me enough.

Suddenly, though, I realized enough was just that in all those years where our lives were overflowing. It sustained us enough. It bonded us enough. If it was enough all those years, why wasn't it enough now? I know I deserved more than enough. I know Mark deserved more than enough. Say "enough" enough times and it just becomes an awkward word. Enough.

"It's funny," I said. "The romantic in me always thought it

would make for a cool love story of sorts. Right? The simple proposition that if you had the chance for one weekend with your first love, would you take it? Decades later. Maybe that will be the first thing I write when I get back at it. It'll be my housewife romance novel. A fairy tale in disguise."

"First off, you are so much more than a housewife. I'm not even sure that's a thing anymore. Secondly, I love the idea of it. Although I'd never want a weekend with my first love. He fumbled through everything."

She made me laugh at that. I suppose not everyone's first love is remembered the same. They get the label, but maybe it's not met with the same sort of sentimentality. I had to be honest with myself, though. I had not remembered the depths of my summer with Tripp like I had written about it. I never mourned it ending because I never allowed it to happen. I buried it like my half-dead hamster, knowing it would perish as soon as I put the dirt on top of it. Cruel. But necessary, I thought. I was eight but already knew it was better to put something out of its misery than to keep it alive, barely breathing. I suppose Tripp was that hamster in ways. The hamster never resurrected. Tripp, on the hand, had been.

Part of me wanted to be that hamster in this moment too. I was in a dark hole. I wanted to close my eyes and fall asleep. Maybe not even wake up. I didn't want to continue to face my day to day. I felt weak not leaving Mark. I felt powerless over the surge of emotions I did not expect or anticipate from the situation with Tripp. I was uncertain about what my future was supposed to look like. It was like a blizzard hit. Trapped inside. Doors blocked by snow. No air to breathe. I was suffocating.

"Why can't I let go, Meg?" She didn't have the answer. Neither of us did.

"I think you struggle because he gave you hope. He showed you that another man could want you and desire you."

"And then burn me." I was quick to reply.

"That part sucks. But you should take away the doubts about yourself being desirable."

She was right. There were good things to be gleaned from what happened. I just could not wrap my head around letting Tripp go. I could not shake him. He was a huge, gaping cavity. It was like I was hemorrhaging heartache. My wounds were fresh.

"It'll get better," she said. "I promise."

I hoped she was right. It was hard enough before Tripp trying to make sense of what the answer to my marriage was. Before Mom died, I had been so confident leaving was the right choice. I knew I wanted to separate then. But Tripp. Stupid, Tripp. He cast his spell a second time. This one, though, had him pulling all the strings, leaving me helpless in its aftermath. He wasn't even in my marriage. But he had somehow become part of the equation. My head was a messed-up space.

"You think I should tell Mark?" I asked.

"About Tripp?"

"About having an affair."

"Why would you do that?" she asked.

"Elicit a response. See if he even cares."

"He will care. He just won't admit it bothers him." She was right, of course.

I thought about how to pose my next question. Maybe I was only asking for my own sense of understanding.

"Did I really cheat anyways?"

Meg laughed.

"Do you remember in college when I was dating that ass-hole, Trevor? He was so hot but had nothing in his brain."

I remembered Trevor. He was one of many boys Meg dated and bedded in Yale's world of secret societies. She came from a wealthy family and attracted offspring of the equally wealthy. It was her powerplay she would say. While I was from a well-to-do East coast family, she was from royalty. And they all knew each other it seemed. For her, though, it wasn't about catching a big fish to keep the family line going. She had older siblings that would do that. She simply enjoyed the game.

"We dated all of fall semester junior year. If I told you that I messed around with Dylan . . ."

I interrupted. "His roommate?"

"That's the one."

"I had no idea."

"No one did. That's the point. No one knew. We never had sex. I mean we did everything but. And God was I tempted. But in my mind, I kept thinking if I slept with him, I'd be cheating on Trevor."

"So, what you're saying is I didn't really cheat?"

"No. I was cheating. I just didn't want to admit that at the time."

"I'm confused."

"I was physically invested in Dylan. I'm not even sure why I didn't sleep with him at that point. Denial, I suppose."

"But I was never physically invested in Tripp. I never actually touched him."

I was trying to rationalize in my mind that maybe I had not cheated. If you never actually physically touch the person, does it make it void, like it never happened? If all the evidence is deleted, doesn't it just go away? I could delete the texts. It would be hard, but I could do it. I knew he would have deleted the pictures I sent. He told me he deleted the videos. It would be as if it never happened.

The virtual tryst. That was the closest we came to physically cheating. We watched each other pleasure ourselves. He was explicit. He was effective. He pleased me without having to touch me. And I pleased him just by being. But there was nothing left behind to indicate it had happened.

Over time, it might begin to feel surreal, like it was just a figment of my imagination. I hoped that would be the case. For now, it was fresh and still felt so real.

I wondered how he rationalized it in his mind. When we first spoke about it, we both acknowledged what we were about to do was cheating. At least the part where we agreed to meet. Maybe his thinking was stop it before we actually touch; if we never touch, it never happened. He would not have been unfaithful because he never touched me.

It would be like fantasizing about another person when you're having sex. Or you watch porn together and get off on that. We have all needed a little help in the bedroom. At least, I hoped I wasn't the only woman in the world who had imagined various hot men in lieu of her husband. It sometimes helped to break up the monotony. Nearly thirty years of sleeping with the same person can do that to you. That does not constitute unfaithful.

Perhaps Tripp was telling himself he stopped before it exploded. It was a momentary indiscretion he could forgive himself for. His wife would never know. And, with time, the memory of me and our brief whatever it was would fade.

The other voice in my head told me it wasn't his first time doing this. He was too good at it. He knew what he wanted. He knew what to say. He knew how to ask. And he knew how to end it. *You weren't that special after all*, it said. *He's just an asshole*, it said. *Be better than that*, it said.

"If it makes you feel better to tell Mark, then do it. He just doesn't need to know everything," she offered.

I left Meg's feeling slightly less bad than when I arrived. The caffeine and conversation had helped ease some of the anxiety I was feeling. She was right that Tripp had given me something.

He reminded me that a man could want me, that I could still be seen as sexy and desirable. I turned him on. I was dangerous. There was this part of me that liked being dangerous. I imagine in the same way that Tripp found it oddly empowering to know I thought about him in private moments. It was hard to let go of that hold he had on me. Inside, I hoped it was killing him too.

A part of me felt I needed to tell Mark. I wanted to be honest with him. I knew I needed to give him some version of the truth in case our relationship survives; in the event, I am too chicken to explore outside my safe little bubble after the crushing blow Tripp caused me.

I wondered if Mark didn't compliment me because he had always been a little insecure about our relationship. That might have been his way of keeping me on a tether without knowing I was attached to something. Did he know deep down that by not giving me affirmations, I would begin to believe I wasn't worthy of them? His lack of acknowledgment a sign that I wasn't pretty enough or funny enough or smart enough to remind that he loved me after all. In the end, though, I never complained or asked for more from him. In my spiraling mind, I began to wonder how much I was to blame for his indifference towards me. The voice: *shut the fuck up.*

That night Mark and I sat on opposite ends of the couch watching an episode of Dateline. It was a convenient episode on deceit and murder.

"If you cheated on me, would you tell me?" I asked him.

"That's a stupid question. I would never cheat on you." I knew that answer before I even asked. A normal human being might have reciprocated the question, if not out of conversational courtesy, but out of curiosity.

"Would you want to know if I did?" I asked for him.

He looked at me as if he was trying to read me, stoic, self-contained.

"Why would you ask that?"

"It's not a hard question. Would you want to know?"

"That's stupid. Of course I would want to know." He paused, reflecting. "Did you?"

I thought about how to phrase it.

"I thought about it. I wanted to. But it didn't happen." Now he knew a part of the truth.

I wanted to tell him to elicit a response. I hoped that maybe he would react on some deeper level that reminded him how much he really did love me. Did I hope he would say that changes everything? I wanted to believe Mark would fight for me even if I did. I wanted to know in that moment he loved me more than just enough.

I should have seen the reaction coming: "But you didn't."

"Not because I didn't want to," I told him. "He called it off."

Still nothing from him. I would have been sick to my stomach if he told me that. Even now, when I wanted out of my marriage, I hated the thought that I would not have been enough for him.

But I would have also had a sense of relief knowing I could get out of the marriage because he did something wrong. Just as I imagine if Tripp and I would have been physically together, that too would have been my ticket out.

But Mark did not want a ticket out. He wanted to keep on pretending, finding reasons that we would be okay, even if I confessed to wanting to be with another man. Even knowing I was not the one who called it off.

"But you didn't," he repeated.

This time, I could see the hurt. I did not need to tell him the things that I did do. The things that all the articles on the internet tell me constitute infidelity. The parts that hurt so deep now because I willingly did them when Tripp asked. I made myself vulnerable. And it cast a shadow of doubt over me like I was taking one giant step back in my forward progress.

"No, Mark, I did not."

He turned back to the TV. I assumed he was digesting what had just been said. He turned to look at me, studied me briefly like he was trying to read me. He touched my foot that was stretched out on the couch in the space between us.

"I'm glad you didn't," he offered as he patted my foot much like you'd pet a dog.

Maybe this revelation was what Mark needed to fight for me. Maybe the hurt from Tripp was what I needed to remind me that maybe, just maybe, being loved enough was good enough. Maybe.

I had confessed, sort of, to Mark. My conscience was not all the way clean, but I did not feel guilty. In ways, his reaction solidified the lack of guilt. Always a man of little words and even less action.

Before I left Meg's earlier that day, she told me I should take the weekend I had planned to spend with Tripp and go do my run anyways. I had a hotel. I had entered the race. And Mark was none the wiser that my original intent had changed. Now I would just go, to go.

"Use it as a kind of 'fuck you I can get past you' opportunity," she said.

And that was exactly what I planned to do.

14

On One Weekend and Lifetimes In Between

I packed my bags on Friday morning to board my flight to Miami. I needed to go away. I went to the race with the intent to find myself again. I did not even tell Maya I was there. That was difficult. I loved the time with her. But I wasn't sure I could contain my grief. I just needed to pretend to be the version of myself I wanted to be. I would start here. The beginning of the beginning, I told myself.

I checked into my hotel room. I didn't like the loneliness of the space. It wasn't like I hadn't spent nights in hotel rooms by myself. It was quite normal when visiting Max or Maya in college on my own.

Today it felt too quiet. Too solitary. I didn't want to spend time alone in my head. I wanted to be doing, discovery, escaping, proving to myself that this could be that 'fuck you' moment.

I would find things to do outside of this space. I'd start by checking in for the run and then head to the beach for some sun. I threw on my swimsuit, grabbed a towel and my beach bag, and headed to registration.

After getting my token T-shirt and bib, I walked to the beach, just steps from my hotel. I loved the hot sand of Florida beaches. I laid out my towel, pulled out a book, and sat myself on the beach. Satisfied. I could already feel forward progress.

For the first time all week, I could feel my body relax. It was a remarkable feeling. I wasn't worried about Mark. I wasn't obsessing over Tripp. I just closed my eyes and took in the fresh salt air, the slight ocean breeze, and the heat that warmed my body over. And I fell asleep.

I awoke what felt like seconds later but had been much longer, as evidenced by the faint shades of pink highlighted around my bikini. My skin was not used to the sun in non-summer months. I should have known better. But I took that deep, restful sleep on the sand as a sign: it was the perfect start to moving on.

I was feeling good. I could feel a bounce in my step, glad that I had found the strength to board that flight. I would not let Tripp hold me back anymore. He had inflicted enough mental damage on me. A quick stop at the hotel to shower, then I would treat myself to a pre-race pasta dinner and a much-needed glass of wine at the Italian restaurant down the block.

Back at the hotel, I got in the elevator feeling alive, ready for this new chapter. I wanted to be back on track, figuring out the pieces of my marriage in the aftermath of Tripp. With Mark, I sometimes felt like a dog. Loyal and true. Never wanting to disappoint my owner, the person who fed me, gave me a roof over my head, let me roam as I pleased. I knew I needed to take ownership, be free of any restraint that held me tethered and tied. Returning home Sunday night refreshed, in charge of my own destiny again, was what this weekend would give me.

The elevator opened at my floor. I could feel my excitement about the future, a smirk finding its way across my face. I turned the corner from the elevator and froze in my tracks. Standing in front of my door, knocking, was Tripp. He turned to me as soon as I stopped. Time froze in that moment, neither of us moving.

My mind was racing a hundred miles an hour. Do I say something clever? Do I run into his arms like I desperately wanted to do? Do I just keep standing here doing nothing waiting for him to do something? I was in a hallway at a hotel. How many options are there, really? Turning around and leaving, the smartest choice for my aching heart, was not on the list.

He smiled that grin. That grin that owned me. I began to walk towards him. I stopped far enough out of reach, feeling a sudden reminder that just days before he said he couldn't.

"How'd you know I'd be here?" I asked.

"I didn't. But maybe I knew you might come anyways."

"I'm that transparent, huh?"

In that moment, he stepped towards me. I could feel his breath, smell his deodorant. He moved his fingers down my arm, gently. His touch gave me goosebumps.

"I told myself I wouldn't relapse. I didn't want to come," he finally admitted.

"But you did."

"I couldn't *not* know. I'd be wondering the rest of my life about this weekend. I can live with the guilt, but I couldn't live with not knowing."

He inched closer, his body brushing mine.

"You're like an addiction."

"I didn't pack any of the things you asked me for," I told him.

He pulled me close as he kissed my neck. I felt my body come alive.

"That's okay. You wouldn't have needed them anyways."

I melted. Every part of me swept away in that moment. Every horrible, awful thought I had about this man and the emotional turmoil he had caused me over the past several days, vanished. All my thoughts about fresh beginnings, forgotten.

There was something romantic in the notion that the chemistry was strong after so many years. Time didn't stand still. We both had a lifetime of other relationships. We knew each other's bodies so well once. Time didn't stand still there either. Both of us matured, wearing time on our exteriors.

I left his embrace long enough to open the door. He followed me, watching to make sure the door shut, locking it as if to ensure I would not escape. I watched as he did, hoping he would not change his mind. He turned to me, grabbed me with intention, and began kissing me.

His kiss was hard. And deep. And like I remembered it. Like I hadn't been kissed in such a long time. A woman never forgets the passion a good kiss holds. When you can feel his intention with every pulse of his tongue, every gentle nibble on your lower lip, every slow kiss that turns to immediacy. It was automatic kissing him.

When he stopped, he pulled my dress up over my head, dropping it to the floor. He moved to my neck with his lips, slowly making his way along my bikini top. He followed the strap with his tongue, stopping long enough to untie my top, letting it fall, exposing my breasts. I gasped for air. He stopped to touch.

"Beautiful. Perfect." And he kissed them, toying with me, slowly then quickly, losing himself in me like I was lost in him.

He made his way down my stomach, once again stopping to follow my bikini line, untying the strings on the sides, allowing my bottoms to fall. I stood there naked in front of Tripp as he took me in. His arousal on full display through his shorts.

In that moment, I was thankful I did not cancel that waxing appointment. It was unpleasant, extremely painful, but felt amazing to be free. The thought of Tripp exploring every inch of my body only to get tangled up in that mess down below would have mortified me. I had rationalized keeping the appointment with the open mind that maybe Mark would like it.

I knew I would have to have sex again with him at some point. He was trying. Maybe he would think it my concession to making things hot in the bedroom again. It might be fun, I told myself, to have him journey back down to a territory he long ago abandoned. Or had I simply closed it for exploration?

Tripp's reaction a basic, "Wow."

I stepped towards him, lifting his shirt off, running my hands over his strong body. I thought it perfect when we were younger, but he had filled out nicely. This was a man's body.

I removed his shorts, stopping long enough to taste him, to put him in my mouth, to toy with him, to make him squirm. He pulled me up to him. We were both naked, skin to beautiful skin. Both of our bodies screaming for the other.

As he explored my body, the same one he knew so well all those years ago, I did not find myself wanting to explain the changes. I had two children. Gravity was something I could no longer defy. My stomach wore the marks. My breasts smaller perhaps and less dense than they once were. My continued love of running accounting for that, no doubt. I never liked the idea of big boobs, although I wondered if he was not a little disappointed. He would not remember those details. There were many I did not remember about him either.

I liked reacquainting myself with his body. Older. More mature. Muscular, but not in a youthful way. Maybe once there was a six pack there. I couldn't recall.

The last few weeks had felt like a blur. At times, he felt real, but mostly it felt like I was playing with a ghost, remembering someone that felt like a figment of my imagination. There were times I could feel his presence like an ethereal spirit through his words or during our virtual tryst. But now he was real, that ghostly vision a tactile human.

His touch so real now. His hands moving freely across my body. He was here in my room with me. If it weren't for the fact that my body ached as he touched me, I might have thought I was still on that beach asleep, dreaming.

But I was wide awake in a bed with Tripp.

His exploration of my body never ending. He toyed with my nipples in back arching ecstasy.

"I like this," he said, referring to my clean slate. He stayed there playing with me, teasing me, gently exploring then growing with intensity. I would orgasm for the first time. And then I would do the same for him.

We laid on the bed in silence, soaking in our own sweat.

"Hi," he said. It made me laugh.

"Hello."

He pulled me on top of him and I straddled him, grabbing his arms and pinning them above his head.

"You look amazing," he told me.

I bent down to kiss him.

"I'm glad you came."

This time, we made love. At first it felt almost desperate, like we were both starving and couldn't feed our appetites fast enough. And then when we were satiated and came back for more, it was deliberate, methodical, lacking desperation but an unbridled passion I'm not sure I'd ever felt before. Ever. I was lost in his touch. The way his hands went from gentle discovery to throbbing, pulsing necessity. The way he made the word slide come alive every time he would tease me before pleasing me. The way his tongue found new ways to touch familiar places. Every part of my body his to explore. Every part of his, a treasure map of discovery.

Maybe sex like this only happens because it's forbidden. Not allowed. Or maybe because you were always amazing in bed and the familiarity and ease of each other made it inevitable.

We didn't need toys. Our bodies finding pleasure in touch and all the ways we could still do that. Orgasms back arching, hand grabbing intense.

"I liked the hand. You're strong."

"Habit," I said, forgetting that I did that. I had learned over the years that I was not always going to orgasm vaginally. I was lucky if it happened. But my clitoral orgasms were intense, and I instinctively have come to help finish the job by applying that extra little bit of pressure. That was something I learned with time and experience. Tripp would not have had that with me.

I could not count how many times we made love that night. It felt as if we flowed from one place to another, like we only stopped long enough to allow our bodies to reset.

In one of those moments, we were in an embrace on the couch. He was playing with my hair. "I like you blonde."

I smiled at him as I ran my hand across the side of his face. "I know. My hair is not what it once was," he added.

"No. But it means I can see your face better. And I really like your face."

"Were we always this intense as lovers?" he asked.

"Probably in those moments. At that age. We were. You were the first boy I slept with. I ate you up teaching me about sex and understanding my own body. And yours, of course." In that moment, he rolled me over, pinning me beneath his strong body. He kissed my neck. I could feel him hardening beneath me.

"God, I'm a good teacher." And I moaned as I felt him enter me. "I don't think my body will ever tire of you."

I watched him as he moved slowly over me, deliberate in his movement, savoring each pulsation.

"I know mine won't," I said. I knew I would hold on to this night for the rest of my life.

We would shower, making love for the last time then. I was lost in Tripp. My mind had never been more present in a moment. I knew this wouldn't be forever, that it would end, but I didn't want to remember that part.

When we finally settled, our bodies exhausted, fulfilled, and simultaneously awoken, he held me in his arms. Our naked bodies still perfect together. Our fingers intertwined. My hands felt old to me, scarred, and worn. One of the few things I felt betrayed my age. He traced the scars.

"Scars are stories," I said.

"Always with us," he said softly.

I looked at him as he stared at mine. Then he looked at me for a long moment. I wondered what he was searching for.

"You think there's a song for this?" he asked.

"Us? Now?"

"Yea."

I thought about it.

"I'll know it when I hear it," I said.

Tripp and I talked for hours. It wasn't just the sex that was amazing. I wanted it to be only about that. At least, that's what I told myself. But it was hard not to fall back into what suddenly felt so familiar. He gave me small glimpses into his loneliness. And I shared with him the parts of me that felt empty. Much like our lovemaking, conversation was fluid, enjoyable, and without judgment or condemnation. We were breaking the rules of marriage. That was not lost on us.

"When you go home, will you be able to pretend this didn't happen?" I asked.

"I'm not going to lie, Jenn. I will try. I have to. You?"

"My situation is different from yours. And I have to figure my shit out."

"I want you to be happy. I wish I could give you that."

"I know. I know you can't." I paused, watching him as he held me. "You gave me a gift today. You reminded me of the woman I am." I kissed his chest slowly, breathing him in, tasting the lingering sweat.

We were both broken in parts. Being in this moment made us whole, if not just for a little while.

I woke up and reached for Tripp. The space next to me was empty. I called for him, but there was no answer. I got up, put some clothes on, went to pee, and brushed my teeth. Walking back, I noticed his clothes were gone as well as the duffle bag he had brought with him. I felt myself panic a little. Had I dreamed the whole thing? Confused, I walked towards the coffee maker. I needed caffeine to think. And there, beside the machine, was a folded-up piece of paper with my name on the outside.

I opened the paper and read the letter. A hollow pit was growing in my stomach. I wanted to throw up. I read it again, torturing myself with his words:

Dear Jenn,

A long hand note because a text would not do. But saying the words to you in person would be impossible. I watched you sleeping this morning. I know you always hated that, but I couldn't take my eyes off you. It was as if you weren't real. I studied the lines on your face, wondering what things made you smile and laugh all these years, wishing deep down that I could have been there to watch them become part of you over time. You were beautiful then and are even more beautiful now. It sounds cliché, I know, but you took my breath away. It pained me knowing what I had to do. I realized that you are dangerous for me. I regret nothing about last night. And wish we could have this morning. But I cannot. The pull towards you is too great. Know that I loved you once so deeply it scarred my heart and a small part of you has always been there. But I cannot. Or I won't. Be happy, Jenn. I will always think of you, but I cannot do this. And

I think you know and understand why. You always made me weak. And all these years later, it's finally time for me to be strong.

Tripp

I crumpled the letter in my hand as waves of sadness convulsed through my body. I cried, wailing in sorrow. Or maybe it was self-pity. I don't know how long I lay on the bed curled up in a ball, suffering. Unable to breathe. Hating myself for doing it.

The race went on while I cried. I should have mustered the courage to run to spite Tripp. To show I was still strong after being broken. But he crushed me unexpectedly. I was not prepared to see him, be with him, then be left by him. All three within twenty-four hours and without any warning.

Second chances. I believed in my heart they existed. I didn't believe you magically picked up where you left off. Decades of life happened in between. The second chance was to start anew.

A second chance with your first love. Everything was different. The only thing that remained was some small part that knew it was not finished when it ended. Over the past few weeks, it became clearer to me why I had buried Tripp so deep within myself. The story was unfinished. I tucked it away so that maybe someday those memories might be recovered or rediscovered.

At eighteen, I would not have thought that possible. In my mid-fifties, I recognized it as fact. The pain of today would have been significantly less, assuming I would have let him in at all, had I just thrown him out with the trash like I did all the others who came after him. Now he was a stinky reminder of young love.

I headed home. Doubt about my life on full display. That one voice screaming Mark never would do that to you. The other one whispering that was beautiful and look at the woman you still are.

Maybe it was all a dream anyways. It felt surreal. Like it never even happened. Maybe the better phrase is beautiful nightmare. An oxymoron if there ever was one.

Once again, I stood at the front door to walk in. This time totally lost and confused. I wasn't ready to go in yet. I turned around, got in my car, and drove to Meg's house, hoping she would be there. I could have called, but I didn't know where to begin.

I knocked on her door. Craig answered. He was a perceptive man. He could read me, clearly registering I was hurting. He let me in, hugged me, and called for Meg.

"Geez, Jenn, you look like shit."

It made me laugh.

"Seems to be a theme when I walk in your door. I feel like shit. I can't go home yet." I followed her towards the kitchen where she pulled out a bottle of red wine and two glasses. I sat, she poured. I took a sip and shared my weekend.

I started with a simple, "Tripp showed up."

Her jaw dropped.

"Jesus fucking Christ. And . . ."

"It was so much more than I could have imagined. But I woke up and he was gone. Left me a note. That was it. At least that was better than those texts."

"Which he obviously did not mean."

"No. He meant them. But I think he needed some sort of closure. Or it was a game. I don't know."

"It wasn't a game. Clearly, you were very real to him."

"I feel so stupid feeling like this. I'm a grown woman and

I'm acting like a stupid teenager having her heart broken."

In all honesty, I didn't know what that felt like. In all my relationships, I was always the one that broke up. If I sensed a boy might be over me, I'd be over him first. If the timing was a little off or a boy had some strange quirks, I'd be running the other way. It was always easy for me to get up and go. But I did generally feel bad about it afterwards. I wasn't mean. I just didn't want to stay in a relationship if there was no purpose.

"Maybe you never really mourned that relationship ending. I mean, to be fair, I've known you since freshman year of college and I can't ever remember you mentioning Tripp."

That revelation was not lost on me. Even in my diaries I didn't dwell on the breakup. I had new fish to catch. I just simply moved on.

"Wow. I think you're so right." I was digesting that. "So thirty-some fucking years later, I'm mourning a breakup from when I was eighteen? Jesus, what kind of freak am I?" Really. Was it normal what was happening to me?

"You're not a freak. I think you were so in the moment back then, you never looked back. But I do think it's normal to grieve, be sad, depressed after you break up with someone, even if you're the one breaking up. And your first love? I cried every day for weeks after my first love and I broke up."

"Well, now you're really making me feel like shit."

"No. I think you've just been hit with this blast from the past and became overwhelmed by everything. You let yourself feel again." She poured more wine into our emptying glasses. "I know this hurts like hell, but I'm proud of you for putting yourself out there."

Maybe Tripp hadn't been playing a game with me. He weakened knowing I might be nearby. It was one last chance to kick in the door of opportunity before he knew it would be closed to him. By him. Weak, embattled, heartbroken me knew that door would always be left slightly ajar.

I had tormented him enough that he was willing to risk it all to have that weekend with me. An afterthought, maybe. The pull to me too much. Maybe I had more power than I thought.

If I told myself that, maybe I would stop feeling like shit.

We quickly polished off that bottle of wine during the course of our conversation. Meg went to open another. We weren't done talking, but we needed to be.

"I need to get home. Mark's expecting me."

"I know. Hopefully, he doesn't ask too many questions to-night."

"He usually doesn't."

She rolled her eyes at his general lack of interest. Tonight, though, I did not want to answer any questions. I wanted to continue to grieve, wallow in self-pity, beat myself up more for being an insensitive seventeen-year-old.

"How was it by the way? The sex?"

I took a deep breath, remembering the magic of the night before. The countless hours we had spent reacquainting our-selves with our bodies. And then discovering new things about each other. Our tastes had evolved. Our ability to appreciate the intensity of it in that moment something we did not have when we were younger. As adults, we had learned what pas-sion was and how to channel that into each other. We were simultaneously able to be selfish and satisfied while allowing the other person to feel the same. At this point in our lives, we knew how to be lovers and appreciate the magnitude of those moments.

You do not simply fill a void, discount gaps in time, and expect things to be like they were. Even if it was unfinished business. We were so young. And I had forgotten so much of that relationship. But the sex was always great. Tripp was a thoughtful lover then and a passionate lover now. Evolution.

I took a deep breath, trying to hold back tears.

"Unreal. He was unreal, Meg. A beautiful man with a beautiful heart who loved me once, reminded me of that. And now I'm broken." I wiped a tear from my eye. "But I would do it all over again just to feel his touch."

She gave me a hug. "Sucks that first love is wasted on the young, doesn't it?"

She was right. And with that sentiment in my head, I went home to Mark. I would face his avoidance head on.

I found him watching TV. I went and sat next to him on the couch. He did not attempt to kiss me or even reach for me.

"How was your run?" he asked without looking from the TV.

"Slow." I lied. "I'm getting too old to race anymore."

"You tried, though. That's good."

I tried. *I just fucking cheated on you. My heart is broken in a million pieces. You can't even look at me and see my swollen eyes from crying. Or even smell the alcohol on my breath.*

This was Mark supporting me. Enabling me. Making me want to run away.

"I'm tired. Long day." I got up from the couch. "I'll see you in the morning."

"I'll be up soon."

"Good night."

"Night."

I readied for bed, saddened by the reflection of myself I saw in the mirror. I had come so far, but this weekend was more than I had ever imagined. I had fallen, taken a step back in my forward progress.

I got in bed, closed my eyes, and felt myself remembering, playing that night over in my mind, not wanting to let go. His touch still so fresh on my skin. His lips, his breath, his presence. I wanted to reach for him. But he was gone. And I knew there would never be another time for us. I was lucky, maybe, that I even had that opportunity. He could have hated me forever for all those years ago. Some people can carry grudges like that.

But I did not believe in regrets. I knew that in my life, I made the right decision all those years ago. Tripp and I had both done all the things we were supposed to do. Our paths were to intersect once just long enough to know a special love. That love fueled by the knowledge there was always going to be an end where our paths would go different directions. I learned what it meant to be loved unconditionally and completely, not to doubt or fear I wasn't good enough. But it never could have been forever because I was too young and was just beginning to live. We both were.

All these years later for our paths to cross again was unexpected. They say people come into your life for a reason. I couldn't get past what that was supposed to be this time.

We met again on the other side of our evolution. We were grown-ups. Full-blown adults with lifetimes lived. The memories should have been faded, serving only to provide joyful glimpses of our previous life. But there was something between us. The pull inevitable. The timing imperfect.

Decades do not simply bridge seamlessly like a gap in employment. You do not go back in time and believe you're going to pick up where you left off. There are holes. There are changes. There are questions. Why go back at all? Do you go back because what you shared was so intense it left a mark on your heart and psyche? Was it unfinished? Or did it just end imperfectly?

I knew the answer was imperfectly. We were victims of the clock ticking at a different rate for us, never able to synchronize or stay in place long enough to tick together. Twice in a lifetime is a cruel twist of fate, I thought.

It was beautiful but ultimately brutal having Tripp come to me. I wanted it more than anything. But I had suffered so much that week prior, questioning myself. Now, I was crushed to the core. It wasn't the hope of a future with Tripp. I might have envisioned it, but I never considered it more than a fantasy.

I went through a mental checklist, asking myself if I would have considered myself capable of having this reaction. Until the moments when I revisited those memories through my diaries and then reconnected with Tripp, I thought myself immune to a reaction like this. I had not thought about Tripp in so long. I no longer knew what I was capable of or if I was even strong enough to handle second chances in the first place.

I wondered if I should come clean with Mark. He seemed oblivious to my pain. In ways, I had already confessed to him that I thought of having an affair. Ironically, before the physical part. Deep down, I knew doing it would have crushed him. It may have sealed my fate in our marriage, been the actual ticket out. But I knew if I told him that Tripp had a change of heart, just showed up unannounced, that I did not plan this one, he still would have been broken because I did it anyway.

I couldn't bring myself to say more. The hurt would be much. And if I found myself resigned to staying, it would be a black cloud. For now, I had caused him enough pain.

The next several months were a struggle. I could not shake Tripp. The things that I did for him. That was the hardest part for me. I shared so much with him. I gave him every part of me. We had been intimate in every way. His text messages to me were so erotic, so perfect in their execution. A man wanting to *slide* into me. I am sure I will never hear that word the same again. I pleasured in exploring every part of him and him exploring me. In the end, though, he would get more from me than I asked of him.

I knew we both had unfinished business with each other. But less like a business arrangement where both parties have something to gain, this felt like a game with one winner and one loser.

I lost. I felt like I had been used, like I was the pawn in his game. He had already made me doubt before he had come for me. Then he came. He gave me sex. I said that was all I wanted. And it was perfect in every way possible. Except the ending.

I let myself feel things for Tripp beyond just wanting his touch again. I felt silly and childish. A mature woman in her fifties unable to delineate fantasy from reality. I could hear Mark taunting me that fairy tales aren't real; there is no happily ever after. He would remind me that the original Grimm fairy tales all had morbid undertones. He was right.

I regressed after our night together. I doubted myself. Questioned why I would leave something that was safe and secure. I told myself that Tripp was not the man I thought he was.

He was like many other married men who strayed for a moment but found too much comfort in his family and life at home. I knew he could not have been totally happy in his relationship; even I knew I did not hold that much power over him based on a relationship that happened decades ago. I wanted to find good in him again. I was disappointed that I allowed myself to be vulnerable. More than anything, I wondered why I didn't feel remorse or more sorrow when I broke up with him the first time. Was I that cold and heartless? Was I like the Grinch who had to grow into his heart? Was this what true heartache felt like and I was experiencing it for the first time at my age?

Maybe first love is wasted on the young for a reason after all. They have the ability to let go and move on. And sometimes just forget all together. Youth. A gift we don't appreciate until it's no longer ours.

I found myself in a masochistic state. I would read and re-read his erotic texts to me. Even after the hurt, they still made me feel wanted, desired, needed, even with knowing how it ended. He would do all those things to me even more perfectly than he wrote of them. But his words ultimately were tormenting me. I could feel his touch through them. I could feel his breath, smell him. His words were all of him. I needed Tripp gone. I realized that for me to move forward, I had to start letting go.

I sent Tripp one final text: "I can't shake you. And it sucks."

I knew he would not reply.

Then I started deleting his texts. That was painful. It was all I was ever going to have. Deleting them meant having no more reminders that Tripp ever happened.

Deleted.

Crushed once more.

Tomorrow a new beginning. I hoped. I will always wonder if our story would have ended differently if time had not been our enemy. But I needed to move on. I was determined to move forward even if it meant I occasionally fell backwards.

15

On Graduation and Vacation

Moving forward. Pretending that I was fine. I had to find a way because standing still was not what I wanted to be doing. There have been times I wished I had a full-time job to preoccupy myself. Maybe I would not have found myself questioning so much in my marriage. I would have been content being busy in my life, helping others, making a difference, forgetting that I had needs.

I knew all of Mark's characteristics. Why were my needs suddenly so different? But they weren't. The needs were always there. They just found a way to stay hidden in the shadows of chaos. Life had been chaotic with Mark. We had never known normal until both kids were gone from home. Normal. What was that even?

Normal meant no one needed me to solve the world's woes on a daily basis. Normal meant waking up and not having to hurry somewhere, be someplace. Normal meant I could start doing things for me again. It meant I could start writing. It meant I could learn to paint if I really wanted to. I didn't, but it was an option none the less. Normal meant I could be me. But, stupid me didn't like normal and was confused by the person she was supposed to be in the face of normal.

The voices would battle. They'd tell me it was bullshit. I

have always known that normal meant I could be any version of myself I wanted to be. I would no longer be defined by others' expectations of me. I did my mom job. I raised two brilliant people who are proving themselves competent and capable independent of me (most days anyways). The deviant voice, the one I didn't like because it lacked courage, told me I was foolish to want normal to be anything different than what it had become: routine, expected, lacking emotion or sustenance.

I wanted emotion. I wanted touch. I wanted hot sex or at least more frequent sex. I learned I was very much still capable of that. I wanted validation that my ideas counted, that I would be heard because I had something to offer. I wanted to hear *I love you.*

I wanted to sit on the couch knowing the person I was with was looking at me thinking he's the luckiest man in the world to be by my side. And I wanted to feel the same way. I did not want to be resigned to sitting on opposite ends of the couch with the sporadic glance at the other person. Maybe our eyes connecting on occasion, a long-ago part of him looking familiar. I wanted to be present in that moment.

I wanted to be old and wrinkled and still see that little spark of fire, that he remembered the beauty of me, that I remembered the beauty of him. I wanted to live in a fairy-tale world. I wanted to believe in magic. I wanted to believe that the last decades of my life could be just as meaningful as the first. Different pace. Different motivations. But loved, truly loved. And if that meant by no one, then I would have at least loved myself enough.

I hated using the calendar as justification not to leave, but I knew we needed to stay together, be in the same home, try, until Maya graduated from college. That was just a few months away. I would have hotel reservations to make. Flights to book. Outfits to buy. A party to plan. I would have spring functions with Maya and her sorority. I was determined to create a united front for the world to see. We would not be the talk of Greenwich gossips at tea.

Pictures on Facebook made us look happy. We were a beautiful family. We really were. That part ached. It hurt to look at those pictures knowing they did not tell the real story. No one ever posts the pictures that say, *'I'm struggling'* or *'My life is a confusing piece of shit right now.'* We posted the pictures we wanted the world to see. I looked at the photos and knew the real story: the pictures ripping down the middle, separating Mark and me.

Time began to blur as the days until Maya's graduation neared. As much as I wanted out and away to figure out who I was supposed to be, who I wanted to be for the rest of my life, I sometimes got comfortable with the idea of staying. It was easy to fall victim to self-doubt. The experience with Tripp made me question myself, the risks imposed by leaving, the vulnerability, being gullible, foolish, undisciplined. All things I was not but had been in those moments after Tripp. But I could not fault him completely; self-doubt was always going to be a reality. It was just amplified in the aftermath of Tripp.

Mark and I were still leading independent lives. Together, but not. Side by side, in theory. But the reality said we coexisted. There was no animosity; I didn't hate Mark. I don't even think I resented that we couldn't get past the empty space between us.

I questioned staying or leaving a hundred times a day. I wondered if I deserved my version of happy. Would I be okay living the rest of my life with knowing if I stay, a part of me will always be wondering, hoping, but not living? Happy will be that donut; happy will not be whole.

There were so many days when the sadness overwhelmed me. It would take over and I felt like I was drowning in it. Waves of pain would pound in my heart, pulsing, pushing, throbbing, burning. It was so deep sometimes, and I felt it wanting to explode from my chest. But it didn't manifest itself in any way. Instead, I was left just wondering why I felt this way. I wondered why the life I had been living with the man I swore to love, honor, and cherish for all of my days, wasn't enough. Why now, at this time of my life, when I was on the downward side of life's journey? Why would I even want to consider this? But then I felt it. I felt it pulling. I felt it wanting to pounce on every part of me to remind me these feelings weren't new and that I deserved my own happy even if it meant having to be sad first, maybe even forever . . . and that I would destroy another life in the process.

I was like a pinball, ricocheting all over the place. The sadness would turn to resignation, and I would tell myself I could do it. I could be okay with what it was. I could stay in this marriage. But then I would be reminded why I wasn't sure I could.

I had asked Mark to take some initiative in our marriage. I wanted him to show me that I wasn't just some trophy wife. I wanted him to take an interest in the things I liked and wanted to pursue.

I was asked to write an article about my mom for a Cape Cod community publication. They had reached out requesting a tribute for her. They obviously were not aware of her secrets. Dad couldn't do it. Or wouldn't. But I did. I was quite pleased with myself. I could feel the creative energy start to flow again. I was excited putting words to paper. And I wanted Mark to read it.

I sent it to him at his work email. I figured that would get his attention. I had already told him I was going to write it. I asked him to read it and let me know what he thought before

I sent it off.

I did not receive an email reply. I was already disappointed by that. All he had to do was send me a little thumbs up, say good job, or offer a minor edit. When I asked him about it, he said he didn't have time to read it, but that it was "probably great because you wrote it."

"I just asked for your opinion. I was excited to write something again."

"Sorry. I got busy. And it's your mom. You know what's best."

"That was not the point, Mark. The point was you were supposed to take an interest in something I like to do. I was excited to share it with you."

"I didn't know."

"I told you."

With that, he went to his computer, pulled up the email, and read it.

"Looks good. I wouldn't change anything."

"Of course not," I said.

"What's that mean?"

"It means you'd actually have to think about what I wrote. It's too late anyways. I had to send it this afternoon."

"You didn't tell me that."

"Would it have mattered anyways?"

I walked away from him in that moment, my eyes welling with tears at the blatant disregard for my feelings. But I did not cry. Instead, I found myself pissed and angry with one more reason solidifying why I should leave. Unrealistic expectations met with constant disappointment and the realization that life is too short. At least what is left of it. There are no guarantees of happily ever after. Ever. And I was finding myself fine with that.

I cannot put the entire fault of our marriage getting to where it was on Mark. I could have done things differently earlier on when I started to recognize the void. But I let it go, too. I could have made it clearer what I wanted and needed. I would on occasion tell him that he needed to hug me more or tell me he loved me. Maybe hold my hand. Offer a compliment on his own rather than me asking. I wanted him to show an interest in the things I was doing even if they were trite and boring. He would try for a few days, but it quickly subsided. And I just chalked it up to I wasn't worth doing that for. You can't teach an old dog new tricks. I'd be annoyed but move on because busy was better in those moments.

Mark stayed true to himself in good ways and bad ones. I was not asking Mark to be a different person. I had fallen in love with that person. But there were parts of himself he could have given me in an effort to show his love. I had expectations, and it seems we continually found a way to disappoint each other.

"You don't disappoint me," he said when I brought that up.

"Yes, I do. There are so many times I can see you looking at me like *don't do it* or *don't say it* or just *don't go there*. You fear me and my ways."

I have no filter. I admitted it. I have never had a filter. It was not a condition I acquired over the years. It was me. You loved that about me or cringed. Or, maybe if you're married to me, you accepted that as part of who I was. I have mellowed as I have gotten older. I picked my battles a little more selectively.

"I don't fear you," he said to me. I could hear him mocking me. "And you don't disappoint me. I know that's how you are."

I thought about that.

"How come you've never asked me for anything in our marriage?"

If Mark would have asked me to do something specific for our marriage—an action, behavior, more sex, give him a blow job—I would have tried if it meant it would make us better. But he never asked for anything. So maybe in that respect I really never did disappoint Mark. Because he knew better than to have expectations of me.

"I haven't had anything to ask you for."

"So you're totally happy like it is?" I wanted him to say no. I wanted him to own it. How could he be happy if I wasn't?

"Yes." God dammit. "But I know you aren't. And I'm not sure I can ever get myself out of the hole I'm in."

So now what? I wanted to ask. Mark was complacent. He was fine with what we had. He would be willing to go the rest of his life watching me sit on the fence, deciding if I was going to run for the hills or stay.

I was frustrated and disappointed with Mark's lack of effort to do anything more than the status quo to save our marriage. It infuriated me. And now that he felt he couldn't get out of the hole meant staying the course, being true to his routine, the one where we were two ships constantly passing each other by, but hardly recognizing the other one as friend or foe.

Once again, I found myself in the driver's seat of our marriage. I needed to find a way to get through these next few months. I needed clarity and direction from someone or something other than the voices in my head.

"You need to take a vacation together."

I stared at Tracy in utter shock. We would see her for therapy one more time. A sort of grand gesture on Mark's part since he assumed I was going to do what I wanted anyways. It was his resignation that angered me more than anything. But trying to tell him otherwise was about as useful as a broken record. He didn't want to hear it, and he certainly wasn't going to change anything because he figured the outcome was already determined. But it was his idea to go back for another session with her.

She suggested that we take a vacation together sooner rather than later. It would allow us time away from our everyday lives to reconnect. Taking vacations without our kids was not something we had done since before we had them. I would take trips. Mark would take trips with his buddies or extend conferences here and there. I never joined him because there was always something to do with Max and Maya. We might jointly go visit them when they were in college. I suddenly wondered why we had never taken a vacation when we had the opportunity. Certainly, we could have in the past few years. He never offered it up. Like most things involving planning, I suppose I could have. Why not?

We left the therapy session agreeing to take a trip. Mark actually seemed excited about it. Maybe he thought travel would cure me. I wondered at the irony he did not see: looking outside of himself for my happiness.

I cannot say that I was overly excited about the prospect of vacationing for a week with Mark. We'd have to have sex. We had not been sexual since my night with Tripp. I avoided it, found excuses not to when he made the effort. After being with Tripp, I wondered if I could ever go back to Mark in the bedroom. Sex had become laborious at best and mostly unfulfilling on many levels. But Tripp had broken my heart. And doubts about myself and my potential attractiveness to other men abounded. I tried to tell myself it was not valid. I tried to brush it off as an anomaly of the situation, but my self-esteem still suffered from it.

At least with Mark, there was no doubt. I knew exactly where I stood. Was that better than doubt? Where was that magic eight ball when I needed it? Where was the clarity?

We decided on the Bahamas. There was plenty for us to do

together. We could snorkel, relax on the beach, read, talk to each other. Talking to each other. For a whole week. What would that even look like? Tracy's only rule was we were not allowed to talk about the kids. That was the only thing we ever talked about.

Mark and I shared the same opinions on most things. We brought up politics. That was a short conversation. I was once quite opinionated on all things politics. These days, though, I read the news, kept up on the world, had definite opinions, but no longer had the energy or desire to talk in depth about the state of the world's affairs. Mark agreed.

Mark liked some music, but his tastes were different from mine. He never liked to dance like I did. He preferred heavy metal throwback music. I liked the recent releases on Spotify. Maya was always sending me the latest and greatest songs. Every so often, though, I would find a treasure before she did. My tastes in music had evolved to match the music's current era. But I was always like that. Mark liked the old rock music stations and country. I liked country pop, and we could find agreement on music through that.

"We should go to one of those country music festivals next time there's one," Mark suggested.

"We could fly to California and do Stagecoach," I offered.

"When is that?"

"I'm not sure. Spring probably."

"We should plan on that."

"Okay." I did not offer to look into it. It felt empty since we both knew it was not going to happen.

We had sex the first night we were there. It was nice to see Mark respond to me in a bathing suit. He wasn't a man who liked lingerie. Or, if he was, he had never told me. He always said he liked me naked. And I liked him naked. Funny, though, that men's briefs are what constitute sexy underwear. They never have to worry about being sexy in the bedroom. I liked feeling sexy; I just didn't need to with Mark. Because he wouldn't have noticed.

I wondered if Tripp had found me sexy. Neither of us wore clothes once they came off, and we never stopped. I supposed I didn't need to look sexy in those moments. We were consumed and that sufficed. I was not going to question or beat myself up wondering what Tripp was thinking in those moments. He made love to me like no one else had before. At least not that I can remember. Thirty years with the same man. You forget.

Mark came up behind me, rubbed my butt, grabbed my breasts. Felt robotic. But he was trying, I told myself. I turned to him. And we kissed. For two seconds. Would he even know how to kiss me anymore, truly investing himself in kissing me like he used to? I used to love the way he kissed me. The way Tripp kissed me still lingered. There is no part of kissing that is underrated. Tripp reminded me how much I missed it. People our age were still allowed to enjoy kissing. It wasn't just for younger, new in love couples. It was simple, anticipatory, erotic, essential.

Mark's kiss quickly turned to taking my swimsuit off. I did not bring the one I wore when Tripp came. I would never wear that suit again. It would stay hidden in the depths of my closet along with the lingerie I had bought . . . for him because he had asked me to wear something sexy. God, did I like how he asked me for things. I liked how he had opinions. How he asked if he could do things to me, were there boundaries, was anything off limits.

"There is no part of me that is off limits to you," I texted back when he asked. I was all his, grateful that he wanted to please me in all the ways he could imagine.

Mark discovered that I had waxed. His reaction was actually pleasing.

"You look like a porn star," he said.

"I hope that's good."

He went down on me, going back to a place he had not been in a very long time. And I liked it. Very much, actually. It did not last long before he was inside of me. And a few thrusts later he was finished. I knew the routine. He goes first. I go second. He was good about going the distance there. I was distracted, though. I faked it and he called me on it.

"They don't have to all be big," I lied. He got up from the bed, went to the bathroom to clean himself off, then came back. I got up, went to the bathroom, and finished myself off. Halfway to an orgasm, it was still waiting to happen. In the past year, I had found myself increasingly in that position. My drive for sex and orgasms greater than what was being delivered in the bedroom. I had gotten comfortable with vibrators, knew how to touch myself, and never left disappointed. If I never had sex again, I at least knew I would still be having orgasms.

We would have sex one more time that week. Two times in one week was a huge increase in frequency. We're on an island, barely clothed, hot, feeling sexy. We should be having sex every day, twice, I told myself. We weren't too old for that. All those years when life said we couldn't because kids might walk in, or we were too tired from the day, or we were going opposite directions all summer taxiing kids to their tournaments. We should have been finding that part of ourselves again. I would not buy the narrative we were too old and that people in their fifties weren't having sex. Tripp a reminder that sex could be even better at this age. Stupid Tripp.

The night before we left to go back to the routine of our normal life, I asked Mark how he was feeling. He studied me, trying to read me like one of his law reviews. I'm sure he thought I was as complicated as they were in that instant, trying to interpret the meaning, how to apply it to this moment.

"I tried, Jenn. But I can sense you've already made up your mind."

"So you've given up trying to change it?" It was not wrong of me to want to feel him fight for me. But it was not who he was. He would be the man forever okay with ninety percent.

"All I've ever wanted is for you to be happy. And I wish that happy was with me. But I don't think I can give you that."

I suddenly felt like Mark was giving me permission. I felt a little empty, a little sucker punched. But it was what I wanted; most of me knew that.

"We were amazing together as parents. The part before that was one hundred miles an hour. We've never just really done us before."

"We didn't have kids for two years after we got married. And the years before that—"

I cut him off. "The years before that, Mark, they were a blur. Our paths constantly crossing as I did my corporate thing, and you were building your practice. We were so busy in those moments."

"There's that word you hate again." He looked at me. "Busy."

"I don't want to be happy only when I'm busy anymore. I want to find happy in the moments when I am staring out over the water with empty thoughts. When my mind isn't in a hurry, and I don't have anywhere to be."

"We can do that."

"I don't know if we know how to do that. I have loved you for so long. I will always love you. But I don't think I can do forever anymore."

He turned away.

"I chose you, Mark. And I chose this life. I'm not sure you would have chosen me if I pursued my career elsewhere." Mark liked his version of safe, the one where he didn't have to leave and be tested. I was testing him now, and he was uncomfortable.

"This time, I am choosing me." I didn't always know what

that looked like, but I needed to figure that out. It was time to be about me.

"And you're just going?"

"Just going? For months I have stayed trying to find us. Every time I think maybe, it's like you put up a wall, go back to the way you always are with me. The way that doesn't make me feel like I mean anything to you. God, just once I wish you would look at me like I am the only person in the whole wide world and no one else matters. Just once I wanted to feel like I mattered to you beyond the day to day."

"That's not even realistic."

"Maybe. Not for you. Maybe it isn't for anyone. But I can't be happy in my life wishing I mattered to you . . . I know you tried. I do. And maybe I will regret this decision, but for now, for me, I have to be true to me. For the first time in a long time, I have to do me. It's my turn."

"Okay. Okay. At least you know I tried."

"I know. We tried. Neither of us quit. But we both deserve to be happy for the rest of our lives. And sometimes I feel like we're so fucking old. I do. And I think just give in and stay. But that wouldn't be fair to either of us." I knew it would be hard to say the words that it is over, really truly over.

Mark was thinking. He had something he wanted to say. For a grand orator to be so thoughtful in his word choice meant something profound was coming.

"There are so many things I would do differently if I could. I can see I was wrong to think changing things about myself meant losing ownership. I should have seen them as a way to show my love for you. I could have been less set in my ways."

"I will always love you. And I will always be grateful for the life you gave me. But I will be most grateful if you give me this."

He put his arms around me. Unusual. "I don't want to let you go, Jenn. But I will even if it's the hardest thing I'll ever do to prove to you what you mean to me."

All I could think in that moment was he says the right thing when it's too late. I left it at, "Thank you." I had a heavy heart. I felt tears. But I also felt an overwhelming sense of relief that we had landed on the same page, that we had both tried.

We can live a lifetime. And we can love many. Some loves last forever, others last long enough. Sometimes it's knowing when to let go, move forward, limit resentment that makes the opportunity to live a happier rest of your life key. When was that? If it was at all. I hoped we had found that place. Mark would always be a part of me. I have no regrets, no resentment, just hope that we can find a way to coexist, be happy for the other, and, maybe even over time, be friends. I knew in my heart we could still be that.

"Jesus, we'll have to tell the kids." The reality of the situation suddenly hit Mark.

"It might be awkward, but let's do it after Maya graduates in a few weeks."

He thought deeper. "You don't have to leave right away."

"I know." Presumptuous, I thought, that he thinks I am the one to leave. But I knew he was right. If I wanted to figure out this version of me, whoever she was, I was going to be the one to walk away. It was, after all, my idea. It wasn't like anything was really going to change if I stayed. We functioned independently. Now we would do it with a dark cloud of separation looming over our heads in our own home. No one on the outside could see in. The storm on the inside causing no visible damage to the exterior.

"After she graduates," I repeated under my breath,

wondering where I was going to go and how I was going to do it. He's letting me go. We're separating. I get to move forward and hope that the grass is greener or at least a lesser shade of brown.

I knew in that moment I was not filled with guilt about having been with another man. I was filled with a renewed vigor and even some hope that I could still be attractive and desirable. For my age. There was also a small surge of sadness. The reality the Hail Mary would be dropped in the end zone because I just couldn't make the catch no matter how well thrown.

It was an awkward flight home, knowing that from this moment forward it would be about going through the motions. Moving to separate bedrooms. Crossing paths like roommates. The empty wouldn't change, though. It had been empty even when we were together. Now we would officially have empty space between us rather than the metaphorical one.

We were on autopilot until Maya graduated. Mark moved to the guest bedroom without being asked. I was grateful for that. I found myself looking for him across the bed. I did not find joy in that. It just served as a reminder that my bed would be half full from here on out. There would be lonely mornings, sad nights, sad mornings, lonely nights. I had those in my marriage. There was just a body on the other side of the bed taking up the space. Now there was no body, and that amplified those feelings.

We told the kids about our decision the weekend after Maya's graduation, when we were all briefly home again. I don't imagine telling grown kids their parents are divorcing is any easier than telling younger ones. In a certain sense, I imagine younger kids to be more resilient, less adjusted to life because it's still so frenetic when they're younger. Older kids had become routinized, knew what the expectations of home were because they were done growing.

Max and Maya were adults leading their own lives far from home. Even during college summers, they would stay away at school, working or traveling, visiting friends. We were a pit stop in those moments. That was the way it should have been. If I really thought about it, the nest had been emptying in spurts for years. It had been building, but I had been avoiding the reality. This last year, with Maya's impending graduation, it all came crashing down. I could no longer look at a calendar, using the future as an excuse to avoid the present.

We had spent the day celebrating with family and friends. I wanted the focus to be on Maya, but I felt myself anxious, wanting to scream to the world that this was just a façade, the part with Mark and me not real.

I did not think telling them would be easy. But I also did not think they were totally oblivious. I wasn't sure at what moment to start the conversation, but it had to happen, and Mark left it on my shoulders to break the news. He did not seem in a hurry to change things. Even now he was complacent with our situation.

"Max and Maya, we need to talk." I had a moment when we were all together in the family room. They looked at me, confused. I never made proclamations like that; I usually just started talking. Then they turned to each other, their eyes locking, reminding me they always had a way of understanding each other, knowing what the other was thinking. I missed seeing them together in that moment.

I focused. "I'm sure you've noticed things are a little strained."

"Okay," they said at the same time.

Max offered, "Things are always strained." He had noticed, I thought.

"So I'm just going to say it. Your dad and I are separating." Mark sat there with an empty expression on his face. He was going to be a bystander in this exercise too. The room was silent.

"I know you guys are old enough to understand this. And I'm sure it's going to take some processing, but . . ." I stopped to think about how to say the next part. "Sometimes we realize that we aren't good together anymore. It's not like we don't love each other. We do."

"So why get divorced?" Max said with a biting tone to his voice.

"Because you can love someone, but realize you aren't who you need to be together."

"You mean you, right?" He looked to Dad. "Do you want this, Dad?"

God, I thought, Mark is going to throw me under the bus.

"No, Max, I don't. But I understand it. Your mom and I have been doing our own things for a long time now. We always had you two, but now that it's just us . . ." Mark stopped, and I finished:

"We realize that we need to figure out if we're happier apart."

We told them the usual: we will always love and respect each other, but sometimes letting go is the ultimate way to show someone you care about them. In the end, it would not change our love for them, and we would always be there for them.

"What about Christmas?" Max asked.

"I don't know, Max. But we'll figure it out," I said. That was the dagger to the heart I did not see coming. Holidays. I already anticipated the step back I would be taking in those moments.

Max was less understanding than Maya. I did not expect him to act emotionally. He was always a stoic boy. I never thought he paid attention. He went about his life doing his thing. He functioned independently, checked in with texts daily, called Mark and me regularly. He was my first love, and it broke me to see him wondering about Christmas. In the end, though, I knew he wanted both of us to be happy.

"You okay, Max?" I asked as he headed up to his room.

"I'm shocked. But not shocked, I guess. If I think about it, I can see it. You'll be good, Mom."

"Thanks, sweetie." He hugged me with those wonderfully strong, compassionate arms of his. "Don't ever stop hugging me that way. I love you."

"Love you too." I watched as he walked into his room and shut the door. I heard something smash against the wall. I understood.

"He'll be okay, Mom," Maya said from behind me.

I turned to her. My beautiful Maya. She was an old soul sometimes, wise beyond her years.

"I know. You okay?" I asked.

"I am." We both sat at the foot of the stairs. I rubbed her leg as she put her head on my shoulder.

"I'm not surprised," she finally said. "I have known for years that Dad doesn't see you for the amazing woman you are. I have known you deserve to be loved more than what Dad gives you. I hate that you might not be together, but I think you both deserve to be happy and if that's not together then it's your life and you have to do what you want."

I hugged her hard.

"How'd you get to be so smart and wise about things?"

"I have a college degree." We laughed. I loved her humor. "And I had a really amazing teacher."

Children. They really are gifts.

16

On Potholes in the Road

Sometimes it's healthiest to acknowledge you've run the course. We did our homework. We put in the time. The effort. But despite our best efforts, it was clear that we were going to be starting anew in our fifties. Even he realized that. And I believed it best when both parties came to the same conclusion. We could be an example to our children that we tried. Despite my initial inclination to run and reincarnate myself, we tried for the better part of a year. And then we mutually agreed to separate. We acted like mature adults in the process. We could be proud of ourselves for that.

I was lucky I didn't need to panic about a job and working. But I hated the idea of being reliant on Mark. It took me years to get past not working and having my own source of income. Now I admittedly didn't want to have to work full time. I liked my lifestyle. And I knew that was why so many women stayed. It was convenient. It was safe. I decided *safe* had become my least favorite word.

I was overwhelmed by emptiness. It was a huge hole not just in my heart, but in my head. I was overcome not just by the fear of being alone, but by the thought of what the hell was I supposed to do now? How was I supposed to fill my days? If I stayed, I at least had the one person who shared the last three decades of my life with me. It may not have been perfect, but he was mostly present. Shouldn't that have been good enough?

I had been tripped up along the way by Tripp. He planted a seed of doubt. For every step forward I was taking, I would occasionally coil back. I wanted to be on my own again, figuring out life. I was confident of that part. Most of the time. Occasionally, I was torn inside. Tripp was a contradiction in my head. I hated to admit he was responsible for some of the feelings awoken in me. He made me feel beautiful, strong, and desirable. But he also made me frightened, lacking confidence, skeptical. What if I didn't have the tools to live on my own? What if I walked out that door and I faltered, failed, got cold feet, retracted, and wanted to run back to my safe life? Yes, I admit, if anything was to be learned from my brief time with Tripp, it was that I was still not completely positive that I wanted to be on my own. Mark was releasing me. Separation did not mean forever, I reminded myself. Mark would take me back, I was positive. Win, win. Not.

Ugh, *just be strong and stay the course* I told myself. I had been wrestling with this uneasy feeling for years before Tripp. He was a bump in the road. More like a pothole, really. I knew in my heart and head that this was the road I needed to travel. The potholes threw my alignment off balance, made steering hard, but eventually I would find a way to steer straight again on the road I was meant to be traveling.

During those months of trying, I was able to stop grieving Tripp. I would never be over him. I knew that. But I was able to focus on the task at hand, weighing everything, knowing he was not part of the equation. He never was. Deep down I had reconciled that. That fantasy was just that: fantasy.

I was not being the impulsive me of long ago. I labored and toiled over what to do. I was constantly on the verge of tears but could not cry them. Not since that morning Tripp left the note. I felt like I was being selfish. The one thing I had not been over the years. I gave everything to my family. I had not been selfish during that time, I had to keep reminding myself. Now I was wanting to focus on me and selfish sounded like such a negative word. I wanted to find me again. The me. Who was she? Would I like her? Would I wish for my old life back? I knew I did not have to start with a blank slate. I could keep the parts of me I liked and rediscover the parts of me that were missing, that would make me whole. A man was not necessarily that part.

I kept hearing the voice of reason over and over in my head. The words kept coming back to me: you've only got twenty to thirty years of living left. Take what you've been given. Find the happy in that. I wanted to. But every time I found myself getting there, I would feel that void, that little bit of emptiness that did not allow me to feel whole. The stupid donut that had become the analogy for my life. I was ninety percent. Why wasn't that good enough? *Because the best part of any donut is the donut hole and ninety percent is not one hundred.*

I knew Mark and I had tried. I had been distracted for a fleeting moment at the start of the end. It was a wonderful feeling that was rekindled inside me. One I was excited to have found again. One I wanted to explore. One I had hoped would sustain me in my moments of uncertainty. It made me feel again. So many feelings. And then the heartache. It was a reminder that love and life are like that. We give. We take. We love. We hurt. We recover. We hope.

Hope. I liked that word.

There was a profound mix of emotions that flowed through my heart, mind, and soul when the reality it ended finally set in. I did not believe I failed. Nor did I think myself victorious. I was relieved, yet apprehensive. I was excited, yet petrified. I was happy. I was sad. Above all, I was open to all that might come my way in this next part of my life, the part I didn't expect, never planned for, but maybe always knew was coming.

We had been so busy raising our children, helping them to carve out their niches, find their purpose, find their reasons for being, creating a map for them to circumnavigate their lives. In that process, my life got lost. Now I was on this great big treasure hunt.

With that realization, I found myself unable to hold back the tears. The tears I had been on the verge of crying all these many months. I finally broke down. Mark was letting me go. Tripp had let me go and was not changing his mind. I know I needed him not to anyways. Whatever happened now I needed to figure out without him. He would always be there, a lingering presence, that ghost from the past who would haunt me just a little for the rest of my life.

The tears felt good. I have needed to cry for so long. The real tears. Not like the ones when my mom died. Or when I watched my dad seem lost. Or even when Tripp crushed me. Not when Maya graduated from college. But the real ones that felt like my soul was being cleansed and that opportunity was mine for the taking. I would not let that door close. Whatever stood on the other side, I would face alone, but brave and ready. I wiped those tears away, blew my nose, pulled myself together, and headed for the door.

I never imagined my life starting over in my fifties. The thought of it scared me. It worried me. I had doubts. But I could also feel the excitement deep down that it would be alright in the long run. I knew that this would be a journey. And it would not be easy. I knew I would doubt. I already did. That was normal, I told myself. This time I was okay with feeling normal.

I stood at the door knowing that if I turned, pulled the handle, and walked out, I could not look back. I must move forward, put one foot in front of the other, and head out into the great unknown. If I chose to shut the door behind me, I chose to leave safe, comfortable, and simple.

I knew I would battle the voices in my head for the rest of my life if I did not take this step. The thought of that alone was motivation. I hated hearing those voices arguing the merits of my safe life. Letting the door fall closed behind me was a choice. It meant I could tell those voices to go to hell: *I was not chickenshit.* I was stronger than the negatives. I was the glass half full. The door was open. Choose.

I did just that. I chose. I opened the door and I put one foot in front of the other. I grabbed back for the handle without looking. I had to keep my head forward. I had to be strong for me. I pulled the door shut, hearing the clicking as it engaged closed. I paused. Took a deep breath. Exhaled. And marched blindly towards the unknown that would be my next chapter.

Inside, I realized I needed to be confident in myself, keeping the perspective that I was worth loving. Not because I had been abused. Or that Mark had always only loved me enough. But because there was so much more to me to love. I found her in all its imperfect pieces. And I knew I would persevere. It gave me strength. The great unknown? It scared me shitless. But not being true to myself scared me more.

17

On Road Trips and Liberation

I walked out that front door and landed at Meg's. She had always made it clear that her house would be my sanctuary if I ever left Mark. She didn't want me to have one more reason why I couldn't leave.

"I don't have money to support myself," I'd remind her.

"Stay with me. Craig is good with it. Threw out the *ménage à trois* thing even." We both laughed at that.

With the knowledge that her home would be my halfway house, I packed my car full of the parts of my life that I needed in those next moments. I knocked even though I knew I could just walk in. I wasn't just dropping by for a visit; I would be staying. This time, though, I was not met by "you look like shit."

"You look free, girlfriend."

Those first days and weeks were difficult. I missed my house. I missed familiarity. Fortunately, my routine would not need to change much. I was just waking up as the guest in a friend's house. It would have felt like a vacation except I knew I would not be going home. My new home had yet to be decided. I was working on that daily, thinking about where I could and should go.

I did not have money to support myself was an excuse. I knew I would be fine. Half of what Mark made would be mine, and that would be plenty to live comfortably. I wouldn't be able to buy a big house or live on the ocean, but I would be able to make ends meet. I would not find myself forced back into the corporate world. It would not have wanted me anyways. My education and skills were obsolete at this point. I knew I could find little things along the way. "Busy" work. I laughed at that thought. Busy was what I hated in my marriage, because Mark thought it was the answer to my happiness. The irony that I wanted to be busy in my new normal was not lost on me.

"It's the paradox of life: want what we don't have; need what we didn't want. I made that up. But I'm pretty sure it's a thing," I told Meg and Craig over dinner one night.

"You have to give yourself some time. You may have known you've wanted this, but reality is sometimes harder to digest."

"Let's hope I have a strong stomach."

"I've seen you drink. I know you do." Friendships in the face of discord cannot be overrated. Meg was my rock. She kept me grounded. And more than anything, I knew she was in my corner, cheering for me, advocating for my happiness, especially in those moments when I would find myself questioning the decision I had made.

I woke one morning to Meg cheerfully bouncing in my room.

"I've taken a few days off of work," she proclaimed.

"Good for you," I said as I rolled over, putting the pillow over my head.

"We're going on a girls' trip," Meg announced rather

matter-of-factly, ripping open the curtains, opening the window to let in the humid breeze, a sign that summer was not far off. "You don't get to come here and second guess yourself."

"I'm not second guessing. I'm allowed to feel sad," I said.

"Nope. No pity party at my house. We're going to Nashville for the weekend."

Okay. Not going to lie. I liked the idea of Nashville. I had not been in years. And even then, it had been with Mark and the kids on one of our southern road trips we did, usually centered around Max's lacrosse or Maya's tennis tournaments.

I perked up. "I can do Nashville."

"Good. Our flight's at two." She paused for dramatic effect. "Today."

The party would be in Nashville. Pity was not invited.

Did I get comfortable with safe and simple because it was just that? I didn't worry about the challenges of keeping up. Disappointing each other went by the wayside because accepting that having expectations is counterintuitive to marital accord.

In the process, though, I ended up losing the parts of myself that made me feel most alive, pushed me to be better even at the risk of failure. As my marriage truly began to falter because I did have expectations, there were moments that happened. There were flashes, glimpses, triggers of that person I used to be. And I realized she was still there. Every last little bit of her waiting to be dusted off and put on display.

I felt like I was watching myself in a movie. Suddenly, I was racing against the clock. Wanting to have those feelings again. Feeling that pulsing in places I haven't felt in so long. Then catching myself, wondering what am I thinking? I think

I'm too old for those feelings. I'm past being allowed to experience passion on those levels. But it gnawed at me anyways. I so wanted to know what I was still capable of. I knew that woman was there. She was me. And she needed to experience those things again. Or at least try to find them.

Sex. I discovered it was much like riding a bike. Once you found your balance and your legs started moving, it all came back to you. That uninhibited open to adventure wind in your hair woman you knew once upon a time. I knew from my own past experiences that being with a new man was never the same as another man. They all had their unique way of finding pleasure while attempting to pleasure you.

As we got older, most men had learned that sex was not a one-way street. If they wanted to truly find satisfaction in fornication, they needed to learn to give a little in return. By now, we women had learned what our bodies required, needed, wanted to feel complete. And most men wanted to deliver on those standards as much as they wanted to deliver on their own fulfillment. Simply having an orgasm as a man was no longer the end all be all. Seeing a woman devoid of pleasure was sometimes, for some at least, worse than not climaxing themselves.

Sex in your fifties was not sex in your twenties or even thirties. Bodies moved differently. Felt different. Responded different. What I most enjoyed then had been replaced by something new. That would be the beauty of sex: it can be ever evolving, changing, enhanced, or personalized depending on the situation.

I was excited by the prospect of allowing my body to come alive again. I was no longer holding on to hope that Tripp would magically reappear. I was officially separated from Mark. I was not a married woman cheating on her husband. I wasn't divorced yet, but I allowed myself to believe there was some leeway in defining cheating at this point. I had cheated once. I did not regret it. It challenged me to find my strength more than I ever would have imagined. Those moments with Tripp created doubts about myself, my insecurities, my ability to deal with disappointment, my expectations of men, and my willingness to risk my happiness. It was a laundry list of dirty that I needed to clean. Nashville would be my cleanse I had decided.

There was something about being there that made me feel free and confident, ready to play with the idea that maybe, just maybe, I might be attractive to the opposite sex again. I didn't know if it was the dark rooms, the tinge of alcohol on every breath, the live bands playing familiar songs, the cowboy boots that made every woman and every man sexy, or some massive combination of all those things.

I was glad to have Meg by my side. It had been a long time since either one of us had been the other's wing(wo)man. She wore her wedding ring, making it clear she was not available. To most men, at least. She was a stunning woman and they still paid attention to her. She knew how to turn heads. She never lost that in all the years she had been married. Craig made her feel every bit the woman she was. She was confident in herself and her marriage.

Her confidence worked on me too. I fed off her positive vibe. I really didn't need it, though. I was actually feeling good about myself. I saw men look at me. They liked the yellow dress with the cowboy boots. A young man no older than Max stopped me on the middle of Broadway and, in no uncertain terms, announced, "You should not be allowed in public in that dress. Stunning."

I bit my tongue. I wanted to tell him I was old enough to

be his mother. But, instead, I took it for the compliment it was meant to be. I pulled off that dress regardless of my age. Either that boy's mother had taught him well, or I was playing the part on point of a woman recently set free to figure the world out as whatever version of herself she wanted to be. That was empowering.

We made our way into one of the many bars tightly packed along Broadway. The energy was always positive and happy. Bridal parties, bachelor parties, birthday parties, everyone, everywhere having a party. We were carded. Even if we were clearly old enough, it was nice they asked.

Meg and I found a spot upstairs along the railing looking down on a band playing. We danced in our spot to the music. We were free. No inhibitions. The music. The beat. God, did I miss the high from dancing.

I was lost in that moment, feeling the music flow through my blood. Music and my feet happened automatically. It was easy to find rhythm, to move to the songs as the band played them.

I felt a hand brush my shoulder. I turned to look, realizing it was the man who caught my eye when we first walked upstairs. He was ruggedly handsome. I couldn't stare when we first walked in, but now I had the opportunity to look closer. He was even more attractive up close. He was young, very young. His dark hair combed back with a small piece falling forward into his face. His five o'clock shadow highlighting the face of a man who looked like a chiseled lumberjack. His eyes were dark and mysterious. Strong, defined muscles easily identified through his shirt and legs that said he either lifted a lot of weights or he did something physical for a living. I could have been wrong. But I wanted to imagine something sexier than an office job. He scooted his stool a little closer to me when I turned.

"That dress looks amazing on you."

I beamed. "Thank you."

I felt emboldened, moving a little closer too, with the hope maybe there would be more conversation.

He was nursing a drink. He wasn't in a hurry.

"What you drinking?" I asked, feeling my delivery had that long lost flirtatious tone to it. "Red Bull and vodka."

"Planning on a late night?"

He laughed. "It's been a long couple of days."

I just smiled and told myself good start, and turned back to hear the music.

"Forty-two." I heard him say.

"What?" I turned to him, confused. He leaned in towards me, putting his face near mine, speaking into my ear. I felt his breath as he spoke, which elicited a sense of excitement.

"I'm guessing you're forty-two."

"Oooh, I like you," I teased back. "Fifty-four." I was waiting to lose his attention in that moment. I was a good decade older than his guess. That should have sent him running.

"Wow. You look amazing."

"Thank you." There was a pause. Or maybe I felt like there was one. I was wallowing in that moment. This much younger man had just made my night by telling me I looked amazing and a dozen years younger than I really was.

"How old do you think I am?" he asked. I studied him.

"God, I hope over thirty." He laughed again. I really liked his laugh.

"Thirty-seven," he told me.

"Thank God." I said in no uncertain terms.

We chatted briefly about where we were from and how much we both enjoyed Nashville. At this point, his friends decided it was time to leave. It did make me wonder if maybe they saw me as trouble. Maybe he was married. I was on a nice high that would carry me over for the rest of the trip. I had been noticed. I could see his attraction to me. I felt like a woman worthy of a man's attention again.

I didn't know his name. I didn't want to. I was caught up in the moment. The rush when he brushed up against me. The way I could see him studying me. Undressing me. Wondering what he might uncover. His younger age obvious in his ability to be confident and slightly cocky knowing that he had the full attention of this sexually starved older woman. Still, I felt my own power in being able to engage him and keep his attention. Needless to say, I was liking Nashville.

He went to leave with his friends but not before his arm found its way gently, sexily around my middle. He slid it so perfectly around my waist, almost like he was trying to uncover what he might find under my dress.

"I think thirty-seven-year-old me might be too much for you," he whispered in my ear.

I smiled and whispered back, "I think fifty-four-year-old me might be too much for you."

His reaction to my words made me feel like the most powerful woman in that bar. He grabbed my hand, pulled me to him, and kissed me with such force, passion, and desire. I felt like we were one even in that moment.

"Show me," he breathed in my ear, tickling me with the hair from his five o'clock shadow and just ever so slightly moving my hair. It made me tingle all over.

The voices in my head kicked in. *You're sober. You've had children. There are parts of you when unclothed will look every bit fifty-four.* I wanted to panic. Before I could, Meg slid me the key.

"Go."

I'm not sure if my expression was fear or euphoria. Thirty years. Thirty years: oh shit. And for a brief moment my high was met with a barrage of thoughts.

I knew how to love Tripp. He was part of me. And it came back to me so easily. But God another man? One I did not know. I had two options: be scared and let someone show me, or be unbridled and ask for and take everything I wanted. I was too old for the first. So, I chose to dig in deep for the second. Tripp awoke in me that woman, unlocking that burning desire. She did not want to sleep again.

With the exception of that brief night with Tripp, I had been sleeping with the same man for thirty years of my life. It dawned on me I only knew that anymore. The carelessness of my youth out the door. My confidence locked inside the aging body of a fifty-something-year-old woman.

A frightening thought had crossed my mind in that moment: what if I didn't know how to have sex with another man? I was used to what Mark wanted, knew what brought me satisfaction. It was easy to meet each other's physical needs because we had been doing it for so long. But somewhere along the way something got lost. There was no intimacy. We lost the desire to make each other feel special. Sex became singular in focus: You take care of me, and I take care of you. For Mark and me, the meaning evolved over time. We lost sight of each other along the way. My few exposures through Tripp reminded me that there was still a woman underneath my exterior that wanted—needed—to feel touch again. I had been awoken and I needed that explored, exploited, nurtured, satisfied. Now I found myself being propositioned, summoned by a beautifully rugged specimen of a man who didn't care how old I was. He wanted me. Me.

His friends had gone. If they were trying to protect him, they abandoned him quickly during that kiss. I waved the key, feeling a sense of empowerment. Kissing me again, he repeated those suggestive words, "Show me."

It was a short walk to the hotel. He couldn't keep his hands off me. I wondered what he was looking for. Was he going to stumble upon something that would suddenly turn him off? But I seemed to have the opposite effect.

"God, I love your confidence." Then he would stop and push me up against a wall and kiss me harder, his hand moving up under my dress.

"You are so fucking sexy." This was empowering. When was the last time someone pushed me up against a wall to kiss me?

"It gets better," I teased back. I relished this. He rolled his eyes in delight. I pulled his hand and we walked into the hotel. And it got hot fast.

Somewhere between the lobby and the fifth floor, his fingers found their way under my dress and inside my underwear, gently at first, toying with me. He knew the right spot, the right pressure, the right amount of time. And he knew when to stop and move on. Was this a new thing men did? I couldn't remember a time that a man had found the right spot to touch without a little direction, let alone found *all* the right spots to touch. And as soon as I found myself wanting to moan in sheer delight, his fingers were inside of me, and I wanted to explode. I was not a vocal lover, but every part of me was feeling him. I was aching from desire, and I was not suppressing it. I felt him hard against me.

The elevator door opened, and he slowly moved his fingers from inside me, leaving a trail of my fluids on my leg as he let my dress drop down. He studied me, satisfied that I was enjoying what he had been doing to me.

"This is going to be fun," he said to me.

He walked behind me down the hallway. I could feel his breath on my neck as I scanned the key card. There was something about that bristly stubble against my neck. So rugged. So sexy. I opened the door, and we went in. The door slammed behind us. I hit the light switch and I could see the desire burning in his eyes. I had an effect on this man. It was something I remember having had once upon a time. I thought I was too old for it now. We walked to the bed as I felt him lifting my dress up. I turned around and he slowly finished pulling it off, stopping at my bra, feeling my breasts, kissing the skin that bordered my bra. The dress gone; the bra was next to fall. I stopped to look at myself. These were not the breasts of a young woman. These were the breasts of a woman who had nursed children, who had lost the battle with gravity years ago. A woman who still had nicely shaped breasts, but they told a story rich in history. He kissed them and toyed with them with his tongue. My body was burning as he enjoyed the history lesson my breasts gave.

He ran his tongue from my breasts down to my underwear where he teased me in ways I didn't know possible. He was so slow, deliberate, methodical. I didn't even feel him take my underwear off.

"Sit down," he said. I did as he said and watched as he moved his tongue up my inner thighs while touching my legs. And that tongue would take only seconds to make me climax. That tongue that thrust in ways I had never felt, or at least I did not remember. It was like a great vibrator with varying speeds and pulsing capabilities. And I couldn't stop myself. I didn't want to stop myself. I fell back on the bed.

"Oh my God, I'm sorry." He came up on top of me, his hand moving over my breasts, his lips kissing mine.

"That was just the beginning." I could see he wanted to be inside of me, but I wouldn't let him. I found myself wanting to know what he would feel like inside my mouth. Oral sex: I liked it, but the routine of it had long ago left my bedroom. I couldn't say why other than it didn't fit the moments we had to have sex early on when it was quick and convenient. And over the years it just found a way to leave the bedroom all together. But giving a man a blow job had always been empowering. And I wanted to have that power over this man.

"Wait," I said, as I could feel him wanting to be inside me.

"What?" he asked. I did my best to flip his strong, muscular body to its back. He smiled, knowing what I was thinking.

"It's my turn," I said to him coyly as I began moving my tongue slowly down his chest. And I found him hard and eager when I put him in my mouth. There is nothing romantic about oral sex. It is such a basic concept with a simple goal of satisfaction. It is not making love; there is no emotional component. It is simply a weapon to exercise power over another human being. And such a powerful weapon. He was enjoying it. At least I still knew how to do that. He would not cum, though. He pulled me up to him. "I want to cum inside you." I straddled him, moving slowly at first, sensing his desire to want to go faster, but not letting it happen. I held his arms over his head, controlling the speed, allowing him time to linger on my breasts. I came up for air, let go of his arms, letting him hold my hips, dictating the pace. He studied me as he rhythmically moved inside me. This man knew what he was doing. I closed my eyes as I felt myself climaxing. In a world unfamiliar to me, he would allow me to orgasm first before exploding inside of me. I collapsed on top of him, overwhelmed by what just happened.

I had last had a vaginal orgasm with Tripp that felt like forever ago. And it had been many years before that. Mark had lost the drive to make that happen. It required work and effort in the bedroom. By myself, less motivating. I am not sure, though, if I had ever experienced a vaginal orgasm of that magnitude. And that fast. After the orgasm I just had. I was overwhelmed by sexual gratification. This man. This man had just reminded me of what I was capable of feeling.

I stopped comparing him to anyone. My mind was open to the newness it presented. He was relentless in exploring me. I relished his young body. His muscles still so defined. His hair full. His eyes sparkled with youth. He made me feel like a woman.

I especially liked his sexuality. He was confident in himself and his ability to please me. He was not selfish, something I found surprising. I did not need to tell him what I wanted; he seemed to know. Maybe men are different these days, less selfish. Or better informed. I liked it, whatever it was. All of it.

I never did learn his name. I wanted to keep him a mystery. He would forever be my rugged guy from Wisconsin that drank Red Bull and vodka and thought I was forty-two.

"I never got your name."

"Fifty-four," I said.

"Okay, fifty-four. That was fun. Thirty-seven," he said back playfully.

"That's a cool name."

I got up from the bed, let him look me over once more, and headed to the bathroom. I heard the door shut as he left. And once he did, I let out a schoolgirl's squeal like when the most popular boy says hi to you. I was giddy. I was alive. I was . . . so sore.

There is something about sex with a younger man that makes you lose any doubts or insecurities. Maybe it's because I didn't imagine he would have high expectations of the older woman that couldn't keep up. Or maybe it was that I could be uninhibited and the expectations of me by him were virtually non-existent. I could be whatever, whomever, I wanted to be sexually at that moment. And he had awoken me.

With Tripp there was an emotional connection. There was passion and lust and purpose to having sex together. We were familiar, reacquainting ourselves. With thirty-seven, it was just dangerous, unbridled, uninhibited desire and a WTF attitude. They both reminded me of the kind of woman I could be. I liked both versions of her.

I texted Meg she could come back. Five minutes later the door opened.

"I didn't think that through," she said. "You left and I was wondering where I was supposed to go and where I would sleep."

I laughed at that. She threw herself on the bed. I smiled.
"Well?"
"Holy fucking shit."

Nashville taught me that I needed to allow myself the freedom to be okay to experiment and explore the world again. I would argue with the voices in my head that kept telling me to get over it, you're too old to feel those things again. I knew it was possible and the voices became only occasional whispers I was learning to ignore.

Once word began to spread about my separation, friends would reach out. They would all tell me I'm a catch. Or there are so many men that will be falling at your feet. Words of encouragement; they were supposed to do that. People tell you things they know you want to hear. It's easy for them if they aren't in the moment, if they aren't living that truth in that second.

I found myself adjusting to my new normal of just me. I accepted that I had made the most difficult decision of my life. I tried not to dwell on my choice. I knew inside I was better off alone than pretending to be happy living together.

In my often one-sided conversations with myself, I concluded that it was time for me to go. It didn't matter where I went. I just needed to be away from here. Going to our house on the Cape would be painful. The memories of Tripp were always there, tiny reminders of a past long ago and a brief rekindling in this lifetime. I was not there yet.

I looked at the map, closed my eyes, and played pin the tail on the donkey. That would be the answer. I would rent a bed and breakfast and explore wherever there was for the next month of my life. I would bring my laptop and finally sit down with the ultimate goal of writing that novel I had in bits and pieces on notes and random computer files. I convinced myself I could do it. I was never one to shy away from the challenge. And now more than ever I had to challenge myself, make myself believe I could do whatever I wanted. Shit, I was old. If I didn't do it now, when would I do it?

The old part of me. That's the battle I kept having. It was this obnoxious, irritating voice that kept finding its way into my head. The me I saw in the mirror was still an attractive woman. I was still fit. I was smart. I was witty. But that voice. I needed to squelch it.

I packed my bags, loaded my car, and hit the road. I was nervous and excited. I had no idea what was about to happen. I have always been a planner. The thought of not knowing how the next few weeks of my life were supposed to play out was unsettling. Yes, but necessary.

I couldn't remember the last time I took a road trip by myself. If ever. Silence did not count. The drive home after Mom's funeral felt like I was alone even with Mark in the car. We were driving into conversations and moments that were unresolved at that time. Now I was considered separated. At least we could agree that a trial separation might give us the clarity we needed.

I knew Mark was resigned in the end. I could hear his frustration in our conversations. I had never offered false hope. We were civil. We had never been anything but. Maybe that was a problem in our relationship: We had always been too nice to each other.

There were times when I felt like the back and forth, the attempts to salvage years of being together, and then the ultimate reality that the marriage was over, would never reach the finish line. It was a constant back and forth. We made it, though. We both crossed. I did not feel victorious; I did not set out to defeat Mark. I needed this for me.

I began my journey headed south in late spring. It felt fitting in ways. Spring was about new beginnings, starting fresh. The leaves had already turned a bright shade of green and flowers were in full bloom. A gentle breeze moved calmly through the air. Summer was just a few rains away from stifling with heat and humidity. I loved summer. It meant lazy days, less hustle, long evenings before the sun set, and happy reminders of family. I enjoyed flashing back at the beautiful memories my life had given me in those hours I drove.

I found myself in Myrtle Beach, South Carolina. I rented a cute two-bedroom bungalow adjacent to an old widower's home. Will was in his eighties, not much older than my own dad. He had lost his wife five years ago. They never had children. They had traveled the world together. His eyes lit up whenever he talked about her.

"I love how your eyes sparkle when you remember her," I told him.

He knew my situation. We spoke of my pain and the struggles I had to get to where I was today, far from home in South Carolina.

"Love is not easy. It wasn't always easy for us. But I knew every night when I went to bed just how lucky I was to have this woman by my side." He paused, reflecting. "And I knew even more when she was gone."

"You're lucky to have loved like that."

"Do you know how old I was when I met Gwen?" I thought it a strange question. I assumed they had been married forever, meeting in their twenties, maybe even high school sweethearts.

"I was sixty. I was old. Set in my ways. My job made it difficult to stay in a relationship. And I knew I never wanted kids. I accepted that I was meant to be a bachelor my entire life."

"Wow. You weren't married that long then?"

"Almost twenty years. She was a little older than I was. She had been married before. Lost her husband to cancer after twenty years together. She had a daughter, but she passed away young. She had been alone a long time. Gwen was sad when I met her. Maybe that's how we found each other. Two sad souls needing saving." He laughed at that. Then he looked at me. "I didn't know I needed saving. Until Gwen."

It was a beautiful story. And a valuable reminder to me that love doesn't have to be defined by age, rules, or preconceived notions. Love happens.

My time in Myrtle Beach was just what I needed to find focus. I had started writing a novel. I had ideas for magazine articles I wanted to submit. I was reading books that I had bought but never had the time or energy to read. I would journal when I found myself lonely, missing safe. It was a different void than the one I had at home. Unlike the donut my life had been, it was a hole, an empty space I knew I could fill with time. I would transform into a jelly donut, full and bursting with flavor.

I did short runs on the beach in the morning. Most mornings I would set out as the beautiful orange hues started to light up the sky. It was the most beautiful time of day. It always had been for me.

Evenings I took long, slow walks along the water's edge. I invited Will to accompany me. He would do so on occasion. He said I walked too fast. I think he was becoming attached to me. While he appreciated my company, he knew quiet was just a few days away from being reality again. I understood that. I promised I would stay in touch after I left.

I was sad when my month at Will's bungalow was over. I had found a confidant in him. He had taught me a lot about life, love, and the choices we make. Everyone has a story, I reminded myself. My parents' story was unexpected. Will's story short, but perfect in its telling. My own story only partially written.

Life happens in parts and pieces. It's only when it's over that anyone can look back and tell the full story. There were so many chapters to every person. When we're living them, we don't always know if this is the last chapter. Or how many more chapters will still be written. I never imagined this chapter of my life. But I get to keep on with my story.

That's some deep shit, I told myself.

In what felt like an ironic twist of fate, divorce papers arrived on my 55th birthday. It had been nearly a year since I first opened the door on this journey.

There was no part of the divorce process that was easy. Even the parts I had imagined. The liberation. The freedom. But it was also filled with sadness. In those months we were separated, I came to appreciate that Mark and I did the best we could. We were not meant to love each other as a married couple forever. I knew in my heart I would have felt growing resentment and bitterness had we stayed together. The fear of an empty life with him was greater than not knowing what the last years of my life might be like rediscovering, perhaps even reinventing, myself.

After camping out at Meg's, the Nashville adventure, and my month in Myrtle Beach, I came back to Greenwich. I found a small cottage far enough away from the home I had lived in for over twenty years. My big, beautiful house that was the cornerstone of my existence had been sold. Mark was renting a condo not far from his office. Greenwich was still my home, though. The place I raised my children. It was ideal for me to explore from. I could rely on Meg to keep me from relapsing or doing something impulsive or impetuous.

I found myself moving forward able to slowly piece my life together. I had finally stopped listening to the excuses life kept throwing me. I was living.

18

On Bittersweet Conclusions

Tripp was the part of me I had the hardest part reconciling. I wished I was my younger self. The version of me that dropped boys like flies because there might have been someone better. I never stopped wishing he would reach out, saying he regretted the decision. I wanted a redo with him. I wanted that grand romance. I wanted to get to be the one that lived the story. I wanted to be the fairy tale. A part of me always wished for that.

I would keep asking myself why. Why did this man have such a hold over me? Why couldn't I leave him in the past where he belonged? Why couldn't I simply bury him like I did all those years ago? Was I that weak? That desperate? That sad and lonely? I hated these emotions. I had mad sex with thirty-seven. I knew I was capable of more than the memory of Tripp.

I wanted to believe it was just about the sex with Tripp. The way he touched me. The way his eyes burned through me. But more than that, it was the way he could still read me even after decades apart.

There was meaningful conversation that came with such ease. Even after all those years, there were no holes, no awkward pauses. We flowed, sometimes saying the same thing, like we could read each other's mind, but also open to a different point of view. I missed those moments, forgot how much being with someone who understood me added so much value to life and love. Even if I couldn't have it with him again, I was reminded in those glimpses he gave me. Tripp made me whole then. "Ha," I laughed out loud as I thought that. He was the jelly filling once.

The memories of Tripp that came flooding back began to slowly subside like the tide as I put one foot in front of the other in the name of forward progress. There were little reminders here and there. But I moved on, knowing that he and I were once significant in ways we never fully appreciated until we reconnected. The reminders I could be loved so deeply and love in return was the beauty that only first love truly captures in all its rawness, innocence, and frailty. He once said to me we should all be so lucky to have a love like that. He was right.

The greatest gift he gave me was to love me. To teach me what love was. For that, he will always own a piece of my heart. He does not go away anymore. My heart felt heavy at times when I thought about my marriage being over, with a good fight I could be proud of, together with the realization that Tripp and I would always be that couple that never got to finish. We would always be that story that didn't get to have an organic ending because our endings were always the victim of timing. The emotions. The feelings. So intense. So real. So raw. So true. So young to know any different until decades later, when lifetimes had taught us real love. In those moments, we could look back, recognize them, and yearn to feel them all over again because they were still there. All it took was a little nudge, a little coincidence. Then fate intervened. Cruel when it plays the same trick on you twice.

It had been nearly a year since reconnecting with Tripp. He was finally beginning to feel more distant, like a far-off ship on the horizon that can't be made out quite clearly. While Tripp never fully adopted sharing his life on social media, he did post an occasional reminder that he was living his life. I tried hard not to read into the pictures, wondering if he was faking that smile, or if he was really fine with the choice he made to keep his family together. I wanted to be happy for him. That would become somewhat easier as I explored in my own life, and the reality that we once again crossed paths at the wrong time sat concretely in my heart and mind. As time went on, I tried to bury him, but ultimately realized he would always be a part of me. Now, perhaps, more than ever.

It was the music that made it difficult at times. Tripp and I had always had that. It was a part of our first summer and it was a part of our reconnection. For all my forward progress, all it took was one song to send me over the edge again.

You can listen to a song a hundred times and never really hear it. Then one day the song stops being background noise and you actually process the lyrics. This was that song. The words resonated deeply. Once I actually heard them.

I finally had the answer to the last thing Tripp asked me. I remember so clearly his last question of me: *You think there's a song for this?* The song for us in that moment. I said I'd know it when I heard it. I had been hearing the song for months as background noise, never listening to what was actually being said. It was just another pretty Ed Sheeran song on one of my many playlists.

But when I hit play this time, I knew this was the song. Every word true. It was like the song had been written for us.

Tainted memories. Feeling a ghost just when you want to let go. Cards stacked against us. A love that will never leave. Inability to erase us. And he would never be lost on me. God, how did I miss that? Our song: "Overpass Graffiti."

I broke down and sent him the song. One last text, I told myself. It was simple.

"I found the song. I think you'll understand." I attached a link. I hit send. I did not expect, or even really want a response, but Tripp did reply.

"I like the words. A very meaningful song."

Sometimes I just wished my heart would stop beating.

I needed to let any connection to Tripp go just as much as I needed to let any guilt about Mark go if I had any hope of moving forward. After I saw he read it, I made the difficult decision to delete him from my contacts. And I removed him from my Facebook.

The ghost that was always just a little too close this past year needed to be laid to rest. So I did. With the utmost pain in my heart.

I had always said I would write a novel when I had time to focus my energy on it. I had the time now. I needed the distraction from my own life. I had been scribbling furiously, typing endlessly as a barrage of thoughts came flooding into my head. It is what I did in those months after Mark and I separated, when I wasn't sure what I was supposed to do, with whom I was to do it, and what my real purpose was anymore.

I decided I would start small by writing a short story. In the end, I found myself writing about the opportunity to spend one weekend with your first love at the back half of your life. It was the story of Tripp and me. More or less. An indirect version of it. It was how I would cope with all the emotions that time with him had stirred in me. The process was cathartic. There were things I needed to say. I wanted to use it as a stepping stone for what was yet to come in my life.

I submitted it to magazines and found myself a published writer a few short months later. It was a beautiful story, and I had told it as I wanted to remember it. It was the catalyst for me to begin writing more. I had so many ideas I had tucked away over the years. I was excited to tackle those now that this was behind me. I had accomplished something for me. Under my name. Unattached to anyone else. I felt liberated.

After the article ran, I sent Tripp a copy with a note to him:

Dear Tripp,

So often I wanted to hate you for coming back into my life. It was sometimes better not knowing or being connected. I never set out wanting more from you. And when you wanted more from me, I eagerly accepted. You were so familiar, and it was so easy. That in itself was strange. And then we crossed all the lines before it became too much—for you. I know you say you didn't see it that way. You were just exploring something. I was sad for a long time that I let that happen. And I'm resigned that you will always be this aching part of my heart that I buried so long ago but that is now so real.

Yes, I want to hate you. But our few weeks of playing with fire and that one beautiful night were enough to help me write this story. I could never hate you. Not even a little. I do not believe that the pull of our past gave me that much power over you to make you cross all the lines we did. I know you loved me once and it became real for you too.

I believe in happy endings. I wish ours could have ended differently. In a different place and time, maybe. I hope you are being loved in all the ways you should. You can't fake happy. Not forever at least.

Wishing you the best,

Jenn

I folded the letter, placed it in the envelope, and sealed it closed. I tucked it inside the pages of the magazine. And I mailed them. I felt a sense of relief having done that. At least for myself. A little passive-aggressive. Maybe. I am not sure that I thought he would understand. But it did not matter if he did. This was about me.

19

On Dating Apps and Running Clubs

I had wiped my hands clean of Tripp the best way I knew how. And I stayed true to my plan to move forward in life without looking back at the what-might-have-been/what-could-have-been moments.

I had decided I needed to put myself out there. I was determined to prove Tracy wrong. I knew all the good ones could not be taken. However, the prospect of dating was daunting. But I wasn't one to be deterred. I was open to navigating a dating landscape that looked so foreign. Like anything I did, I would not do it half ass. I threw myself into the saturated dating market where there was no shortage of men eager to date.

I started by checking out the dating sites. I asked Maya's advice, even though I generally thought women in their early twenties had different intentions than women in their fifties. That was only partially true. Turns out there was a dating app for every kind of situation. If I wanted to hook up (I did not), there was one. If I wanted something more religious, there was one. If I wanted a guy on a tractor, there was one. Relationships, yes. Friendship, that too. Older men, yup. Younger men seeking older women, you bet. There was something for every conceivable situation.

I tried them. So many of them. I created profiles. Filled out countless questionnaires. Said I only wanted men over six feet tall but got matched with men shorter than me anyways. Didn't want smokers (was shocked that people still smoke), but even they would show up in my matches. Some men looked amazing in their pictures, young, lean, fit. Some even matched their photos. Most did not. Men did not photograph as well in their fifties. It was entertaining at times.

I found myself having fun anticipating what the date might look like. I liked dressing nice, putting on heels, doing my hair, feeling pretty. I got that much out of it. It was rare that I found myself wanting to go out on second dates. A few times I made it to three. On a few occasions, I even allowed myself to have sex. A one-night stand at my age. I laughed at the reality I never thought that would happen again. Ever. Oddly, not all men wanted to have sex. And not all men were good in bed. Or maybe I wasn't. I may not have been interested enough; simply curious I suppose. I controlled the narrative, and that was empowering.

Tripp and thirty-seven had brought out the woman in me. Two completely different men, but they both showed me what my body could do and feel. They had set the bar for this next part of my life. I didn't feel myself in a hurry or desperate to find someone who might come close to the bar they set. I had no expectation that anyone would ever surpass it. But I knew I never wanted that anyways. Tripp would always be what he was: the gold standard.

Once I got over the need to feel like I could still be attractive to men, I found myself less eager to be dating all the time. It was stressful. Sometimes felt juvenile.

I learned I was still desirable. That men could want me. And that there were still some good ones out there. Thank God the therapist had been wrong on that account.

However, I found myself okay not needing to be with

someone all the time. I did enjoy the companionship. It was fun to date on occasion.

As time went on, I moved off the dating apps altogether. I wasn't looking for love or feeling that I needed it all the time. If it was going to happen, it would happen organically.

Above all, I wanted to be doing the things I wanted to be doing without being defined by anyone else's expectations of me. Men on apps had expectations. I wasn't ready for those yet.

I traded in dating apps for the same running club that Meg made me join thirty years ago. I voluntarily joined this time. I would no longer be the one setting the pace and running at the front. I would be the pokey old fart (as we called them back then). But pokey old farts were nice people with fun stories to tell. They liked to get a beer after Friday runs and meet for coffee after Sunday ones. Some were married. Some were single. They all became my friends. Running had always been my medicine. Now more than ever, I suppose.

I thought about my mom at times when I was sowing my wild oats in the name of sexual emancipation in my fifties. Maybe I could understand her a little better now. She did not have the option to get out. I'm not sure she would have been strong enough, but I don't know that either. She will always be an enigma, but I understood her emptiness despite being with a man who loved her. My dad couldn't fill her void, just like Mark couldn't fill mine. I don't pretend to know what she really felt during those years, but I understood her desire to be fulfilled on a physical level, wanting to feel yourself attractive and desirable. She wanted to be a woman not just a mom, and society made that hard. There were times I wished she was still here so I could hear her story. Parts of us weren't that different after all, and my disdain for what she did to my dad was replaced by sadness for not knowing my mother better.

I had one relatively steady relationship in those years after Mark and after the trace thoughts of Tripp subsided to the occasional trigger. He became just another memory. One that was still beautiful despite the pain. Jefferson was a nice, unforeseen transition from married to divorced to free-to-be me.

Jefferson Davis Rutherford III was an acquaintance from Greenwich. While his name was noble, his wife was the one with the financial power. Our sons had played lacrosse together through high school. He was married to an obnoxious woman named Buffy. She was the epitome of East coast high society. We would not have run in the same circles if not for our boys. In fact, I'm not sure that Buffy actually ever stepped foot on the field to watch a game, preferring to stay nestled inside the climate-controlled sanctuary of her Range Rover.

Jefferson and I found ourselves alone at a bar one night, recognizing the other as familiar but never really having had opportunity for conversation. He had heard I was divorced, asked how I was doing.

"Really well, actually," I said, telling the truth. I was in a good place.

"That's good." He paused. "I always admired you."

"Why?" I wondered.

"Because you didn't get caught up in all the drama. You never thought you were better than anyone else."

"Mission accomplished," I blurted, raising my drink as if to say cheers to that.

"How's Buffy, by the way?" I did not know the status of his marriage. And at this point I was beginning to be a bit savvier when men were trying to hit on me.

"Honest answer or the one everyone wants to hear?" I found him sincere. I started studying him more. I never noticed what an attractive man he was. I suppose when your wife steals all the attention, you get lost in the shadows.

"Honest."

"She's a selfish bitch."

"Okay then."

"Too much information?"

"Nope. Just surprised by the candor."

Over the next couple of hours, he poured his heart out to me. I learned that men can be stuck in marriages just like women. They don't all possess the financial means or courage to leave a marriage, either. Sometimes they have to pick safe too. For many years, Jefferson had been stuck with a woman who knew she had the power over him, to emasculate him, to make him miserable. She withheld sex. He wasn't sure if she was having an affair or if she wasn't secretly a lesbian. He just knew that if he left her, she would ruin him. Living a miserable life with Buffy meant being less than a man, he admitted. But she had manipulated the children and their friends and made the prospect of living independent virtually impossible. I felt bad for him in ways, but at the same time I could understand. I just never thought those things happened to men.

I liked Jefferson. I liked that he was honest. I liked that he had seen me during those years when I felt no one had noticed. I liked his vulnerability and ability to own it. He didn't blame anyone else for his situation. He was genuinely a likable man in a crappy situation.

Jefferson became my lover that night. Neither of us wanting more from the other during those times than the physical companionship it provided. It was kind of nice. I will not lie. Sex for the sake of sex. Made me appreciate those college years where meaningless sex was the norm. Once it was clearly established that neither of us wanted more from the other, he would become a trusted friend. We had formed a mutually beneficial relationship. I would never have imagined that.

My new normal became a rhythm over the years. I dated. I had sex. I didn't settle. I lived in those moments regretting none of my decisions even in some dark, lonely moments.

I never felt sorry for myself. I found groups with like interests and found friendships amongst women who shared my journey. Just knowing I was not alone in leaving a seemingly perfect marriage gave me support in those moments when I might have felt a tinge of self-pity. I was grateful to have had my strength and courage to step into the great unknown instead of staying for the sake of lifestyle and appearances. And I was most certainly not one of those women who was bitter in her divorce. Alone at times. But I reconciled that as my decision. I was living. Doing me. I was being the woman I knew I was. I had found her again.

I held my head high, played loud music, and danced.

20

On Long Enough

My Dad died. There is no eloquent way to put it. I was lucky to have spent the last few days of his life with him. I know that he had found love after Mom died. He was never lonely with Carol by his side. She adored him. And he adored her. I found comfort in knowing that however long my dad would still be alive, he would feel the love he so deserved. Carol was true to him until his last breath. I was so grateful for her. She cared for him. She doted on him. She loved him in all the ways that my mother did not. It was fitting Carol would die within a few weeks of Dad. They had both lived long lives. Her son told me he thought she died of a broken heart. I found a strange comfort in knowing that someone loved Dad enough to want to be with him in death.

Dad knew he was dying. He had developed pneumonia after a bad fall. He would tell me it was his time and that he was fine with it. He told me he had been the happiest he had ever been these last few years. He did not go so far as to say it was because Mom was gone. He never would have said that. Dad was not a man of regrets. He lived a full life and felt himself lucky to have loved three times: his first wife, Mom, and Carol.

I cherished those moments with him in the end. I loved our conversations and the ease with which he spoke of things. Since Mom's passing, he was free to think, do, and say as he pleased without worry or fear of being reprimanded for saying the wrong thing. He told me how proud of me he was. He knew that my decision to leave Mark was a grueling and devastating one to make. He wanted me happy.

"All I have ever wanted for my children is their happiness," he said to me one night before fading off to sleep. "No one should endure sadness when there is happy to be had," he said, squeezing my hand in his. "You have always been my world, Jenn. Be happy in yours."

He would not wake up the next morning. Those words were his greatest gift to me in death. I have held them close to my heart ever since.

Mark had found a way to move forward too. After our initial separation, things were strained and awkward. I know he had resented me initially for breaking up our perfect world. But as time progressed, he saw the things I had been missing. We found a way to be friends. We talked regularly about life. About the kids. He remarried a nice woman who is much more like him than I ever was. It was ironic at first that he would be the one to find love again, especially since he was not the one setting out to change his world. I was happy in my heart knowing that he was not alone.

It has been five years since that night with Tripp. I played out those moments in my head hundreds of times. At some point I just resigned myself to the fact I was never going to be able to totally let that go. He had reminded me of a love so deep from a lifetime ago. But, beyond that, he reminded me of the woman I once was, that I longed to be again. I resented him for that, but only because I realized that I never stopped loving him all those years. It was the power of first love, I told myself. We're not supposed to forget those. They shape us, form us, and remind us that love can be uniquely beautiful in its most raw, honest, and emotional way.

I stopped trying to fight the memory of him. Instead, I hung on to that brief weekend where we found each other again. The ghost from my long-ago past made his way to me, released me from the gallows, showed me the power of his love, and then left me aching at a depth I had not experienced before then. At my age, to have a broken heart felt a million times worse than when I was young, when we simply suffered a few days before moving on to the next crush.

I had realized much over the past few years. I even found myself able to look at how things were with Tripp on a philosophical level.

I knew that occasionally two people's paths might cross, if only briefly, so that they may become acquainted. And sometimes they cross long enough to become meaningful. But then time comes rushing in and the pressure to move forward down that road wins. You go your way; they go theirs. Sometimes your lives even run parallel without ever knowing it. Then you forget.

You eventually live your life not really wondering if you'll ever see that person again. You become thankful for that time and the memories they gave you, the feelings you felt, and the emotions you experienced. They become distant reminders on the highway of life.

I came to understand that people come into our life for a reason and sometimes disappear just as quickly for reasons not always understood or wanted. But every so often, our paths find a way to intersect once more. We can live lifetimes in between, then suddenly find ourselves at the crossroads again when we least expect it. The question became do we stop long enough to love again, or do we keep driving not wanting to tempt fate?

Tripp and I would tempt fate in those moments we found our lives intersecting. He would teach me I was worth it in the end, even if he couldn't choose me.

Our second chance was a fleeting moment of indiscretion, at least on his part. He ran a red light, breaking hard when he realized the impact that could have on his life. He wasn't ready beyond what he gave me. At first, that was false hope. Then it was doubt about myself, my desirability, my potential gullibility with men. Ultimately, I knew he had never stopped loving me either and that being with me in another place and time would have been the perfect ending to our love story. If only I told myself. But I tried not to dwell or wallow in self-pity.

I long ago stopped trying so hard to stay so kept together with the thought that maybe love would happen again for me, and I would need to be this perfect version of myself. Somewhere over time that illusion of myself disappeared, and I became more okay with the natural version of me: the one with wrinkles and shades of gray and snowy white. The body I worked so hard for a little softer again, but still fit. I just stopped worrying so much about needing to be that perfect naked body should that opportunity come again. At this age, a man would need to love all of me equally not just sexually. I celebrated turning sixty with an open mind and an open heart.

So many years since the divorce. So many hits and misses, trials, and tribulations. I moved back to our summer home after Dad died. Jason didn't want the house and all its perceived aches and pains. I liked the history. I liked the feeling that this was where I belonged, after all. It had always been a happy place for me.

Jason and I had a long talk the evening after Dad's funeral.

Cali and their two kids actually came for this funeral. It surprised me. She was the same cold woman I had always known her to be.

"So, does Cali actually really hate me that much?" I asked after two glasses of wine long after Cali and the kids had gone to bed.

"She thinks you hate her," he answered.

"I don't hate her. She just never says much."

"You do know it's hard to get a word in around you at times?" he reminded me.

"I know I can be a bit overbearing. But, geez, she's been married to you for over twenty years. You think she would have figured me out by now."

"Maybe." He paused and gave some extra thought to his next words. "We aren't you and Mark. I know she loves me. And I love her. No one needs to know that or even see beyond me and Cali. Don't you get that, Jenn?"

In that moment, I realized Jason was happy in his marriage. It didn't matter what I saw or perceived because it wasn't their reality. We had two completely different marriages. Mine looked perfect on the outside; his was perfect on the inside. For the first time, I envied my brother's marriage to Cali. It warmed my heart at the same time to know he had no doubts about his marriage. I hoped that Cali felt the same way too.

When I finally settled on the Cape several months after Dad's death, I was good with myself. My children were successfully living their lives. Both Max and Maya had married, and each had a son. I doted on those boys. My grandchildren provided joy in those times we shared together. I was writing. I had made new friends. I was living in those moments, content knowing I had made the right choices in my life; that life cannot be lived with regrets.

Yes, I wished time had worked differently sometimes. But it ticked to its own beat, lacking consideration for those seconds, minutes, or hours that, had they been a little faster or a little slower, might have changed the trajectory of life on so many levels. I was satisfied in one place now no longer feeling like I needed to run from something or searching for some great unknown, anything to give me purpose. I was a content woman.

I sat on my porch looking out over the water in front of me as the sun began its gentle assent to daylight. It was still my favorite time of day before the noise and the thoughts of the day filled my head. It had always been my time to reflect, dream, just be.

I had been so lost in that morning I did not hear a car drive up. I did not hear footsteps as they turned the corner. I did not see him until he stood at the foot of the porch steps where I was sitting. He was older. But he was still Tripp. And he still made my heart skip a beat the same as it did those years ago when we briefly reconnected, the same way it did that first summer a lifetime ago.

I had a million questions swimming through my head, but my voice remained mute just like the first time I saw him as a man and not a boy. He smiled that boyish smirk which had remained despite the years. He walked up the steps to me. I stood in anticipation, my heart beating quickly like a nervous schoolgirl.

"Tripp," was all I could muster.

He stood in front of me, took my coffee mug and placed it carefully on the banister beside us. He continued to hold my hand. And with the other, he stroked the hair from my face and lingered on my neck as he tucked the curl behind my ear.

I stared into his beautiful blue eyes as they studied me. I wondered if he was trying to find the old me in there or if he had been disappointed with how I had aged after all. Confident me but always still with some reservation.

"God, you're still so beautiful."

I wanted to tell him he was too. That there had never been a more beautiful man to me. But I couldn't. I was simultaneously scared of him breaking my heart again and hopeful that he would fill it. I could feel the rush.

"What are you doing here, Tripp?"

"Can we talk?"

I motioned for him to sit on the steps.

"Coffee?" I asked.

"That'd be great." He handed me my coffee mug, brushing his hand on mine as he did. His touch lingered on my skin. I went inside, poured a cup of coffee for him, and topped mine up. My hands were shaking, but my thoughts were strangely blank. I was in that moment not looking forward or back.

When I returned, he began to share with me about the last few years and how he struggled since he left me in Miami. I studied him as he spoke, watching as his mood lightened the more he shared.

"That morning I left before you woke was the hardest thing I ever did. I watched you and found myself wondering how I could have felt so much for you in such a short amount of time that first summer. I thought maybe when you know it has an ending, even if you hoped it wouldn't, it makes everything that much more intense. But I knew in that moment in Miami all those years later that was one of those times too. I knew then how easy it would be to love you again.

"Falling asleep with you in my arms was everything I ever imagined. But I awoke to fear. I panicked. I never wanted to leave your side again. I saw the end with you, just like I had seen it all those years ago. But time. God, I hated time.

Sometimes I even resented it.

"I stared at you for a long time before I forced myself to get up, watching you as I dressed. I knew it wasn't just about sex between us. You reminded me of what I was capable of feeling and that you were more than just a memory. What we had was always so real. It was more than I could bear. Two times in our lives we would be together. And two times the ending would be dictated by circumstances out of our control. Fucking, goddam time. I hated it.

"You have always been there, Jenn. You were right when you wrote I couldn't fake happy. I guess I wanted to believe my family vacations would be enough to fill the emptiness the rest of the time. My kids, Jenn. God, I wanted it for them. But I just couldn't put you away."

He told me about his kids. He had always been reserved letting me in beyond the pictures on Facebook. "Kids never quite get the credit they deserve for being resilient. Or maybe mine just had adapted enough through nannies and daycare while we both pursued our careers."

His honesty made him even more endearing to me. I knew it wasn't easy for him to make these decisions, which he did without a guarantee that I would be waiting for him once he did. With that knowledge, I knew this was a decision he was making for himself, much like I had done all those years ago.

"Did your wife see it coming? Did she know?" I asked.

"Maybe. She was disappointed but I don't fault her for having been so driven. We put in so many years specializing in our fields. I never wanted or expected her to be a full-time mom. That was not her thing. I rationalized that we made up for lost time through those family vacations. For a few weeks a year, we focused on us. The rest of the time, we pretended. I tried telling her that I felt like an afterthought most days."

"How'd she take that?" I reached out to him, stroking his arm as I did.

He snickered. "She said I should keep busy."

"That's kind of harsh."

"That was her answer."

"That was Mark's answer for me too. But I was just a mom."

"Just a mom? That's funny. I doubt you ever *just* did anything." He looked at me intently as I watched him talk. "I just realized that we weren't going the same direction in life. And that I was going to be miserable pretending until she was ready to be in the same place, if ever."

"I am sorry, Tripp. None of us ever sets out with the idea it won't last."

"You're right."

He reached inside his coat pocket and pulled out the article with the note I'd written and handed them to me. Our eyes locked and did not break. Then I turned to the note and reread my words. I looked over to him when I finished. "That was kind of harsh in retrospect," I admitted.

"I didn't want to hurt you, but it was obvious I did. I felt the knives stabbing me. I swear I tasted your bitterness and could feel your pain." I was mesmerized by his words, not wanting to interrupt him, afraid he would stop talking. "It was impossible for me not to want to explore you. And from the moment I saw you I knew I would be in trouble. You had reopened those wounds and the feelings I thought I remembered were mild compared to what you unleashed."

I wondered if Tripp had rehearsed what he would say to me. How did he know I'd be here? That I would even want to see him again especially after all these years? He knew the answer to that too.

"Turn the card over." I did as he said and saw two hand-drawn hearts overlapping.

"It looks like a Venn diagram."

"In hearts. But yes. We may have led separate lives, Jenn,

but where we intersect, it's overflowing. What I always loved about you was that you saw me for me. You weren't impressed by where I went to college or by my profession later on. And you understood my tastes in music. You got every part of me."

One half of the diagram had the word "medicine" while the other half had the word "writing" and in the middle was "music."

I remembered that conversation as we lay in bed in Miami.

"It was always music and medicine for me, you said."

"And you said it was always writing and music. I remember. And then I started thinking of all the other things we had in common. We were more alike than different."

He looked at me before continuing. "But there was always more than that I felt. And when we reconnected, it all came back, and I wanted so much to be able to pick up where life made us stop. It's always been right there in front of me."

My heart was pounding outside of my chest. It hurt knowing that I caused him pain too, and that wanting me would make him see what he had been pretending all along. I never wanted him to be unhappy in his choices. I never wished him ill will. But I always hoped he would find his way to me.

"I would listen to *our* song." I looked at him uncertain which one he meant. "The one you sent me by Ed Sheeran."

"It was perfect, wasn't it?"

"I listened to that song hundreds of times. Just to feel you. I didn't love the melody, but I loved the words." That made me smile. I forgot what a music critic he was. I wasn't a musician. I just liked music that made me feel emotions of all kinds. That he found a way to critique the song in this romantic moment felt fitting simply because it was Tripp.

"There were so many songs that triggered you. Not even just recently, but throughout my life," he would tell me. "There was always a song for you, Jenn. Always. I wanted you to go away in my mind. I wanted to be okay with my life, the one I had carefully crafted and chosen. But you reminded me of the man I liked being." He stopped and reflected out over the water. I could see he was choked up.

"I'm sorry, Jenn, that I hurt you. All I have ever done is love you even when I didn't want to."

He pulled me to him, gently kissed my lips for only a moment. And then he said the words I had known in my heart I had waited a lifetime to hear:

"It's you. It's always been you. And it still won't be long enough to love you."

Maybe it wouldn't be long enough. But it would be ours. Finally on the same path with no foreseeable intersections begging us to choose opposite directions. This time we were in the same car, going the same speed, heading to the same place, giddy like the young lovers we once were, but with the realization time does not stand still or wait. Our love would be like bookends with a beginning and an end that was uniquely ours, but with stories in between that were shared with others. We would have the rest of our lives together to tell each other the parts that made us who we became, independent of the other.

We sat on that front porch together and watched as the sun rose. Both our hearts full in the knowledge that we had been given that chance to love each other again.

I looked at him. "Do you remember all those years ago when you asked me how this ends?"

He smiled, remembering that long-ago conversation when we had first reconnected. "I do. You said you didn't know."

I studied his eyes as they looked at me, waiting for more. "With you. It was always going to end with you."

He kissed me longer, more intentionally. Then I rested my head on his shoulder and could hear the beating of our hearts ticking in perfect unison. The stars, the earth, the moon, the seconds, minutes, hours, perfectly aligned if just for long enough.

About the Author

Kirsten Pursell is an American author. *Long Enough to Love You* is her fourth novel. Previous works include her memoir, *On Becoming Me: Memoir of an 80's Teenager*, and two additional novels: *Harvard* and *Company Clown*. She lives in Oceanside, California.

Visit Kirsten online at: www.kirstenpursell.com.

About Atmosphere Press

Atmosphere Press is an independent, full-service publisher for excellent books in all genres and for all audiences. Learn more about what we do at atmospherepress.com.

We encourage you to check out some of Atmosphere's latest releases, which are available at Amazon.com and via order from your local bookstore:

Hidden In The Shadows, a novel by A.D. Vancise

Hidden Shadow, a novel by Jennifer Bourland

The Songs of My Family, a novel by Jillian Arena

The Ridiculous Man, a novel by Frank J. Connor

The Wisdom of Winter, a novel by Annie Seyler

Beyond the Hostile Sky: Part One, a novel by Karen J Laakko

Failed States, a novel by Justin O'Donnell

Amaranth, a novel by Samantha Davenport

The Lay-off House, a novel by David Rogers Jr.

Stranded, a novel by KristaLyn A. Vetovich

The Hand of Midnight, a novel by D.R. Selkirk

Almost Indestructible, a novel by E R Sandfire

Pythia in the Basement, a novel by Alejandro Marron

The Lighthouse, a novel by Karin Ciholas

A World Without Men, a novel by Randall Moore

Other Me, a novel by Elen Lewis

The Weber House, a novel by Mark Lance

Made in United States
North Haven, CT
27 March 2023

34599995R00157